COLLECTED WRITINGS

Vol 24

DEDWYDD S.H. JONES

ISBN 978-0-9957601-8-9
Copyright ©2017 Dedwydd S.H.Jones

A CIP record for this book is available from the British Library

This work is a work of fiction. Names and characters are the product of the
author's imagination and any resemblance to actual persons, living or dead is
entirely coincidental.

Published by
Llyfrau Cambria Books, Wales, United Kingdom.
Cambria Books is a division of
The Cambria Publishing Co-operative Ltd

Discover our other books at: www.cambriabooks.co.uk

Cover design by William Gurney

DEDICATION

This volume is in memory of my father, Major Francis Jones, the late Herald Extraordinary of Wales. Before he died, he passed on to me a sheaf of old documents. These two stories, *The Box Tree* and *The Tower was too High,* were among them. They were inscribed, "reminiscences of a Grandfather, for dear Caroline, my granddaughter." They are published here for the first time.

"People do not die immediately, but remain bathed in a sort of aura of life which bears no relation to true immortality, but through which they continue to occupy our thoughts as when they were alive. It is as though they were travelling abroad."
Remembrance of Things Past
Marcel Proust

"If no one answers to the call, then walk alone, walk alone."
Rabindrath Tagore

'TOTUS MUNDUS AGIT HISTRIONEM' ('We are all Players.')
Notice outside the Globe Theatre, South Bank, 1603-1614

I am eternally grateful to Maruti M. Morajkar for all his kind help and support.

CONTENTS

The Tower was too high

On a fine Autumn afternoon, in the reign of the first Hanoverian, three ladies sat in a panelled room within the manor house of Kilkiffeth, enjoying cakes and honey, and occasionally sipping syllabub from small glass jugs that stood on the table before them. They were sisters – Gwenllian, Gwenfron and Tanglwst – whose names sounded like the opening line of a lyric, so they had been told by Mr Dryden himself whom they had met on the only visit they had ever made to London, years before.

The sisters looked very alike, red-haired, blue-eyed, short – none was much over five feet high – and extremely fat. In saying this, one is not being ungallant, one merely states the truth; they were, physically, animated dumplings in dresses. They had pink faces, their eyes twinkled and the sweetest little dimples accompanied their smiles and simperings. Although none would see their fiftieth birthday again, they were wonderfully preserved, and to a casual observer, appeared to be the most amiable, good-natured trio who ever existed. They always went about together, and when speaking, had a habit of clasping their hands held to the breast, for all the world just like 'religeuses.'

The eldest, Gwenllian, was clearly the dominating member of the sisterhood. Slightly taller and more muscular than the others, animated by a family pride, that would have made a Spanish Grandee seem the most modest of beings, she always dressed as if about to make a visit to, say, the Mayor of Newport or the Lord Lieutenant. A slight limp, the legacy of a fall from pony-back in her younger days, in no way restricted her movements, and her activity was proverbial. 'As busy as Gwenllian Kilkiffeth' passed into the language of the district. She now sat upright in her chair, her plump form clad in a silken, looped-up gown, a flounced skirt, and perched on her flaring red hair, a high, mauve-coloured fontage, fashionable among the great ladies of those days. More homely garb covered Gwenfron and Tanglwst – wine-red

1

housecoats with loose sleeves, laced at the wrists, and round blue-bonnets which stood like haloes on their heads, wholly concealing their luxuriant curls. An acute observer would have noticed that despite their roly-poly appearance, their movements were lithe and brisk, giving the impression of well-trained Caucasian tumblers dressed up for the day.

In fact, their looks wholly belied their nature. It was only when they spoke that a re-appraisal became necessary. Gwenllian's rasping tones, Gwenfron's harsh, unmusical utterances and Tanglwst's deep, guttural grunts, soon shattered the pleasant illusion created by their almost angelic faces. Indeed, they were vestals of uncommon acidity. Their diction was abrupt, imperious, even aggressive. Servants obeyed their least orders with alacrity; their business Manager trembled at the sight of them and the family attorney carried out their instructions with a speed wholly at variance with the normal practice of his profession. Intelligent and alert, their whole lives were devoted to one object – the accumulation of riches, an exercise at which they had been as successful as the shrewdest Lombard street banker. They were widely respected, although somewhat feared, and the most confident of men, not to mention women, were most circumspect in their dealings with the formidable trio.

Their parents had died when the four children – there was also a brother – were under ten years of age, and during their minority, they were cared for by a childless uncle and aunt, to whom they were greatly attached.

Background and breeding entitled them primacy among their peers. Several reasons had influenced the founder of the family, Llewellyn ap Cyhylyn, a famous war-leader of the time of the Norman invasion, to choose Kilkiffeth as his main homestead. It stood in the centre of his vast Pembrokeshire estate. A little distance from below the house, on a spur above the river Gwaun, stood a defensive camp fortified by fosse and rampart, a refuge for man and beast in times of trouble. High up on the south rose Kilkiffeth mountain over 1000 feet high, at the top of which stood a small structure, where in olden days, sentinels watched for the approach of marauders from Morfil and Puncheston, Fishguard, Dinas and the upper Gwaun valley, but now used as a hut for shepherds who attended the flocks that grazed its sparse pastures. On the slope almost midway between these two posts stood the fortified house of Kilkiffeth with its high tower, now undergoing basic alterations. We do not know whether the founder had any poetry in his soul, probably not, but he had established himself in an enchanted land; on the north loomed the craggy hills of Dinas, Llanllawer, and Llanychllwydog, crowned by cairns of ancient chieftains, their lower slopes shrouded in a shaggy mantle of forest trees; on the south side the gentler rolling hills of Casfuwch, Morfil, Kilkiffeth and Cilgelynen, covered in heather and golden gorse and dotted with white-washed farms and cottages. Between them lay the Vale of Gwaun, richly wooded, sheltering the old mansion of Pontfaen, three churches and a holy well, all dedicated to St David, and the hamlet of Llanychaer where the Lord's mill ground the grain harvested from the stubborn soil by hardy hill-farmers. It was a Mabinogion sort of country and one would not have been surprised to see Twrch Trwyth emerging from the thickets or hear the hunting horn of Pwyll Pendefig himself.

In the Welsh tradition, the sisters were given to ancestor-worship. On the paternal side, they descended from Llewelyn ap Cyhylyn, mentioned earlier, and he in turn traced his lineage to the early princes of West Wales. One forbear had gone on Crusade with Richard the Lion-Heart, another had fought at Agincourt, another had received Henry VII at Milford, and all had added to the acres and coffers of Kilkiffith. They had shown more caution than partisanship during the Civil War so that their wings had not been singed by the Commonwealth nor clipped by the Restoration. They were a canny, knowing breed, made to last, like seasoned oak.

Although unmarried, the sisters had not lacked suitors. Mr Warren of Trewern had made several bids to win the hand of Gwenllian. Mr ap Rhys of Treicert had bargained for Gwenfron, and Mr Phillips of Haythog, a very grand gentleman indeed, had laid siege to Tanglwst. The fair ladies proved most critical, finicky, and difficult, even from a young age, and despite the urgings of trustees and guardians, refused to accept any arrangement that did not wholly meet with their approval. After coming of age, they continued to display an independent attitude, and squire after squire had to retire, utterly discomfited, their suites usually foundering on the jagged rocks of finance. They remained unattached, heart-whole, eminently respectable ladies of impregnable virginity. But it was the conduct of the brother that sealed their committal to a life of spinsterhood.

This was Harry, in whom every ingredient that goes to produce a ne'er-do-well, was concentrated. Of middle height, slightly built, dark in colouring, bright of eye, taking after his mother (a Laugharne of Llanreithan), in temperament and outlook the direct opposite of his sisters, weak-willed but wilful and headstrong when it came to his personal desires. From early years, he had proved a torment to his family, a problem that increased with his growth. He was expelled from Haverfordwest School for fighting with his Euclid teacher. While still under age, he had abducted a young ward but was caught before much damage was done, and only through the intervention of powerful friends and relatives did he escape the punishment that less privileged men would have received. A mere youth, he tippled in taverns, diced and gambled. Efforts had been made to govern him. The Vicar, the rural Dean, even the Archdeacon, had striven to convince him of the folly of his ways, and he had been prayed for publically with much fervour by a Puritan preacher in Fishguard. Prayers, cajolings, threats, all were spurned.

When he attained his majority, all restraint was cast to the winds. For the first time in the long history of the family, the acres of Kilkiffeth became pawns on the checkerboard of the money-lenders. Mortgages and bonds filled the charter chest, and even the dowries of the sisters were placed in jeopardy. Finding Pembrokeshire too hot to hold him, Harry took the road to London to seek employment where profit could be made without undue exertion, where he would be safe from Sheriffs' writs, the

4

fury of fathers of injured ladies, and beyond the reproaches of sisters and kinsfolk whose indulgence he had exhausted.

His gay, engaging manners soon brought him friends, among them leading lawyers, Mr Chaffinch and Mr Progers, no less. Through their interest, he obtained a minor Court post of indeterminate nature, by all accounts not dissimilar to that of his sponsors. Even there he proved so wayward that he found himself obliged to relinquish his appointment. Harry was by no means unintelligent, and with the help of friends managed to receive a desk at the Navy Office. Finding life here far too prosaic for his liking, he soon resigned, and returned to the delights of the gaming table and other activities of a more dubious kind. The climax came when he stood trial for his life on suspicion of having been involved in the hold-up of a stagecoach but was sufficiently fortunate to be acquitted. He showed a cat-like capacity for falling on his feet. However, this last escapade determined him to return to lie low for a while. The profligate was not long at Kilkiffeth. His nature could not be changed, his disastrous career, apparently, could not be checked. He took to heavier drinking, revelled in the pleasures of low life, quarrelled with his sisters – on one occasion chasing them through the rambling house with a loaded pistol in his hand – so that, gradually, few would have anything to do with him, even his tap-room friends and companions. The Vicar of Llanychaer who had long despaired of the prodigal's soul, had bitter battles with him over the matter of tithes. The good man dubbed him, 'Homo Kilkiffethiensis,' and when asked by his churchwarden what this meant, answered sadly, "A complete worldling, a heathen". At this stage, the peccant squire decided to travel overseas, and having mortgaged everything he could, set off one fine morning for the port of Bristol. Thereafter, a cloud of mystery enshrouds him, perhaps mercifully, and all that could be gleaned was that the "Swallow", the brig on which he embarked, had foundered on a reef off the coast of Virginia. When the news of the shipwreck reached Wales, it was assumed that Harry had perished. Few tears were shed over his fate, no one mourned him, apart from a few dark-eyed lasses whose compliance had formerly been tempered by the guineas of Kilkiffith, and his name was rarely mentioned except by the more respectable parents when admonishing difficult sons, and by the disreputable who occasionally regaled their friends in the dram-shops with hilarious tales of the pranks of the well-born sinner.

Accordingly, the estate was placed in the full and absolute possession of the sisters, as co-heiresses. They immediately set about restoring the fortunes of their house. Their stubborn pride, acquisitive habits and firmness of purpose, fitted them for the performance of the formidable task that lay before them. By careful husbandry, due economy and sound advice, they steadily winched the estate out of the morass of debt into which their improvident brother had plunged it, and two decades later Kilkiffith once more stood on firm financial foundations. The sisters were justly proud of their achievement and, having at long last savoured the satisfaction of solvency, devoted their lives to the further accumulation of land and wealth, and the status that accompanies such projects. They still enjoyed robust help and their energy was in no way diminished. They were now, in effect, married to Kilkiffith. Hopeful suitors ceased their forays, and distant relatives studied the remainderships of the family entail with a quiet relish.

As the sisters sat sipping their syllabub, they talked mainly of domestic concerns. On that day, the huge house was strangely quiet, for all the servants had gone to Puncheston Fair, an annual event that could not be denied if servants were to be retained at all. The three mistresses had grumbled but had given permission as they always did in the end.

"I'm not sure whether we should allow Griffy Hughes to remain at Cilrhedin," said Gwenllian, "he is mighty improvident... and all those children."

"Don't forget he always pays the rent," croaked Tanglwst.

"That is what matters,' added Gwenfron.

"I suppose so," sighed Gwenllian, "he is certainly better than Jack of Lodor in that respect. Jack's lease has only three years to go, and then he must go too."

"Quite so, quite so," chorused the others.

"Jack's the last tenant to whom **he** gave a lease," commented Tanglwst meaningfully. The sisters never referred to their brother by name, and the passing of time had failed to mollify the resentment they felt towards the one who had nearly destroyed the patrimony their exertions had saved.

"This is somewhat off-taste," said Tanglwst, raising her jug and smacking her lips, "I must speak to Meg again. You've got to be after them all the time."

"Yes, all the time," the others agreed.

"Good to be without them for a day anyway. Always chatter, chatter and breaking things."

"I hope the maids will return home without hap. You know what I mean. Remember Jane last year?"

"Yes. Twins. That old Dick the Garn. At it every whip-stitch and him married too."

"The married ones are the worst, they say."

Mistress Tanglwst rose with a sigh that may have been of resignation or envy, and walked to the window. After gazing out for a moment, she said, "Well, they've had good weather for the Fair. Marry, look, someone's coming!"

The others quickly joined her and they stood looking with intense curiosity at the figure of a man who was even then unlatching the gate.

"Who can he be?" asked Gwenfron a little anxiously, "he looks uncommonly shabby. A tramp? Shall I call the mastiff?"

"No," replied Gwenllian, "You and Tanglwst go to the door, and I'll fetch the blunderbuss. Don't worry, you know how well I shoot." And she swept away with limping majesty, her head upheld as if bearing a peacock's crest, her train flowing behind her. Gwenfron and Tanglwst followed her into the hall, then moved to the door with decision. Determination and courage had never been lacking in the family.' The sisters would have faced the hords of the devil without flinching. Tanglwst opened the door and with her sister stood on the threshold of the Tudor porch. By now the stranger had crossed the path that led from the gate, and came forward with a nonchalant, confident air until he stood three or four feet from the entrance. Taking off a hat that sported a small cockade, he gave a sweeping bow in the manner of a gentleman, and said, "ladies, your humble servant to command." His voice was hoarse and rasping, not unlike the sisters'.

Although of only average height and shabbily clad, the visitor nevertheless presented a striking figure. He held his head high, a pair of small light blue eyes gazed from a face that bore the marks of violent encounters. His nose had been broken and inclined slightly to the left, a great scar ran from his furrowed, sun-bronzed forehead down to his unshaven chin and gave the whole face a slightly sinister expression. His clothes, tattered and faded, had, evidently, once been the height of fashion - a red, three-quarter coat with long buttoned cuffs, decorated with embroidered flowers and butterflies, and a blue waistcoat richly embellished; but, in contrast, loose working men's trews covered his legs. His worn, dusty shoes showed he had walked a long way. His neck-cloth was loosely tied, and like his wig, was of a dirty grey colour. A dagger in his belt completed the ensemble of what may justly be described as a devil-may-care, dangerous swaggerer.

He looks a dissolute rogue, yet somehow, a gentleman, mused Gwenfron. He can hardly have come to beg, what can he want? Behind them, peering out from the shadowed inner hall, Gwenllian was more impressed by the stranger's air than the details of his dress, and, as a sudden twinge of apprehension passed through her mind, her forefinger slid forward towards the trigger of the blunderbus. The sisters stood still, their plump features showed no emotion, their small blue eyes watching warily. Tanglwst broke the silence.

"Good day, sir. What brings you here? Have you walked far?"

"I have come to Kilkiffeth because my sisters need their brother to protect them and to relieve them of the burdens and trials of governing an estate. Gwenllian, Gwenfron, Tanglwst, do you not remember your own brother? I am Harry, this my house,

8

these lands are my domain. I have often longed for them in the wild parts of the world, and now I have returned to my true inheritance."

Three pairs of eyes opened wider, lips became compressed, hands clenched, horrible realisation dawned in their eyes. But whatever dire emotions that might have been aroused, the sisters soon had them firmly under control. The grunts and gutteral tones of earlier days were readily buttered over, but their previous confidence had received a nasty shock. 'Harry!' a name that had not been uttered at Kilkiffeth for over twenty years, and the memory of it - a tolling bell that recalled shame, distress, scandal, discredit and near bankruptcy. It was then that Gwenllian, always the leader in such situations, fair or foul, took charge. Putting down the blunderbuss on the hall coffer, she stepped towards him.

"Our brother is long dead. We do not know you. We are not afraid of you. You are an imposter."

"No need to be afraid, Gwenllian, yes, you are Gwenllian. Let me enter and I shall prove to you that I am indeed your brother, in spite of my altered appearance. If I fail, I shall go away and never trouble you more. I have never hurt a lady whatever my shortcomings."

Gwenllian motioned to her sisters to stand aside.

"Come in, sir. And we may perhaps learn who you really are."

He bowed, walked past the curtseying sisters and entered the hall. "There is little change here." He walked around " ...the old charter chest... the helmet dented at Crecy... the pikes and bills of our retainers... the maps of master Speed... the arras our father brought from Brussels... the antlers of the last stag killed in Cwm Cerwyn. Ah, the floor rug, that is new." He paused, "I congratulate you on your stewardship, good sisters." He gave a light-hearted laugh, "it's good to be home!"

"He could have given you a description of our hall to you," mused Gwenllian, "you seem to have a good enough memory."

"Words are no title deeds," Tanglwst managed to put in.

"Very well. Then I shall now proceed to produce proof. Before

9

I left this house all those years ago, I hid three objects. No one knows what they are or where they are, except me. Come, sisters, you can see how well I know my way around here." He led them along the dark passage-way towards the back of the house. The emerged into a small courtyard, where an angry mastiff bayed frantically and tugged against the great chain that kept him within bounds.

"Your gallant protector?" Harry asked sarcastically.

"We can protect ourselves perfectly well, thank you," came curtly from Gwenllian.

Leaving the courtyard, they entered the walled garden beyond. Harry came to a halt by a line of apple trees. "Now let me see," he said, and began counting them. He moved forward. "Yes the fifth tree. Here. Before I left, I hammered the iron tooth of a harrow into the fork up there. The tree has grown somewhat but I think I can still locate it." He hoisted himself up and pointed "behold, fair ladies, there it is, red with rust." The sisters craned their necks up. Yes, there was no denying his words. The head of the iron tooth, now red with rust, lay embedded but still visible in the bark.

"What madness is this?!" gasped Tanglwst, aghast. Gwenllian shook her head.

"What? You still doubt me? Then let us go to the cooking pots." He walked confidently into the stone-flagged kitchen followed by the three disturbed sisters. He stopped at the wide hearth, still hung with cooking vessels. "See here," he said, with a light smile, "the beam over the inglenook. See there, a hole left by one of the drills. See. Now plugged with sawdust. Inside there is a steel skewer for roasts, placed there especially by me." He picked up a knife and scraped out the plug. "Look, Gwenllian," he said. Gwenllian slowly looked. Sure enough, inside the hole, lay a steel skewer, exposed to view. The sisters shrank back. "There, you see. No one but your brother could have known these things." Gwenllian recovering, answering sharply, "All of these things could have been told to you," Harry waved the needle under her nose, "then let us go into the parlour!" The sisters followed,

10

getting more and more perturbed. Harry marched up to the glass-fronted bookshelf, opened it and selected a leather-bound volume, "My old History of the Saints!" he announced with a laugh. "Now watch!" He held it tightly and slowly peeled off the spine, then shook it. A gold ring fell with a tinkle onto the table. "Look at the initials," he said. "I know that ring," gasped Gwenllian, "It's Mam's wedding ring. She left it to…Harry…after she passed on." "Now," said Harry, "do you think I would ever tell a secret like that to anyone" he said looking upwards with a pious expression, "a sacred secret, and to a stranger? Betray our mother, and I mean **our** mother." The sisters examined the ring one by one, their breaths now coming faster and faster. Gwenllian stared at the hated face of her brother, scenes from the past flashed across her inner eye, Harry's drunkenness, his frauds, his thefts, seductions, the writs, distraints, shame and flight, and to have snatched victory from the jaws of that defeat!? And now to lose it all again, – she tensed herself for action, all her old determination and fight re-asserted itself. Lose it all again? Never! Her responses were now brisk and business-like, as if she had decided something of vital importance.

"It seems indeed that you are our long-lost brother." Her sisters sensed the change in her. They stared, what was she up to? She smiled and dimpled at him as in the days of their youthful innocence. The sisters followed suit. It was as if they were welcoming home a long lost gentle lover or husband. "Please forgive us for not recognising you just now," she pleaded prettily, "it has been nearly twenty years and you have changed, so much more, well, distinguished, brother. And you look as if you've been in the wars too." Harry greeted this remark with a vigorous nod, and traced the scar on his face. "But we will make amends," Gwenllian went on. Welcome, dear brother! We shall prepare you the best meal you've had since you were last here. Sisters, to the kitchen! Harry, upstairs, wash for supper!" He laughed. Orders again? Fine. But she'd soon discover who the real master was. Gwenllian ushered him through the hall to his room. As she returned to the hall, her eyes fell on the great shield with its broad

11

swords, the ramping lion on their crest and the strange knotted device her ancestor won as the French King's champion on the Jousting fields of Picardy. 'Happy the Brave' the family motto shone above the shield. Well, this was another battlefield in another country but she was determined to be as much a winner as her ancient forbears had been.

The dinner proved a great success. The three sisters seemed moved by a desire to atone for all their doubts and suspicions and their plump little forms exuded kindness and sisterly care. Their brother replied with descriptions of his daring-do days - he had hunted, bison, beaver and bear in Hudson Bay, he had been captured by Corsairs in Algerciras, fought with Rooke at Gibralter, sailed to India, was employed at the Court of the Sultan of Camphor, and on his departure, had been loaded with spices, jewels, gold and silver amulets and bracelets, and a gold dagger. "By God" he shouted, "I had enough money to buy all of Britain." He thumped the table and finally turned on Gwenllian, "Hell, haven't you got anything to drink in the house?" he finally declared.

"Now," said Gwenllian quietly to her sisters, "off you go to bed. Your brother and I have lots of things to discuss." The girls trooped out. War, they felt certain, was about to break out.

"So," opened Gwenllian, "you amassed a fortune, no doubt."

"Many fortunes as I've just told you, and I enjoyed them hugely while I had them. Every last jewel. But when I arrived at your door, I frankly admit I had not one penny left to my name. But I had always consoled myself with the fact that, whatever the ups and downs, I always had Kilkeffith.

"Well" asked Gwenllian," smiling, "and what plans do you have now, Harry?"

"I have given some thought to the matter. I propose to marry and live here. At the moment this house, **my** house, is dead, but by the powers, I will restore it to life." As he went on his voice became harsher, colder, more arrogant and vengeful. "I will lease the old farms out to numbers of my old friends – Jemmy Hughes, Black Dai, Jack the Rising. And not forgetting Moll of Morfil. This will be a happy house, as in the old days."

"But what about us," asked Gwenllian softly, "your sisters, where will we live?"

"You three, you have enjoyed my estate with all its profits for over thirty years without thought of me! And a cold welcome on my return. You are in debt to me now! I can't share this household, you will keep your portions, of course, that is the law, nothing I can do about that, but I will allow you to live in one of the worker's cottages on the estate..."

Gwenllian stood up abruptly, "No, no, never!" she started, then her tone changed, "but perhaps it is all just as well," she went on with a steadiness her sisters knew meant only one thing, trouble. "We can discuss details later. But first a view of your estate, let's walk down to the old Tower, where we used to play, still in ruins, you can only get to it through the old mansion next door, and that's falling to pieces too. The builders have started on the Tower, they say it's too high."

Harry hardly took in a word. His thoughts were all centred on the coming happy days. "But I've got a bank loan, and it's being properly restored, made safe. You can view all your acres from there, north and south, east and west. All yours."

"Yes!" grunted Harry, "All mine!" My God, he thought, she's gone soft, a real push over.

"You need a walk after that supper." she urged him.

"Yes, I suppose," Harry replied, puzzled both by his sister's sudden retreat and her cool self-control. And the ruined Tower and mansion, he thought, what a waste of money!

The house itself was early Tudor but the tower at the Western end was a relic of its Mediaeval past when it was both a look-out and a place of refuge. It had been incorporated into the mansion and both buildings had remained as one, throughout the ages. The house was four floors high, but the tower soared above it like an Italian campanile. Most of the flooring had long perished but the central staircase was still in place and led up to the locked door which led into the tower, then a further climb to the leaded roof-top and the stunning view of the vast green estate. The builders had already dismantled four lines of the brickwork. Piles of rubble were had been left, ready for disposal. The debris was simply tipped down the inside of the Tower, where it would be mortared over when the job was finished, to save transport costs, an economy Gwenllian had suggested, and which had been at once accepted.

As they approached the Tower, Harry cheered up. "God, but my old London friends are going to love all this when they visit! I'll give a Tower warming party that will be the talk of the County!" Gwenllian nodded and smiled as if in approval.

They entered the mansion and climbed up to the locked door, which Gwenllian opened with her pass-key, and they were soon at the top of the Tower. The builders had left piles of material scattered about the planks and had constructed a single rail around the central opening, where the rubble was being dumped. Harry looked over the dismantled battlements, and was at once struck by the extent of his holdings. He had forgotten how wealthy he was and what a brave show it could put on for him! But the Tower was too high. He estimated it should be lowered by at least twenty feet. Gwenllian was right. But what did he care? It was all being paid for. God, his sister was an odd one. Just lost her home and still full of the joys of Spring. He couldn't wait to see the back of the sisters and take in the view all by himself. Yes, he thrilled, and all mine!

The slanting rays of the sunlit up the scenic magic of the Presseleys, gilding the heights of Dinas, Trellan, Carn Ingli and Killfillin and bathing the mansion and tower with glowing rosy light. What a panorama thought Gwenllian, thank god for my good work.

Harry pointed at a farmstead in the distance, "Isn't that the farm of Mynydd Melin?"

"Yes," Gwenllian responded calmly, "You sold it once. We bought it back."

"Really? And isn't that Cluncath Farm?"

"Yes, you sold it once and we brought it back."

"You don't say. And isn't that Trellwyn Fawr, on the slopes

14

over there?"

"Yes, you sold it to old Vaughan of Pontfaen and he's the only one who never sold it back." She went on, "Look at the wonderful views out there, we're so lucky to be alive, and then see down there," she pointed at the wide hole with the railings, "can't see a thing, so deep and dark!"

Harry peered down into the pitch-black space. "So deep and dark..." he repeated. These were the last words he ever spoke. Gwenllian had worked it out during dinner. She has recently seen an illustration of a horrendous murder in the local almanac. She now stood close behind her brother, reached down quickly, gripped the loose bottoms of his trousers, then heaved upwards with all her strength. Harry gave one terrified yell, reached out for the rail as he fell, his hands scraped the masonry and dragged the railing after him. After a few seconds came a thump and a clatter. Then silence. Gwenllian knew exactly what to do. She now proceeded to pitch all the waiting debris into the well, covering the corpse - the stone slates, the sawed off rafters, the corbels, the dressed stones, broken masonry, and perforated sheets of lead. She then dusted off her hands and retraced her steps down, re-locked the door, smiling all the way.

It was dark when she arrived home. Her sisters were waiting upstairs, telescopes out. They had had a glorious view of their sister on the Tower. Now together again they viewed the lovely landscape in the moonlight and the last resting place of their demonic brother. Kilkiffeth was safe at last. The three gentle ladies dimpled comfortingly at each other just as in the old days. Next morning they were up early to carry on viewing the good work on the Tower, yes, and Gwenllian made sure the height was lowered by exactly twenty feet before the last capping of mortar. They all agreed, including the builders, that the Tower had always been much too high.

The Box-Tree

I was about five years of age when I first became acquainted with Pryfyn Enoch, or perhaps it would be more correct to say - conscious of his unseen might and potential capacity for meting out swift punishment to erring humanity, for I never saw him in the flesh despite long vigils waiting for him to emerge from his lair in the box-tree growing in the garden of my mother's old home, the farm of Clawddcam.

The garden lay behind the house. One side was bounded by the dwelling house and the dairy, the other three sides by high-topped hedges, necessary bulwarks protecting it from the savage gales that swept inland from the channel beyond the headland of St. David's. During the summer the garden was a veritable sun-trap, and from its rich warm soil sprang a variety of vegetables, fruits, herbs and flowers, all contributing to the attractions of the dining table of the farmhouse. Although small, measuring roughly some thirty paces by forty, it was so admirably planned and cultivated that its output exceeded that of many a garden twice its size. Every inch supported some sort of growth.

Flowers grew in profusion, providing a colourful pageant for human eyes and a feast without end for the bees that poured from the conical hives beneath the shelter of the walls. Along the borders, and in carefully tended parterres, grew lavender, violets, daffodils and primroses, white roses entwined around a few rickety arches raised by the hands of some unskilled enthusiast. Herbs grew in orderly abundance – mint, marjoram, parsley, thyme, and sage used to flavour the steaming 'cawl' – speciality of Clawddcam's kitchen, and wormwood which provided a bitter tea to cure many a childish ailment. In the hedge grew agrimony 'good for them that have naughty livers,' I once read in an Elizabethan manuscript, vervain, said to have been used by the Druids to combat plague, camomile whose flowers could be made

16

into a poultice to rout toothache, elecampane that cured kidney troubles in people and coughs in horses, and the joyous little celandine whose sole purpose seemed to be to bring pleasure into our remote rural world. An impetus to herb cultivation in the district had been provided by the Reverend Mr Lloyd, sometime Vicar of Llanreithan and Llandeloy, a devotee of Culpeper, who shortly after his arrival, electrified the parishioners by his addiction to sandwiches made from dandelion leaves and an appetite for plants and grasses traditionally reserved for farm animals. Apple trees, gooseberry, raspberry and currant bushes produced generous harvests. Beds of leeks and cabbages provide more homely fare and there were a few rows of early potatoes in the western end of the garden, the main crop being grown in the potato-field some distance away. Neat paths, their surface hardened by reddish ashes from generations of coal fires, ran between the plots.

An embowered cloister, a Garden of Eden, you might say. Not quite. For in this haven of flower and fruit and colour, crouched a hidden terror whose malevolence was directed particularly at small boys of just my age.

Most of the fruit grew in the eastern end, its main feature, a glorious strawberry – bed. At the edge of this attractive territory grew the box-tree, some twelve feet or more in height, whose dark, glossy, evergreen leaves retained their glistening brightness throughout the year, summer and winter. The Box is uncommon in these parts. It is the heaviest of European woods, and if placed in water, it will sink like a stone. An early writer speaks of the tree as one of 'great beautie' whose wood was 'fitt for dagger haftes.' I could never learn who planted it there, and it was very old when I was a boy.

Predatory instincts awaken quickly in the young, especially at the prospect of a succulent dish. As a toddler, I used to walk around the garden, somewhat timid and well-behaved, clasping my mother's hand. As I grew, I became more unruly and adventurous, and when about five, suddenly became aware of the charms of the strawberry-bed. However, I lacked the hypocrisy that, alas maturity and sophistication bring in their wake, and my intentions, if not stated in so many words, were certainly telegraphed by my behaviour. The family became uneasily aware of the presence of a rogue elephant, albeit a diminutive one, which, could he get into the garden unperceived, would soon wreak devastation among the good things earmarked for the table. I had been observed gazing wistfully over the wicket gate leading to the garden, and caught trying to clamber over one of the high hedges. I was soon stopped dead in my predatory tracks, not by sermon or spanking, but by a far more effective deterrent.

I soon learnt the garden of Clawddcam contained a monster, by the side of which the awful Guardian of the Hesperides was no more than a frolicsome pup. The name of this fearsome being, so they told me, was Pryfyn Enoch.

Pryfyn Enoch seemed to have been capable of changing his form, at least, so I concluded after hearing detailed descriptions from various members of the family. To one, he appeared as a small, tawny, bristly, four-legged creature, possessing a singularly long lasso-like tongue with which he dragged his prey into the range of his powerful jaws. Another said he had three eyes and six legs – one informant gave him ten legs and fifty claws - claiming he could kick and leap like a kangaroo. My dear empirical grandmother agreed with all versions. An old serving-man, whose grey hair and solemn visage vouched for his veracity, went so far as to tell me he had actually seen a severed hand lying near the box-tree, sole remains of some juvenile gadabout who had tried to raid the strawberry bed.

His lair was the heart of the box-tree, his life dedicated to the protection of the fruit. All agreed he was completely harmless so long as one did not take the fruit, especially the strawberries, without my grandmother's permission. One could walk and play along the paths, around the bushes, indeed around the box-tree itself, without incurring the custodian's wrath.

Later, it dawned on me that this strange creature seemed to be totally unknown outside the family. I mentioned Pryfyn Enoch to my fellows at Sunday School and to some grown-ups on neighbouring farms, but they had never heard of him, and a few were frankly sceptical. But I knew the doubting Thomases were quite wrong, quite ill-informed. To me Pryfyn Enoch was as real as the box-tree in which it lurked, as real as the luscious fruit its ceaseless vigilance protected.

I spent long hours among the ferns on the top of the hedge, I crouched behind the privet near the wicket gate, I gazed from a window overlooking the garden, hoping I might espy Pryfyn Enoch emerge from his leafy den. But he never moved, and my vigils were in vain. I usually entered the garden as bold as a grenadier, but as I approached the box-tree my courage wavered and waned. I peered cautiously into its dark heart, and on one occasion, fled headlong, believing I had glimpsed a pair of baleful eyes glaring at me from among its leaves.

In those early days I lived at Llandeloy, some two miles away, and my visits to Clawddcam averaged about once a week. It was only in summer and harvest-time that the name of Pryfyn Enoch was invoked. In the Winter and unproductive seasons, he apparently hibernated for there was no fruit to guard. As I grew older, faint doubts arose in my mind, not of the animal's existence, but of his efficiency. On one occasion, and the bushes heavily laden, I momentarily forgot all about the sinister sentinel, and plucked at the forbidden fruit. Realisation of the mortal peril came immediately, and I tore frantically from the scene of my temerity until I reached the safety of the farm-yard, for he would never leave the confines of the garden. I was amazed to realise I was alive at all. Perhaps he had been asleep? Or had moved away? When I related the affair, my kinsfolk congratulated me on my providential escape and assured me he was certainly still in residence and would hardly be so tolerant in future. I never tasted his efficiency again.

A few months after my tenth birthday, my parents moved to Goodwick, and my visits to the farm became more desultory. I formed new friendships, new interests and the memory of the guardian of the garden became a topic of laughter rather than consternation. I do not remember exactly when I ceased to believe in Pryfyn Enoch's existence, probably about the same time my belief in Father Xmas evaporated. But while I gave up the latter with reluctance, I gave up the former with relief.

I reached manhood and left the shire of my birth. Now and then I recalled Pryfyn Enoch, smiled to myself, and related the tale to my wife and children, which caused much hilarity. After my return from the war, having encountered among Tunisian djebels and Italian valleys, enemies far more malevolent than Pryfyn Enoch, I made a pilgrimage to those memory-hallowed acres so long held by my ancestors, pathways I had trod as a child, hedgerows where I had found nests of wren and robin and finch, streams where sticklebacks had succumbed to my youthful cunning, moorland where I had once shot snipe (more by accident than accurate aim), and of course, Clawddcam, home of my early jollities, now owned by my cousin.

The old house itself remained much the same. After some hours around the hospitable hearth, I took a stroll by myself to try to recapture the early raptures and enchantments. Much was changed. The cowshed with its wooden stalls and posts had been 'converted' to meet the requirements of an intrusive government 'Board.' Concrete covered the pebbled causeway in the yard, taps had exiled the pump, the coachhouse sheltered a tractor, the chaff-cutter had disappeared and so had the antiquated scales on which I had seen so much wood, grain, potatoes, and other produce weighed in the distant days of 'mixed farming.' The stables stood silent – the horses I had known, and the descendants of those horses, far, far away as fairyland.

I entered the garden. I will not dwell on the scene. My paradise was lost. The strawberry-bed had vanished, so had the box-tree. I returned to the wicket gate, and standing there watching me, was the ten-year old son of my cousin, a bright lad, wise in the ways of television and smart up-to-date school learning. Smilingly, I asked him, "have you seen Pryfyn Enoch?" He stared and then asked, "is he a footballer or a film-star?" And I knew then that Pryfyn Enoch was dead, dead indeed.

Home Thoughts

"Dylan Thomas Centenary Celebrations in Overdrive!" Western Mail Feb 7th 2014

After forty years, I stood on the Bristol suspension bridge again, rudely staring at my nation, Wales, and was suddenly dumbstruck. For the first time I realised Wales was not just one enormous cow-pat, but consisted of thousands of the little platters, spreading out in all directions, each its own shitty little principality, each possessing its own fortified White Tower - the Town Hall - its own Council-Tax Laundry Department, (robbing the poor to pay the rich), its own Green Hell Makers, Weights and Measures Saboteurs, Pot Hole Planners, Small Print Purveyors and Deceivers , its own mob of soft-brained Aldermen-Yes-Men, full of dress uniforms, always with a royal to lick up to, short fat Mayors, at this moment in time, all backed up by the smashing local Constabulary Marauders, strike breakers to a man! Bless our brave HQ's local heroes, I say, in spite of suffering from ever-present outbreaks of sleeping sickness in all ranks – Croeso Cymru, in the end, a land of near total whisky-amnesia, the whole spreading brownfields giving the world a false impression of the oneness of Wales and the wholesomeness of Welsh respectability - as, yes, it had so deceived me for so long! - whereas there was nothing much there at all, except the big-deal thespians, man - the sham hams - the girl sopranos with their ridiculous homunculae , the insane sheep, dyed-in-the-wool hypocrites, the general tribal myopia and, of course, the entirely satisfactory amounts of drinking and fornicating - not in bits and pieces either, heavy, man! - stuff like that! Why, every Sunday morning the turf itself heaves in every Chapel graveyard as even the dead join in the merry sex-making - O bless those immortal crevices of delight! In a flash, I could perceive all that now, a Damascene vision from the valuable economic asset of a bridge. I was on the road to majestic Splott in Cardiff - now no kidding, man, no hoax in sight, I had been invited by the organs of parochial righteousness to visit the new centres of excellence which the old imperial satrapies and protectorates of Taffswazia offered the well-oiled anglefied traveller, not such as me, for I am Tom Tell Truth, the old Demetian himself, but they knew not the monuments of the Dylan Marlais Thomases, the scattered Sons of the Wave over the land of my ancestors, the pale lurkers of poesy, were here or there. So I said to the mask in disguise from the Order of Deep Nodders in the Department of Pointless Commotion, "I'll come and have a look, then," and I went and here am I!

As I skidded to a halt outside Splott's electrifying emporium, the worthies of Wales, lined up on the marble itself, gave one mighty fart to speed me on my way. What the hell, wrong address! - they'd tried to frame me already, put me off their foul scent, the worms in the Welsh canker, but I was determined never to be scooped up like a lump of icy vanilla from a cart! They'd learn! They'd soon find out! I realised at once that it was Swansea I was supposed to be going to, see, where all the sweaty lucubrations was, laced with the top magic of the Mabinogion, and all the stunning creative crescendoes of Gwalia, all packaged for overseas trade, a penny for a three-pack - Dylan Drops, Elixers of Marlais the Tommoscine Mushrooms, if you please, variously named as you can pretty well tell, in the faggots and cheese Market, next to Salubrious Passage where all the brilliant Taff shitterati still hang out. (What a lot is packed into those few words there!) A tall Officer of the Extemporaneous Drama Volunteers awaited me - a man blessed with various ranks and titles, Commissar Curator, Able Intern, Cast Eradicator, all first class, of course, to go with the glittering stars, sashes and orders on his mighty breast, a frequent sight in those nauseous dens of cow-patted veniality - golden pensions blessing every one. And why not? Was he not a fine-grained person, of very few knots, a worthy representative of the old Welsh Arts Cloaca, an ancient body well known for its kindly, light-hearted outlook on Man and

Mankind. Why my Co-convener Co-conceptualist, that was his moniker formal-like, could swear one-thousand miles an hour without attracting the odium of the podium, his charm was that strong. But what did it for him was the fact that he was also Tyrant of the Ten Thousand Sycophants of Splott, the Crowned King-Emperor of Welsh Wallets, First Secretary Manipulator of Public Pelf and, low blow here - Official Sultan of Sarcasm in the Halls of Eastern Ease – little wonder there was so much power in his head!

A cab belched past. I glanced in astonishment, for on its doors were writ the words, "Do not go gentle..." and on Tacsi number 15 behind, late as usual, "Rage, rage against the..." then three brazen tourist charabancs, with their deadly blind spots at the ready, scrawled to bits; pale white delivery vans with a lot to say but nothing to deliver; fire-engines with their obedient tenders, every inch of each winch scripted like hell! What biro-tyro had come up with all this Parnassian flim-flam? Bless you, Dylan, through it all, you patriot of Llareggub, you Lord of Libation, you Messiah of the Enlarged Pentameter, you remained tipsy to a man! I noted there were banners in the wind at every egress with the name DT signed on them in huge ink. Oh, what rich hollows within, I thought, what egregious place- names without! TV screens were lit up higher up, like in Times Square, USA, showing *Under Milk Pudding* with Elizabeth Taylor in, all the time. There were discarded brochures fluttering about too, trod-on- poesy for the masses at every step. The Llareggub verses recited by the Rev Ely Jenkins were stamped on pennants which streamed in the firmament, all over the how-green-was-my valley of night-soil Wales, in every crook and nanny. Then, damn me, a flyer flew up and flapped me in the face. I read it out, "No-Welsh-writer-can-earn-his-bread-in-Wales-unless-he-pulls-the-forelock.-Wales-is -the Land-of-my-Fathers' –and-they-can-keep-it!" I waggled the message to my Guide. He exploded, "Haven't had one of those for years. Ignore it. Some damnable rotter. Never D T's! Take no notice, it is an unforgivable swindle and all wrong. Dung on it!"

He chucked it back into the treacherous eddies with a flick of an elegant wrist. Meanwhile, whichever way I looked I was positively drowning in the super delirious Dylanomania I was dying for. My brillcreamed Mentor suddenly bellowed at me as we swept up glittering Cwmdonkin Drive, "Wales has changed! Look around, look you. Have you ever seen so many stale Welsh-cake souvenir delicatessens, or second hand condom machines, traditional Tampax boutiques, genitalia done in slate for sale on the pavement, and daffodil quims fluttering in the breeze, we have now proclaimed it all over Silurian territory itself - Mam-Wales is a sex-machine cum Drama Panorama of one thousand and one years of age, more than it took for even Helen to launch just one of her perfect faces! Bitch! Look!" The man pointed, "Gaze on my civil slaves from HQ struggling to get in, the turnstiles bobbing up and down, they are the only ones who can afford the prices, even with buckets–full of lickspittle thrown in."

The Fab Facilitator shone with pride, smoothed down his head, waved his arms in conviction mode, his eyes a steely glow, as in the grip of sheer masturbation.

"We have purchased up the entire approaches and Hall of Residence of early Dylan," he went on, grinding his teeth and pounding his palm, "and converted it into a permanent exhibition pavilion and promenade of Dylan's boyhood muse of paradise, Xana-dewi. People, sing your heart out!" He threw another switch which revealed a vista of Dylan at Collonus, Bangor, the World - an old man with bloody eyes, a classic tragedy of antique Llanelly! Such is it!

Now to the piece of resistance! My crafty Dominator reversed two levers, and I saw at once it uncovered the subtle conker heights of the new Imperium of Wales. He gripped me forcefully by the finger, and enunciated, "here are my Vestibules of Tremendousness, each apse, alcove, nave, colonnade, gazebo, billiard saloon and slave quarter owe their very existence to little old magnificent me! These are the external manifestations of the great I am; inside, my teeming brain-box boils and bubbles, the very heart and semen of my own personalised transparent cavern in there, the Mother of all Vestibules, man, eco me!" How he swelled up, how his bare chest quivered as he took out his Main Man baton and waved it at the ewe-eyed sheep in the voters' booths of Gwent. How far above all was he, how muscular yet delicate was his very stance! "And don't you ever forget it," he thundered to a close, overcome by saliva and slyness. "Yes," he asseverated on, "each worm-hole is a permanent sort of grave-rave, and all due to Wales the Brave, namely, me again! Like I said, didn't I? Yippie-aye a!"

I did not venture to contradict him as he introduced me to anther vast ante-chamber of Tremendousness, "bigger than the Reichstag one of mighty German Adolf!" he carolled, "Zeig heil! Ich bin my own do-it-yourself apotheosis, and do not you ever forget that either!" He grunted as he switched on the two-hundred or so huge swasticoed chandeliers. I stepped back in awe and gasped at what I saw. Ranged ahead of me stood what looked like a whole reserve series of new expansive Mexican cave entrances, fresh, well placed, full and rounded as hell, with the sound of captive Aztec humming-birds rising from gilded cages somewhere in the distance.

"Makes the hell-hole of the Boulevard Hall of the British Museum look like a bird box!" he trilled. "What a sight and sound for the old language of our drooling Taffo-thicko OAP's!" he snapped out, revealing his contempt for the ordinary man in Queens Gate Mews, and me as well. I had just celebrated my eighty-second birthday. First rate snake in the ass!

So this spread was it! I was at last confronted by the immense authentic quality of Wales's one thousand and one cultivated Arts Empires, for those curving thresholds were picked out in slab Victorian brown, the colour of the Great Stink, but then I saw the speckled brownages were spread out in delicious little mini-dollops like the larger picture; the whole site seemed that of an exploded mammoth, a vista of whirring brown fragments and turdy oscillations in every direction, from bored hole to bored hole, all with the unmistakable stamp of Wales, the puce dragon on a yellow background with untrimmed nails, belching out fake flames held aloft by the over bare-ing Saint Trinian blouses of Splott, with the elusive Prime of Primes, the arch-creator Dylan hisself, supping a quart at the Mythical Beast Pub in the posh Uplands of Swansea where the likes of him and me do dwell..."

"...I should think so - I don't think!" he muttered out loud, a pathetic sarcasm, now in the public domain, condemning him forever!

"Those rugby barrels of theirs up there, are always near-by," I uttered instead, "they have 'dear is my country to me' inscribed all over them!"

"One of my best lines," my frothing Literary Installator burbled out and motioned me onwards on this quite devastating tour of Greater Taffia, probing into each mind-blowing catacomb for his Sultan's sake – he felt so important, I could see that, and that was vital! - him chattering like a rat trying fuck a bat the while, while I bent my arm at his knee, clever boots me, O rara avis, I had convinced them all. The duped leader just prattled on and on like an old baby's rattle. The agent provocateur in me urged him on, "as for the disfrenchified voters of Wales and their awareness as just how awful they are, you might as well play a bassoon to an earthworm!" "Bravo!" he brayed and caloo-callayed for a while, then changed the subject to one closer to his ghastly heart - but then remained mute as a mirror. Well, I had to say something, so I said, "Well, you don't say."

"That's because I am yours truly tremendous!" he was tight-lipped back. "Look you on!" he urged and he switched on the automatic Dylan recording in all the accents of the world. The miraculous line was, peculiarly enough, "Do not go gentle into that good night...' first in a Welsh accent, then American, southern style, then Pawnee, Inouit, Patagonian, Galician, Breton, Mann and Jersey, same words, different music, each line a masterpiece. Then, my bouncy SS runic Leader suddenly shrieked and jumped backwards, staring out loud, for the voice had got out of control. These were its very words, a funny spoken at speed non-stop: "Now to DT's favourite-joke!-he-was-in-a-big palace-down-in-the-cellars - trap doors-in-the-floors - he lifts-one-up-and-looks – down-there-a-cellar-full-of-liquid- heifer-diarrhoea - with-all-the-worthies-of-Wales, up-to-their-lips–in-it, singing-in-one- breathless-chorus-their-new-national-anthem, "Please don't make a wave! Please don't make a wave!"

My Mentor stood lips aghast, hands shielding his shocking face, "What a repugnant even thought!" He gagged, staccato-like, "some malefactor from over the border, not DT's favourite joke. The opposite, it was Dylan's most hated funny, I knew him well, don't take any notice, you have a whole lifetime of servility ahead of you. Let's hit the road, man!"

We strolled over to the waiting stages. More gigantic Gothic letterings hung over each germ-free enter sign, notices of an inspirational kind, but softened by less threatening invocations like 'Arbeit Macht Frei,' and above the old Arts Cloaca Hole, 'abandon hope all ye who defecate here - ' to which my Interlocutor gave the distinguished outstretched caesarean salute "Cor, shag a bag, those was the days!" he gushed at his own nostalgia and penetrated the shadows. A sheet of A4 wrapped round his nose, he read it bellowing indignantly, "Palaces-and-mansions, like-stables-and-sties, can still be the haunt, of asses and flies!" Imbloodypossible!" he gnashed his teeth like a polar bear and shredded the blasphemy with his grimy paws. He finally ignored it and passed inside to the next concavity.

I made out at once out a hundred sample cases with toys of lead, decked out in gorgeous pretend-costumes just like my Guide-Deviser's as a Druid. They stood proudly outside replicas of the most decent places of Wales to stay at, like the spot over which the Welsh Arts Cloaca had once squatted, the agate corridors of the Underdone Assembly, the Poets' Teen Latrines, and the sweeping banisters of the Theologium Collegium of Lampeterium where so many of us learned to wank and pray. I noted with awe how my Marvellous Mentor juggled these outstanding figures about, so he could be top gun of every historic champion as he was so moved. Being Honorary Colonel of the Cenotaph Regiment of the Dead was not enough and he promoted himself up as Otto von Valhalla, Boss of all SS Volk,

Reichtag, Germania, the World. Then he gave one little leap of sphincter-like pleasure, and plunged into a short blunt black corridor leading to the inner lecture halls of the Royal Society of Royal Societies. He was there, ape-like Speaker now of the disorderly Arse of Commons, propelling me yet upwards until we rounded a nicotined corner and confronted, for me, a definite odd sight - in the demi-darkness sat a hunched–up figure on a rush-bottomed chair, and that figure was clinging to the belching bubbling boiler of the central heating system, keeping his tootsies warm and his writing finger full of throbbing hot Welsh monometer expletives, just like that, and, I tell you, that braveheart of a bard was scribbling like mad on a school exercise book lots of highly great and original poems, 'Do not go... rage, rage... in my craft,' they were all there already, I could see over his shoulder. "There," commented the Leader, in very undertones, "is here, where Dylan wrote his verse in deep midwinter. He never fell off that chair. And the waste-paper basket was never wasted, such was the fairy fluency of his cerebellums. Now, we have this whole scene in replica alabaster, the Boiler Poet Scene, it's called, it's proving a great little seller too, the humbleness of him appeals to all benighted humanity outside us, I'd say. I'll get a set for you, half price, don't you worry. But there are other choice choices too. Look, the Dylan in posture series, Dylan puking, retching, honking, flicking ink, jerkin', burpin, spluttering, peeing into the sands of time, all hand-painted ; here, eating jelly-babies while reading school-boy detective yarns; more Dylan pix here, saluting me, signing my books for me, a rare distinction there, and look, old Mr President Carter's changed the US flag for Dylan, to - 'E pluribus, ME!", the 'me' being 'me' of course. Voila then, a mere selection of the Beatitudues of Wales in the Dylanosphere, a showcase for the outer reaches of the cosmos!" He paused. "I have prepared this box for you." He gave me it officially, and in it went into my back-pack quite openly and I read it out, "Dylan-is-shaving-now, lather on his-chin, the-razor-rasping, the-furious strokes, the eyes bathed in alcohol, the flushed cheeks soaked in beer, the guttural

28

muttering, the wet head full of horrors, his mirror reflects yet cannot hold the frightful apparition of a mortal brother..."

"Never go on"! he yelled turbulently.

"...that's Jacques Chessex!" I broke out," I'd recognise him a mile upwind among the vines."

"Disgusting outburst whatever the cost!" said my now unsentimental Firing Squad Addict, "toss that Swiss garbage aside in a heap."

"But he won the Prix Goncourt with it once upon a time!" I stood up for my principles, however brave, "the first non-Frenchman ever to win that cordon bleu trophy."

"Fackin bit of froggy tinsel! Fackin' tripehound!" he belched voluminously, "god help the triple agent when I catch up with him. But now come and see some proper fame!" He darted down a side-tunnel, marked "Fans!" Before me again up-rose the whole of St Trinian's girl Prefects, guys, swelling out like soiled blouses on a line - all under the jaundiced eyes of phosphorescent skies, I may add! So romantic!"

"God!" he simply shouted out of the blue, and plucked up a figurine and picked it, "Pig snot and cats piss, what is this again? Regard the bloody thing - a blasted Congo adulterated vegetarian pigmy, I do declare, with apple-eating cannibals of the East Indies, rotten to the core! With bits of fruity-tutti stuck on! Revolting! Off! Off! What presumption! How did they sneak in?"

"Never mind, " I riposted more verbiage to dispel his questioning glance – "fleshpots galore in these glaring ducal ponds, swan songs for pens, evaporation for ink, home of the disappeared I'd say. Hey, look at the Ayahtola Bin Dylans there waving their most recent trimeters, not a single Koran in sight! See, the entire population of *Under Milk Pudding*, in bloody gilt, gold lame, in..." he cut right across my penetrating consonants.

"*Our* personal uniforms!" he hissed, intensely outraged, "ours to wear out. How did they get them on in here? I'm pulling them all off, I'm putting them out beyond the Pale!" He rejected them in piles. "Hell, where from did they come? Nothing to do with you, is it!?"

29

"Never in a Satan of sinful Sundays!" I protested like a vampire teenager in heat.

"Fine, then! They belong only to the Cellar of Duff Mementoes!" He hurled the final offending items to the ground, and quite rightly too, pissed all over them.

"Now back to the brown purlieus of Dylan," he chimed in, and with one fell sweep across a map, pinned down the endless artistic dust-bowls of Wales in choice periods, "parishes and hundreds, Marcher Lords and Bastards, one thousand Chieftains of the Peak, so to speak, twenty two nation states, 69 Presidential Candidates, all singing like chains in the sea, ..." he smirked like a politician, satisfied with his marvellous quote - yes, he knew he was as humorous as the stars above. "A moveable feast day for me," he commented indicating some of Dylan's global fanatics on the screen, "note the Apache Recitation Warriors, the Zulu Impi Soneteers, with their yodelling lady-girl male matrons, the Blackfoot Spearwomen, the Maori Majorettes, swinging sexameters to a man, the entire Pawnee nation, experts in the dreaded trochee, all descendents of Geronimo, who could spot a mixed metaphor from the face of an Alpine glacier - Mr Humphries there, who took over from the great Capone, Chicago branch, specialist, in private of course, of the bra-wearing CIA Directors of the St David's day Massacre! How they all lay down their arms, and legs, for Dylan! This here was after Dylan's last Lecher Tour, long before he had those final 987 whiskies - I'm talking bottles, of course." Then I put in, I had to say something round about Dylan on his Thirtieth Birthday to the outer moons of Jupiter, else I was done for, "Creator of supernova orders of odes!" I proclaimed, "which rise out the crotch of perspiration over down by up there, the domestic boiler stance! And listen," I perorated, "buddy boy, those who came to scoff, remained to drink!" I ejaculated out with it at the end. My Gilded Praetorian, now heaped up with his chains of office, roared his approval and dragged me out, passing, as we went, a young boy reading classics. He chanted as we passed, "Peace-will-be-and-soul be free, Who February's stone takes up, Wise is he and serene will be, Who drinks for an Amethyst Cup!"

"The amethyst is a prophylactic against drunkenness," I hastened to add.

"Twice as loathsome!"" shot out my Censor, and flattened the academic lad with a top upper cut, "shit in a bin, it is no sin to have a taste for gin! Bollocks to the lot of them!" and he barrelled us into another green and pleasant cavern, boasting Wales's chief architectural delights, a panorama of pebble-dash abortions, the very House on a Breakback of Rocks, the spine-tingling Writing Shed, the exquisite shape of the perfectly formed Boat House, with the dilapidated, owl-haunted, ivy-covered Castle Towers close by, where lived the all-Welsh novelist Richard Hughes - actually something true, at last. My Guide pointed at the chicken-coop, ticky-tacky torture-chambers, "see there, well, the Leader of the Opposition has sworn that by the end of this century every family will have a Shed of Excellence like that, in every front parlour, and those of higher civic rank like me, a boat house replica, however far from the sea it may be, and for high-flyers like me again, an entire Cwmdonkin Drive blown up out of all proportion so I can piss on it after a big binge, and a second mini one, done down, so it can fit into my toilet as I praise the great constructivist, Dylan, the Vitruvius of the block, with my trousers down about my balls and cock!"

"What was your prior name?" I asked the seedy, vulgar creep.

"Dame Armitage Shanks," he moued shyly, a beacon in all that gloom. "You'll find me every night at the Bible and Black Manhattan Cocktail Bar near the giant capstan."

"And the dread thing," I hurried on becoming more aware as I went on, "is that sets of these toys are the veritable mental core of the admirable Parochialees, and Mediocraties – and the 'crachach', the crach, or scabs, as our leaders are known in the English tongue, the bosses, the leading shafts of darkness of our government, forever clothed in their silver dungarees, castrator scissors always in hand..."

He was turning white with my transpirations, when I interjected in to stop him short, "hey, look at that flashing metaphor on the heights!" Look, above Liz Taylor. I spelled the words coming out, "I-am-a- Welshman-who-does-not live-in-his-own-country-because- I -still-want-to eat-and- drink!"

"That's not DT's again! Perish the thought!" my Sultan of Sarcasm growled and waved his index finger, indicating the more heroic replicas of DT's, "these are the real Dylans!" He cursed the lying lumiere up there again, "that most notorious trick-blinking is not for true believers right here in Splott," he yelped, "whoever is doing this to me is a dead hunted duck, I promise all our more bigoted clients. Tight-arsed. You'll see! But onwards now to something healthier and much more normal, our Awardees Awards. He rapidly condemned out of hand the furtive postal services and the nasty telegrams, "hey, you up there, you don't put me off with your dirty diatribes, you messengers from the dead, no escapegoats in my old pals act! Hey, Twm or Tom, you gotta move on! You see the Ambulatory gift packs here, brown envelopes crammed with crinkly greens, random as hell, especially for the last late artists. This is how the protocol works - Gareth, Dai, Luned, here passing by haplessly, see, are given 500 pounds in broad daylight, like that, like that, like that, simple hand outs, no receipts anywhere, just first names will do for Accounts, your wallets can rest easy - all awardees must be anonymous to keep it fair and free, - and tickets for the white-suited first night penguins, over down by the Opera pissoires. But how to control any buggering toy nay-sayers, those disgusting slips of the tongue, wretched denizens of used toilet paper, how!? Lo, see, over down by up there, my Berserker Grenadiers on the Barrack Square, down there my shocking troops on their flanks, the fearsome Ossificator Animators, one burp from you during the main aria means one touch of their deadly pacific wands, and you instantly become stone, mere stone, like in the ground, muddied, defuncted, deaded, goned. Plus our brave Lank Skirmisher Probers, our Ten Logistic Commandments over there, with their mortal Animators and Obfuscatorial Squads, to keep the climate calm, the cuckooes in their nests, the radicals down the plughole, and the Tremendous, US, always ahead. Yes, innovative events are never 'Everests' for me. Why, just one poem of my lot modified the frontiers of Albania forever - that was due mainly to the one thousandth and one Spenserian Stanza, never to be trifled with. But behind the pomp and power, Opera nose-dived, for example, but my recently impressed Rock Re-animators moved in and the rot moved out, bloody vagabond-vanguards, the long-haired, tennis-shoe pervert wearers, down with their obscene 'e' mails– I have the potency to reduce them to the condition of reddish terracotta twerps! And I would remind you," there was no blocking his muddy stream, "that it is humiliating for a man of my standing to put a mouse on trial for manslaughter..."

"...no, it is not!" I finished for him. He stood, his whole body agape, ears cocked for the faint voices, tenor and bass, floating over the surges of the sea. "Please don't make a ..."

"...never! Cut that out forever!" he went on bended knee and covered his ears. "That's not just an order, it's do or die!"

The anthem hovered a moment or two in the air like a sick helicopter. My Mentor sprang about, giving ordures to down below.

"Throw in the Ossificators en masse!" my still grotty batty eminence grise trumpeted, and in a second the lead figurines froze even more solidly and went still.

"There they go, the stiffs," he carolled, "they will be dispatched to the Carousel of Agony at dawn and tortured back to life in the hideous Memory of Nightmare Arcades, the tomb of the Liberties of Wales!"

God, he looked so bloody in the limelight, I have to say, but he seemed to be drawing to some kind of conclusion. Overall, in spite of bureaucratic excesses and blotting paper landslides, I was happy to be a witness to so many familiar strange phenomena - the awesome profile of the lava-bread of Wales, for example, still more elevated, still more bronzed, and so much more tomorrow, and all bear the hue of dew on a bog in smog on her face, Mam-Cymru's to a 't', – bravo Mammo!" Well, in spite of snipings, metal and mental, expulsions and poison gas attempts, it was nice to know I'd had a glimpse of the true Taffucks of life, however worrisome. 'Twas the overall tremendousnesses of it wot done it - the Mexican cave entrances, the inky yellowing banners, the greyish rigid figurines set in concrete, the handsome brown envelopes, the silly jejune Gueveras, the rancid home-grown voters cast aside, the smart post-cards of Offa's Dyke, the Hadrian's Wall of Wales, keeping all other opinions out forever. But I saw him peering around, smelling out the turncoat deadly-nightshade Trotsky-Quisling. Who was it really who had fucked up the malodorous jamboree of the glorious, multifarious Dylan centenary Celebrations announced in The Western Mail? I saw the question writ across his veined orbs. We now stood in mutual suspicious valedictory suspense on the suspension bridge. I pointed out the howgreens of my nation over there and admitted my guilt, open as a Venus fly-trap for a dunce to drop into! It did. His face was immediately wreathed with viciousness and he glared at me with his expression, "so you are the two-faced flapping labial back-slider, the crimson stab in the back as well - the Indian in the woodpile!?" he asserted agressively, aside on every side, "Twm the toilet tissue traitor all along! I told them in Cardiff to fart you in the opposite direction, just in case, but they would not listen. And you have been opening my postscripts, I can tell by your quotations, I have I hit the nipple on the ripple, am I right?" He pointed with sharpened eyes and yelled over the sand-bars far below, "Aux Armes, Aux Armes, mes braves, on parade, full battle order, my Obscurantists, Obfuscators, Berserkers, Nitpickers, Ossicators and tall-in-the-saddle security skirmishers, gold pilferers, false prophets, hangers on, scrap iron hunters, marvellous mayoralties, all tremendous sods of the capital's Splott machine, now, I urge you like mad, all unite under the banner of the Ales of Wales, in the White Towers, never to allow another alien miscreant-emigrate like this peasant penny-whistle-blower Twm the Useless, herein or in there."

"Yes," I sang out, back, "the people of Wales will one day definitely comprehend all the brown droppings of Splott Hall, their rich greed blazoned on every bank statement, and all its foregoing, it will out! So for now, my Guardian Pimp of all Ordures, my belle Dame Armitage, Queen of the U Bends, in your typical ghastly Poet Centenary Year, hail and fuck off!"

He turned puce and marched off, shuffling nevertheless. His dim words echoed across the usual Channel, dead as toe-nail parings. His day was done OK, but not his new anthem and the coming waves! And the land of my Fathers was still over by there, just like me! Staring hard again at Wales, the final vision came to me:

'My dream is done, my agony spent,
Old Tom Tell Truth for you was meant,
So take Twm's part, truth has no end,
And learn the ways of the heart.'

Ivor Thespis (Obit.)

Take my cousin Ivor Thespis, a barrel-chested pacifist, fine-featured nationalist, speaker of the ancient Welsh tongue, thunderous basso profundo, most tuneful nevertheless, also known as 'the Cardie ram', a non-stopper; friend of the benevolent Boatman, well known to Groundsmen everywhere, always receptive to the Fading of the Day, with good humour, accept him, quite mad or eminently sane, all the while winning every gold medal going at the eisteddfodau, for bass and baritone indeed; double first in physics and maths from Aberystwyth University, the highest score ever, was at once head-hunted by the British Atomic Commission and inducted into the deadly secret Harwell plant, which Ivor christened 'the Poisoned Eden of Lloegre' - all splendid, of course - except for one minor obstacle - five girl-friends, each for one night of the week, Sat and Sun for singing, but that was not enough, the singing I mean.

Well, one day Ivor leaves work from the lethal labs of Harwell, and sleeps around very much, and misplaces his briefcase with all the up-to-date heavy water blue-prints, a gift to all enemies of whatever hue. Red emergency alert! - the suited snoops were out like forests on the move. How they searched, all his girlfriends on top, and finally came up with the briefcase, found under the bed of Friday's floozie, next to the piss-pot (they had them in those days!)

The full Commission gave evidence, Ivor had signed the Official Secrets Act after all, but the atomic ingredient remained under lock and key. However, Ivor gave the final message to the Bench: "Listen, m'Lud, I have a few words for the rest of the world – wars, including nuclear standoffs, should be fought only by old men like yourself, for it is your jealousies which cause wars, and all the while the flesh of one little finger of yours was considered more precious than all the millions of gallons of blood spilled on Flanders field and in every other broken shire. Furthermore, the ordinary troop in the street has to fight for those who are never in the fray - you white-haired wreckers, you!

However, I do agree with conscription, but only for those between 45 and 80. Let the oldies have the wars and youth the peace!" he repeated to me on the steps outside the government's loyal courts of Justice, "Do not worry," he went on, "we are all born into rags and ruins. 'And how does that help?' you might ask. Well, I have no fuckin' idea. But off I go now, I have five nights of arias and arousels to make." He strode off singing Boris Goudonov all the way. (Special Branch subsequently trailed him for twenty years to this very day without finding a single false chord.) Well, after his five farewell nights of huffing and puffing, he cycled to Sadler's Wells and passed the audition.

He ended up on the stage of Munich's State Opera, still uncrowned Prince of the basso profundos, beloved and believed by all, never unhappy in death, a most sane, lively and melodious cousin alright! Ten out of ten, Ivor! Take to him too, please!

The Strange Adventures of Demetrius Jones (2)

I awoke with a start. I knew exactly where I was, although I had no map of my Gallic Odysseys. I, Demetrius Jones, soldier by misfortune, swear this is true. That noise again disturbing my slumbers, a kind of rustling and panting in the undergrowth. And again! What was it? A pale shaft of moonlight bathed the waters of the mighty river Rhone as it rushed past me, sparkles glinting on the mini-waves, not twenty yards from my little encampment. The rain had stopped, leaving a damp ghastly twilight over the whole scene. I was sitting up on my military ground-sheet with my back-pack as pillow, the hitch-hikers essential equipment, comfy but now just a bit discomfiting. There again. A huge shadow within the shadows seemed to detach itself from the bushes and spread itself over my space. I froze! No, it couldn't be! I could make it out now, a four-legged creature with a huge gaping gargoyle's dog's head, orbs blazing, muzzle flecked with froth. From the shades, the same rustling panting sounds, as two other identical beasts slunk out and joined their companion in blood. The identical trio now sat side by side, slavering in the silvery gloom like some beasts escaped from an invisible caravanserai of wild polecats, tusked boars, and performing elephants to steal the show. The three beasts remained seated still as stone two yards from my feet, looking fixedly over at the other bank. I saw their fur was blanched white, their legs and tails tipped with red, their eyes now changed to raw as after weeping. In unison, they suddenly threw back their heads and howled at the moon, a most unearthly salutation! Shit and damnation, I froze again, yes, it was, the sounds of the Hounds of Annwn, the Guardians of Hellgate! Had I been appointed the prey, the next to go? Were they after me? But without turning their hideous dripping muzzles, or giving a single look in my direction, they arose as one and loped down the reed-covered bank and sank without a splash, melting into the waves, leaving not a ripple behind. Was it a waking vision, a fearful dream, a visitation from the infernal regions. Why had they called? Did they have a message for me? Why had they left without a sign? A demon card? A curse? I would never have imagined the ferocious Celtic Familiars of Death would have visited this peaceful place of waters and greenery – and me! I mulled it over until I realized I would never find an answer. I rolled up my possessions and clambered to the safety of the track above, leading to the main road. I watched the horizon rise until the black and rosy dawn restored a degree of humour, irony and quiet to my spirits. The images faded as I stretched my limbs ready for another day's hike. After thirty minutes of brisk walking along the cracked, worn highway, I stumbled across a milestone in the long grass of the verge, 'Vers le Nord,' it proclaimed, and since this was where I wanted to go, I took that route. To make no point at all, I sat on the stone, a reminder of better days. It was then I heard the soft footfalls behind me. If I hadn't turned, the individual I beheld would now have been at my side. He was about my height but nothing like my rugby weight, twelve stone. He was fifty or so with the sharp features of a ferret's, eyes narrowed to slits with a sly sidelong look. One side of his face was decorated with a criss-cross of old scars. He was wearing the obligatory blue workers' jacket, with a striped naval T shirt, flared corduroy trousers, dusty shoes worn down at the heel. His black beret was pulled down one side so that most of his head was concealed. He was evidently a tramp or thief of some sort, possibly on the run, considering the remoteness of the place. What had the Hounds of Annwn prepared me for now? A distant baying of dogs filtered through the trees. Christ, were those beasts still around?! The man held up his hand, and with fake bonhomie, sang out, "Bonjour, m'sier," and laughed. "Dogs in trees. Your dogs? "I nodded. "Ou va tu?" obviously a testing question. I was broad and burly, possibly too much for a physical assault. "Je vais ..." I replied in school French, and gestured vaguely northwards. "...Lyons, excellent," he swiftly replied," moi aussi." He now stared pointedly at my watch, an army multiple-dialled time-

39

piece, heavy as lead but it had served me well on my lost labyrinthine journeyings. "Good shop in Lyons," he went on in French pigeon, "give good money. Give watch, I see you at big post office, restante place, good price..." To emphasize his offer, took out a pocket knife, flicked it open and began paring his finger-nails. I reacted without thinking. I had a vision of my mother, at dinner table, I saw myself in full flood, flourishing my knife about. In a trice, my mother had waved one hand above my head, evidently to distract me, at the same time, gripping the muscle between my forefinger and thumb. At once I felt an excruciating numbness in the palm of my hand, I could not move it. With a quick twist, the handle was in her hand. She waved it under my nose, no nonsense from this top P.E. and Tai Kwondo practioner. "Now..." she practised the movements with me. "But don't ever play about with knives," she concluded," you might get hurt," and handed the knife back to me. In a second, I had reacted, one wave of the hand, one twist, and the knife was in my hand. The Matelot took a step back in alarm and astonishment, the knife was pointing directly at his belly. Like my old Ma, I abruptly reversed the point, snapped the blade shut, and handed it back to him, "ne joue pas avec les couteaux, ca pourrait etre dangereux." The man paused, pointing shakenly at the distant baying in the woods. Now I saw he was actually afraid - of the beasts or of me, I will never know. He accepted the weapon cautiously, glancing sideways away from me. I shooed him off as if a pup had messed my boots. He retreated backwards down the road, keeping a slant eye on me. Again, like my Ma, I put my hands on my hips, did the shooing motion and took a step towards him. He accelerated to the bend in the road and disappeared, certain, it seemed, he had just encountered a lunatic knife-grinder with hidden hunting dogs as back up. This soldier, thought I, salutes his Ma! But what would she have done about the Hounds?

I resumed my trek northwards. I heard the familiar sounds of a revving car behind me. I turned and was nearly run down by a silent vast blue Cadillac saloon. It accelerated past me continued for a minute or two then ground to a halt. I approached the front door. I could hear hill-billy music which the driver turned off as soon as she had me in her sights. She was female alright, craning her neck to see me, she seemed reassured and wheeled down the window. "Sorry. Which way you going?" a pleasant if fruity voice, mid-Atlantic, definitely not American, with dark glasses, tilted down so she could see me, grey-blond hair, about 40 or so, dressed in a loose T shirt and shorts. By her side laughed a girl, evidently her daughter, the similarity of their laughter was quite charming. "Hi!" she trilled and grinned in a very friendly way. Was she actually trying to come on to me? Impossible! The interior car light shone down onto her skin, giving it an inviting erotic glow. About 19, in T shirt, too, with the Chrysler building aloft, mini-skirt, thrusting breasts, bulging puppy fat body, well shaped, with definite promise of prime sexual hi-jinks. Don't know why, but I can always tell. "I'm going northwards, Lyons." I said.

"So are we! Hop in, plenty of room." He slid into the capacious seat, as indicated. The interior was vast, enough for a dozen people. The girl reached over and threw my pack into the back. "I'm Marilyn," she laughed, "get the name, Monroe," and dug me playfully in the ribs, "Hop in. Mom was so bored, she wanted someone else to talk to. Such vile weather, you can't see your hand in front of your ass. Play on Mom." To my enormous surprise, the divine tones of Mozart's Violin concerto in A came on. Marilyn switched it off. "We all gotta talk now," she declared. Mom put the purring automobile into gear and moved off smoothly. Hey, thought Demetrius, am I lucky or something, were the fates being propitious? Anything, as long as it wasn't those bloody hounds. I noticed the air conditioning was cooling me down. Marilyn immediately turned it up.

"You going to Paris?" asked Marilyn.

"Got to catch a train."

"You know Paris?"

"We're going to call you 'Rock'" put in Mom "because you look like him."

41

"OK with me," laughed the new 'Rock'.

"You even move like him," added Marilyn.

"Show him, honey" Mom urged, "you know."

The sun intermittently shone down through the windscreen on two pairs of bare stretched thighs, one on the far side, the other much too close to me for comfort. Marilyn reached up to the Chrysler picture and pulled up the T shirt. Her breasts bulged out, drooping yet taut. 'Rock' felt his prick harden, even more so as she reached down and began to caress his rapidly growing friendly monster.

"Let me look," she cooed, giggling and flushed, wriggling down on the plush seat.

"We're on the autoroute now." Mom interjected, pulling into the main lane, "on our way, straight through, go on Honey!" Honey slid off the seat until she was kneeling on the car mat, unzipping my shorts the while. She thrust her wet muzzle into my gaping flies and began licking rapidly, sucking on my risen prick, gasping more by the second. 'Rock' swore that she was already having a great come. He noticed Mom had turned on the air system even higher, and soon all three of us were gasping in the heat. 'Rock' could no longer hold back and came copiously over Marilyn's face and lips, the spunk hanging there in great suspended drools. From the front came Mom's sexy cheer. 'Rock' saw she was watching it all in the rear view mirror. Marilyn, showing no remorse, merely paused, whipping off her shorts and black panties, kept up the fleshy sucking until I was hard again. My erect prick was swivelled, rubbed, bounced inside the tight flesh of her pink vag until he galloped irresistibly into a spunk-laden orgasm. More cheers from Mom in the front. 'Rock' suddenly gasped, God, it was getting hot as an oven. I saw Marilyn was affected too, she climbed off the floor and fell into my arms, her mouth insistently sucking on my nipples. I floated off as on a cloud, pleasured and relaxed, still wondering from on high what in the hell was going on. Mom switched on the radio again. To my astonishment, I heard the opening bars of 'Lark Ascending' until it disappeared out of sight and sound. Silence. I saw that Marilyn had actually fallen asleep. I dozed off with her. I awoke abruptly, as from a long dream, a wide sleep, the wipers sweeping onwards. How long had I been sleeping, I had no idea. Where were the girls? I blinked and felt that familiar glow in my crotch and found I was dying for more. I looked around. The girls had stopped at a petrol station. Mom and Marilyn were standing by the pump Attendant, laughing loudly. Mom finished, paid the Attendant and walked back to the car. They waved and cheered when they saw their 'Rock' peering through the side window. To my surprise, Marilyn jingled the car keys and proceeded to get into the driving seat. As if on cue, Mom immediately pushed me onto the back seats, deftly stripped off my shorts and began giving the same lingual treatment Marilyn had just meted out, tearing off her clothes the while. Her build was, magnificent, bundles of yielding, quivering flesh, her breasts twice the size of Marilyn's, bounded up and down slapping my belly as she sucked. I saw I had not done her justice – she was a natural blond, and luxurious with it, up to her belly button. Her orgasm, not surprisingly, was a replica of her daughter's – short yelps of intense pleasure prolonged for minutes after the apex, very mutually exciting. I withdrew my electric stick, now pink at the head after all the gravitational thrustings, and slumped back, tousled and sweating, Mom licked away, with M's grinning lecherous face still urging her on. Her face blurred for a moment, then vanished. After a long blank space or dark void, the discordant uncontrollable barking of terriers on the radio distorted the air. I covered my ears. "Please, please switch it off," I begged. "So, you're awake at last," put in Marilyn, "we missed you." Both burst into suggestive laughter. "It's just a novelty disc," explained Mom, "they are barking in chorus," successive single barks came from the radio. "And guess what they're singing!? 'Happy birthday to you...' with the unholy cacophony switched off, the two repeated the chorus a number of times, even more discordantly.

"No...," groaned I."

"Don't you like dogs?" demanded Mom.

43

"Not today, thanks."

"They're just goddam dogs."

"Not that lot! Shoot them. It's been a fabulous trip I'll never forget. Don't spoil it." The two ladies cheered in appreciation of the compliment and gave each other lotsa high fives. Marilyn jumped into the back seat, and buried her mouth into her Mom's crotch, searching again for her ideal of unguent heaven. Again came the swap. Mom pounced on her daughter, her daughter pounced back and together then went into 69 Laocoon wrestling positions non-stop, until finally both lifted their heads, beaming and very pleased. Mom resumed her racing posture at the front and accelerated off the forecourt, scene of a classic sexual encounter. Meanwhile, I, Demetrius, wondered if this was really was of this globe or in some Land of Apples in the divine firmament 'Otherwhere,' with Eve, a place we all search for so sadly and so tenaciously for, a rare slice of peace and quiet. And was I, thus drenched in oils of vag, really speeding northwards through ruined nations to some kind of terminus in the sky. Well, it was true, I did have a train to catch but I didn't know about the other thing. Mom now suddenly gave a shout and pointed. Marilyn raised her juicy lips, licked and stared, transfixed through the thickening mist which had arrived but minutes before. What was passing now, going south, a seemingly endless convoy of military vehicles, three-ton Bedford lorries, 15 cwt trucks, self-propelled field cannon, Bren Gun Carriers, Dispatch Riders riding up and down the column, trying to keep order? The whole line resembled a metallic funeral cortege with all the participants, human and machine, going for scrap, the end game of all armies, I suppose. The girls began cheering and waving to the troops packed into the back of the trucks. Mom switched on. I heard 'Lark Descending...' Vaughan Williams?! Was my mind in terminal disorder? Then again, silence. What was going on?

"The troops - Daddy's men, I bet," said Marilyn.

"I almost recognise some of them," Mom said, licking her lips.

Each vehicle loomed out of the fog and passed with a watery

44

whoosh, as if taken out by an unseen earthquake into some dark endless tunnel.

"Bless you, Daddy O," Marilyn prayed fervently as the last troops sped by, "we're all coming soon!"

Mom displayed her liking for me again, glancing at my crotch in the mirror, but I was beyond either her, for a moment, and this Soldier by Misfortune, drained among the triangular bushes of lust, began, incredibly, to nod off. But - how about a real bloody Convoy? Where in the hell was it really going, north and east OK, but south, that was where the daisies grew, far from Depot Battalions? And why? Again, I admitted to myself that I did not rightly know. Was it Little Prince oblivion creeping up on me one more time. Mom's shout seemed to come hours later from a long distance, "Look!" We're getting there!" She pointed at the outlines of long admin buildings, wide parking areas, unloading bays and rail heads with coaches poking out from the sheds and an improvised if vast front entrance. Military signposts appeared at every turn and on every building. The RTO, where was it? The Railway Transport Office, strictly for the military of all allied nations, what a laugh! The small newly enlarged station of the village of Versailles now served all traffic going to the East and returning from the East, the freshly laid road was temporary, the only living artery to the battered bastards of Berlin – such as myself!

"There's the Staff Car Park,' cried Mom, pointing through the murk. "No more 'Rock' in this Cadillac I'm afraid."

"Office just over there. Just as Daddy said. Stop, Mom!!" Mom came to an abrupt halt by a new bus stop, 'Staff Cars Only' proclaimed a notice.

"We're coming Daddy-O," Marilyn carolled.

"If I may ask," said I, put off by this giggling look for-the-silver-lining approach to life but "who in the hell is this Daddy-O?"

"He who always gets there ahead of us, "replied Mom, nodding wisely.

"He who is around every corner," added Marilyn.

45

"But what's happened to our glorious fighting men? Station's practically empty."

"They are packed together like human beings, in those very carriages over there. It's always the same. Out now!" ordered Mom. Marilyn grabbed my back pack and threw it onto the pavement.

"Thanks, but let's keep in touch, shall we?" I said, thinking of the hot crotch circus.

"And now tell the nice boy your real name, Princess?"

Marilyn came over all coy with moist poutings and fluttering of eyelashes.

"Princess...??" encouraged Mom.

"...the princess, she, me! who-leaves-no-hole-unfilled-Smith! They went off into peals of identical laughter.

"Yes, now how old do you think the Princess is?" asked Mom.

"No idea, I mean, what's your point?" I was getting a little narked by all these unnecessary enigmas.

"How old are you, Princess?"

"Fourteen and a bit after next birthday," said the Princess casually caressing her crotch.

"There!" said Mom. They embraced and French-kissed right there on the pavement.

I shuddered at the revelation. Never mind randy old Mom, those dates of the Princess meant she was a minor, under age, and I'd just committed numerous sex acts on her. One word from Mom to the MP's patrolling the entrance and I was one last fried carrot. Mom and daughter-in-fornication waved to me, standing there, mouth open, done in. When I'd struggled into my back pack and looked up, the Cadillac had disappeared as wonderfully as it had first appeared.

I stood totally perplexed in the now lashing rain. Had it all really happened, the Matelot, Mom, Princess Marilyn, the glorious sex, the arrival on time due to daddy-O? The Larks going up and down on the radio? And who was actually meeting the game duo? A sugar Daddy Brigadier, a visiting democratic congressman who'd lent his car to them for the weekend, a petrol

46

Attendant, Fate? A travelling mother and daughter lesbian act, a free copulation package, all on the menu? I give up, I swore to myself and moved on. I wandered over to the RTO's Office, bent and flummoxed, still raw in the crotch area, trying to work out the turmoil boiling in my brain.

The trains were drawn up in rows, all sealed and ready to go as the Russians had directed. I saw the whole concourse was practically deserted except for the high numbers of MP's marching around in pairs, looking for trouble. I spotted the ROT, an office on the second floor, from which there was a view of all that went on. That at least had not changed. I pushed open the door. To my surprise, the room was empty except for the Major, in full fighting gear, his Webley 45 hanging in its holster from his belt, at his desk, signing piles of forms. The shelves behind him were for officers to park their gear when they were on leave. There was only one hold-all left. The Major glared at Demetrius.

"So it's bloody Mr Jones. Where in hell have you been? You're late!"

"But Sir, I've got until tomorrow, the twenty second, in fact."

"That's no fact, Mr Jones. Look at my tawdry calendar on the wall there. What does it say? Berlin train: departure, 22nd, 20,00 hours, that is, in ten minutes time."

"But, sir..." I managed.

" ...but me no buts, I was about to sign your AWOL order, Absent without Leave. With this flap on, you would have been cashiered, for cowardice in face of the enemy. Wake up!" He threw the last hold-all at Demetrius. 'Now put on your uniform, all badges of rank on display with regimental insignias, as per usual. I'm IC this Train, and if they've appointed me Commandant, they must be in real trouble. Are you listening? What is the matter with you?"

"I just got a bit lost, sir."

"Lost? Don't tell me you travelled on foot through half of France without a map?!"

"I'd be a fried carrot, sir."

"Exactly! And do not forget your bootlaces. For God's sake,

hurry, Mr Jones, and I've got a signal here for you, your orders, I'll explain on the way, come on!" He grabbed a charged clipboard and marched out. "Come on! And for God's sake wake up, Mr Jones!!"

All I could think of at that moment was that someone had robbed me of twenty-four hours of my precious lifespan, without warning. What footpad was it? Which miscreant? Which sod? - the Hounds, the Matelot, the Staff courtezans, the slut Luck? Someone would have to make up the difference, tho I was not quite sure who. As usual.

I clattered behind the Major as we made our way to the train, an ancient relic from the now old conflict which nobody thought of changing, for after all, such machines had won the war. The Allied chariot had worked up a head of steam which billowed over the platform. Like me, 'Mr Jones,' the magnificent machine awaited the orders of the military donkey.

"You're to meet some convoy or other, at the ruined Bahnof of Tempelhof, red cross stuff, and lead it to HQ, which has now moved."

"To where?"

"God knows, they say under the spectator seating of the 1936 Olympic swimming pool, just ignore it if you think it's loony. On the other hand, that may not be accurate at all, and HQ is nowhere near there. Just exercise your initiative. Ah, here we are." He mounted the steps to the last coach in the convoy, ten supply coaches for the officers and five for 'personnel,' cattle trucks for the troops. It was a victorious French train. The windows were sealed with black-out material.

"Get settled in, and do not ask any more stupid questions."

"What is it really about, sir?"

"Who knows what any flap's about. A flap's a flap! Something about the natives revolting. Ignore it. On the right!" he shouted as I mounted the steps. He shoved the door open and was greeted with the gaping, slavering jaws and manic barking of three huge dogs in wooden cages. They howled all the more when they saw me, I backed out rapidly, slamming the door, but not before I had identified the red markings on ears and paws. Annwn was never far away.

"I said the door on the right, you idiot."

"Why those bloody animals?" I shouted back

"Sniffer dogs. For the likes of you! Soviets insist on it." Carry on, Mr Jones." He turned and faded into the smoke.

I tentatively opened the door to the right and was promptly confronted by a waiter straight out of Monmartre, greasy hair combed flat, a little black waistcoat, buttoned up, apron tied around his waist, napkin over one arm, an extremely ingratiating smile.

"Is Monsieur on Staff?" he asked politely.

"You saw, I'm with the Major."

"You wish for dinner, mon Lieutenant?"

"I do, monsieur," the reciprical 'sir' had done the trick.

"Follow me please, sir."

He ushered me to a freshly laid table. In fact, all the tables were laid immaculately. "It's the war, sir," he said, following my glance at the empty places, "The officers are at a conference."

"Action stations, then!" I was inordinately hungry after all the recent sexual Laocoon wrappings and wrestlings, and needed to recover from the fright in the goods wagon.

"I recommend the Chef's coq-au-vin, sir"

"Then that'll do the trick, monsieur." The Waiter bowed and hurried off.

"'Cockeril against the wine,' I translated. So much for the elegancies of the French language!

I settled into the comfortable plush seat. At last, I thought, a secure berth to mull it all over and to try to work out what was happening to my life, and the weird events of the last few days, in which one day had gone missing - and I still had not found any satisfactory explanation. As for being in time for the train, given the frantic antics of the ladies and the menaces of the Matelot, that really was miraculous. I had been on the brink of disgrace although I had never known it. Ignorance was bliss definitely on this occasion! And now a bit of real French chicken!

The Waiter was at my elbow in an instant, serving the chicken portion in its shiny sauce, tons of petty pois followed, and crisp 'French fries,' plus a full bottle of sparking white wine, poured out for the instant into my waiting glass. What a lovely fruity after taste! I cut a portion and forked it into my mouth. I chewed just once and stopped. This was surely the most delicious leg and wing I had ever tasted. The meat slipped off the bone disintegrating deliciously on my palate. I requested more of this superb French locomotive delicacy, another real novelty had arrived in my life. I had eaten three portions by the time I had finished and felt that no explanation was need for my past life at all.

The coffee failed to keep me awake. I asked the Waiter to compliment the Chef and justly, for this highly satisfied lowly Allied Officer was already drowsing, a happy smile on his face. In a second, I had nodded off, well on the way to another fine slumber.

As from deep space, the train jerked me awake. I dimly remembered the waiter helping me to my bunk. I could now hear footsteps crunching outside my window. I got up and quickly dressed. There was commotion now, with orders and counter orders coming from the corridor. I opened the door. The Major was just outside, bellowing ignored instructions at a crowd of bewildered officers.

"So there you are," he fulminated, "we've stopped short of the platform of the Bahnhoff. Well, don't just stand there, you've got your orders!"

"But, sir, it sounds very confusing. Shouldn't we wait until we know what's going on?" The Major, almost beside himself with fear and anger, seized my arm and dragged me to the door of the carriage, and pointed ahead into the dim light.

"Go along the track until you come to the platform. Your convoy should be waiting at the bottom of the steps of the station. Well, go on, that's an order!"

"Sir, I think it would be better if we waited."

50

"You insubordinate cretin, get going, yes, you, don't you worry we know what you are, you lecherous glutton, get going now, I am giving you an order before the MP's catch up with you." At the words 'MP' I did not hesitate, I jumped down and ran along the track, I noticed no sounds came from the Other Ranks' carriages, weren't they under orders as well? but in the distance, close to the Bahnhoff, I heard a burst of flat hissing machine gun fire - the old, killing Wehrmacht Schmeisser, followed by the hard huge smack and explosive bang – as an old Soviet tank the T34 came into action. The Soviet military had long discarded their obsolete weaponry, only the East German Police, the Stazi still used them - which all meant that the natives were armed and dangerous tonight. Firing had broken out and filled the air in the streets close by. I heard shouting from the train and made out the Major on the track, yelling at the top of his voice. Before I could hear what was happening, from behind the Major rushed three snarling, gaping hounds going like the clappers, this time accoutred for war, spiked collars round their necks. They made a b-line for me. I stood still, why run? - they had me where they wanted, alone and unarmed. When they were but a foot from me, they suddenly divided into two. I could see their distinctive markings, the blood-red weeping eyes, they bounded past me. I could hear their paws scrabbling down the rusting rail steps, and then they were gone, the bleeding Hounds of Annwn! What damn next?! I looked over the rail, thank God! my favourite Corporal Mathews was at the smashed entrance gesticulating wildly up at me. He was at the head of four sagging 15 cwts vehicles, loaded up to their axles. Good for my best NCO! He'd done the pick up! We could be off immediately! Bloody great! I ran down the steps. "Well done, Corporal!"" The Corp acknowledged me with a smart salute. "I think we should move on, sir, shooting's broken out." To emphasize the point, a ricochet whined just below my left ear. A cold thrill went down my spine. This was not as I had expected.

"But, Sir, I don't know the way from here. I was told to wait for your orders!"

"Reverse here, and aim to drive through those builders'

51

bollards."

"But sir, there's no road the other side."

"There is farther up, we'll take the minor roads, less damaged."

"Are you sure, sir?"

"You're getting as bad as me, Corp. There is a road there and there is a house there where I shag my girlfriend every Sunday afternoon."

"Right, sir!"

I looked around at the devastation. "You didn't see any dogs, did you?"

"Dogs, sir...?"

A thunderous roar came from the barrel of the T34 in the next street, the shell hit the corner of the residential building next to the Bahnoff and the entire walls of the apartment block collapsed with a smoky roar. More small arms firing broke out.

"A mad zoo! Mount up, Corp, that's enough for me."

"Me too, sir!"

Thank you, fucking Fate, you whore, you've landed me right in the shit up to my neck in the opening shots of the bloody East German Uprising!

Enjoy the Film...

I t was quite a popular film, but not so popular that it filled the auditorium - 'Welcome Home' something for all the family, something uplifting, something to distract him from the daily grind, anything in fact. He had decided to go to the midday showing, on foot. Few people would sacrifice their lunch hour, for such a film at such a time. The auditorium, he calculated, would be half empty at least, with a minimum of choc-ice slurping and pop-corn popping. Should be just right.

Once inside he paused in the darkness, the trailers were still on. He noticed all the white-head OAP's around, a film trip for our oldies, how sweet, how decent, he thought, not too bad either for sound. The shifting whities were subdued, hunched over their sticks, well on the way into the Grim Reaper's arms, aware of it almost every second of the film, as he was also aware of the fact that a place had also been reserved for himself. So no woe. Just so.

He moved towards the invalid seat at the end behind the back row. He noticed an OAP sitting quietly in his wheelchair beside the fixed cinema seat, the one he always used. No matter. He had never been cautioned for sitting there, after all, he was old enough. He settled down to an hour and a half of moveable anodyne, without a crackle or a fart in sound or sight.

A head suddenly blocked his view of both audience and screen. It was the new Attendant, 'Sonia' writ large on her breast, determined to be as obstructive and officious as possible, as her very important position in the emporium allowed her to be, indeed, required her to be.

"Dammit, she's tracked me here," he thought. "What to do?"

"I'm sorry, sir..." she said, a real dose of oozing spite on her lips - there was a rustle all round, his fellow OAP's knew one of their kind was getting it, literally, in the ear - "...would you mind vacating this seat, sir, it is for Attendants and Invalids only."

He thought rapidly, "Look he said, I mean no offense but the seats are half empty, and the clientele, settled and comfy. Just look at them." That should do it - slight surprise but a composed, even a dignified response from a senior citizen.

"I'm sorry, sir," she replied, harsh and unabashed, "it's health and ..."

He decided on deception, "...look, I have just had a very difficult hip-replacement. I have to stick my leg out like this to relieve the pain. I can only do that from this seat. This is my first trip without my cane." At this point the ancient one next to him came to life, rattled his wheel-chair, sat up, spoke up too, indignant and ready to do battle with this overbearing Plaza Cinema official.

"You heard him," announced the disabled one so everyone could hear, "he's an invalid, like me, I've had the Op and know what it's like, mate. So leave off or I'll call the Manager." Sonia opened her mouth, then clamped it shut and retreated muttering towards the exit, followed by the hisses of the undefeated white brigade at the back.

"Silly fool of a cow," he whispered triumphantly, "thinks if you can't see it, you can't believe it. I just had a double hip-replacement, mate. Don't worry, my wife wheeled me in and she'll wheel me out. She's meeting me afterwards in our car. She's the District Nurse. She'll have a quick look at you, see you're OK, then we'll drive you home. Us 'cripples' have got to stick together, am I right? Now, mate, enjoy the film."

54

Get some in!

areth Jones, 2nd Lt, 62 Company RASC, Berlin, by the grace of God, Orderly Officer, was carrying out his last duty, the Dismounting of the Guard - all twelve of them. He had just finished the barracks inspection. Yes, every bed-space was clean and tidy, and the men at their posts, quiet and unassuming. Very odd. Never mind, in a few minutes when he next marched off the huge parade ground, it would be for the last time.

He gazed through an upper window of the vast building, monumental as a triumphal Arch, but neat as a pin inside and out. The main entrance boasted two huge oak doors, impregnable to any 'dirty commie infiltrator spies' as the paranoid GI garrison officers put it. Lofty, innocent poplars lined the spotless, endless square. This void was where all the VIP parades took place, from the holy Queen's Birthday to the deaths on VE Day. The towering five-storey monster, imposed its own will - only there were a few souls around who regarded it all as some kind of ungodly Teutonic Tower of Babel, a sick fantasy, for the edifice was the former living quarters of the Waffen SS, Liebstandarte Division, Bodyguard of Adolf Hitler.

This unique building-block of the black elite had been spared destruction for the comfort of a Supply Company of eighty men and twelve boy troops of the RASC Guard, and a single 2ND Lt. aged eighteen, who basically had nothing to do with the silly old Cold War just around the corner or a few Nazi inmates ten minutes drive away.

Gareth could hear the Drill Corporal's bellowing voice echoing from the distant Guard Room, "Parade, atten...shun! By the left - quick march!"

Gareth hurried down to meet them as they marched onto the parade ground. "Parade, halt!" the Corporal roared.

The squad smartly formed into two lines of six, rigid as pokers, tho' some with very peculiar smiles on their faces. Why not? Two hundred years ago, in the real world, he had known better and worse senses of humour. For the last time, he inspected his final Guard, cane under arm, cap on straight, with a calm detachment which also spelled 'farewell!' to the world at hand. He noted the slack figures and the bleary eyes of the men, but, as he saw, still smiling, and this after a night of pacing pointlessly up and down for hours – most peculiar.

But no more! Yes, this really was auf wiedersehn, and theirs too. "No charges, Corporal," he ordered. "Sir!" agreed the 'Corp.'

In all his time in the Company Gareth had never charged one troop for infringing any of the myriad, mad, petty regulations which had governed their lives. Thank God, he thought, I leave with a clean conscience and an immaculate bill of health - just.

He gazed at the last of the Guard. So young! The punch ups, thefts, drunkenesses, insubordination, dumb insolence, all ignored by Gareth until the regulations became unnoticeable, indeed. Gareth had actually flattened them out of existence. Yes, he had it worked out, *he* was armed and ridiculous he knew, but wars were caused by bunches of white-haired old men who were jealous of each other. Yes, put *them* in uniform and let *them* fight it out. Let conscription begin at forty-five, and let all youth be banned from ever serving in the bleeding forces of the old!

He caught a movement in the rear rank and saw a sheet from an army orders book flutter to the ground. At the same time, he thought he hear a low guffaw. He moved over and picked up the paper. He slowly smiled as he read the few words written there, "Get some in, Mr Jones!!" - a comment usually reserved for raw recruits and new arrivals with years of de-mob to look forward to. When he folded up the paper, still grinning, there came an abrupt, mounting cacophony from all sides - the windows of the five storeys of the former SS hell hole, were rattled open in one drill-like movement. This was followed by an explosion of hilarious shouted goodbyes, "get some ins!" by the dozen, comradely blessings at their best, followed by universal 'hurrahs' and a tidal waving of arms and berets.

"Squad, Present Arms!" yelled the Corporal above the

laughter and plaudits.

'What's this?' thought the blessed and rare Second Lieutenant Jones, the 'Present' was only for Senior Officers, such as Major Generals - not the lowest of the low, like Second Lieutenants! The heads of the entire company now stuck out of the window-frames, all sang one discordant, heart-warming , last chorus, "Get some time in Mr Jones! Get some in!" The Corporal gave his final order too, "Squad, dismiss!" The Guard marched off, saluting Mr Jones as they passed - they to the Guard Room, the Second Lieutenant to the Offiicers' Mess, well named, and the pleasant 62 Company, all 80 of them, back to their bed - spaces in the cavernous devil's den.

Thirty years later when he was looking through his life's mementoes, he discovered that in all his years in the military, the only memorial he had retained was the order paper with the words 'Get some in, Mr Jones!!' written on it, a precious document indeed. He wondered how many of his men had survived it, as he had - just. Yes, 'Get some in!' was absolutely right!

The End of Hannibal

Tom Byrne hurried down home from the Underground. Christ, even the slabs on the pavement seemed menacing. Everything gone wrong, his job, down the plughole, just because he'd shagged the manager's wife just once at that crazy office Xmas party or maybe because he couldn't fit in anywhere and was resistant to every make of computer. Those disabilities had now returned and with a vengeance.

They had arranged for his recent abrupt notice the day before. His wife had gone mad with disappointment and had refused to talk to him over meals, before and after too. He tripped over a crack in the paving, swore loudly and pressed onwards.

What would his wife do now? Thank God she was still at work. Would she really leave him? Surely wives didn't piss off just because of a shortage of bread. Why half his friends were in the same hole. Or because she thought there was no more fun in the house. Hell, what did she want? The Blue Danube playing all day? But damn, what if they were behind on the stinky Mortgage, down on the central heating, up on the overdraft, shiftless future no doubt, a hopeless CV all round , when all said and done. God, the grovelling job rounds again, something he had never learned to do in the last 32 years, what a life! Gutted, absolutely gutted.

He shoved open the garden gate and stamped towards the front door. On his left was the fence with the missing flat, damn, the bloody dog again finding a way through. His enemy, Hannibal, was a wild tempered Pembrokeshire corgi, a right royal hound with a right royal temper. For almost 10 years it had been at war with him. He had tried everything bar poison - noise pollution complaints to the council, neighbour conciliation exercises, pet management, all fruitless. He had even suggested moving the cast-iron antique railings on the far side of his neighbour's garden, they would have stopped a Panzer Tiger tank. Even his neighbour, Bill, had agreed, but the Council had cited railings of historic interest and the matter was dropped. But no, they remained in place and the furious dog, Hannibal never managed to tear a way through.

Hannibal was doddering now, but his hostility against Tom remained undiminished. As if roused by the thumps on the slabs of the drive, the canine mortal enemy sprang snarling into sight, darted through the open slat and made for Tom's unprotected ankle.

What a bleeding day!! He yelled out loud as he felt Hannibal's teeth nip his ankle bone. Then all his frustrations boiled up and appeared to dwell in his right boot. With all the desperation of utter hopelessness, he lashed out with all his strength. His toe-cap hit Hannibal under the chest with a sound of a balloon exploding.

The dog's whole body catapulted over the slatted hedge and hit the iron railings on the far side with a shocking smack. The body flopped down into the border, quivered a few times, then lay still as a stone.

Tom gaped. Was Hannibal dead!? His life's most deadly enemy, apart from the wife? God, he looked around, had his neighbour witnessed the end of Bill's beloved foul-tempered four-footer? He had to flee the bloody scene at once. He was sure and shockingly so that he had ended the life of his prime enemy, and all by accident. No one could blame him. It was a massive heart-attack, the poor doggy was snow-white practically.

He stood behind the front door in a turmoil. Was the hell hound really deported? He heard footsteps from the next drive. He opened the door a crack and peeked outside. It was then he heard the howl of grief, followed by wild gnashings of teeth and beating of breasts. His neighbour was on his knees before the inert corpse, weepings and wailings rising and falling. He attempted to hold the dead mutt in his arms.

Tom looked around wildly, grabbed the empty carton in the hall used for groceries and ran outside waving the cardboard coffin. With unaccustomed energy, he leapt over the hedge.

"No!" he shouted," into the box!" bent down and placed Hannibal tenderly in his last place of rest with the smell of oranges.

"A proper burial, Bill, OK?" It was then he heard his wife's car pull up, the familiar car door slamming and her footsteps approaching. They paused for moment at the hedge. Tom kept his head lowered, stroking dead Hannibal. What a heart-breaking scene it must be! Bill gave another whole series of heaves, clutched Tom, and said through his sobs, "Tom, Tom, thank you Tom from the bottom of my heart. No one could have a neighbour as fine and decent as you, thank you."

A Bucket of Hot Water

D avid fell out of the car as it came to an abrupt halt in front of his house. He was hoisted back to his feet by his three army mates, all in the same condition, to varying degrees, cheerful and triumphant. The Four Youthful Musquetiers had enjoyed a huge a ceremonial curry but David was not used to such fiery vindaloos. He bent over again clutching his stomach and groaned. He was dying to get inside. The four Potential Officer Cadets had, the day before, passed the fearsome W.O.S.B, the War Office Selection Board Test, which qualified them for officer Training, a vital step towards a privileged mess-life with batmen galore, but preceded by months of hell-drills and murderous aimless route marches. His father, the crusty, trusty old Major, had tutored them for the vital war Office interviews and they owed him one mighty big one. After all, thought the Major, he had once been in the same hole and had also managed to crawl out, with a little help from his friends. The Major had, hilariously, taken them through the three phases of the elusive 'dumb insolence' charge and how to counter it, a question the examining officiating officers had actually asked. "Keep your noses clean, your words short," the Major had given his final contradictory order, "and your mouths shut." The four heroes, all of eighteen years of age or so, wet as a pint behind the ears, had just enjoyed their last feast of tipples and rare eats before the next noisy weapons training time-table, but this time as semi-commissioned beings! As the car pulled away to cheers and mock salutes, David staggered up the steps and tip-toed into the hall, glancing up at the top of the stairs, where he could make out faint glimmers from under the father's study door - but he dared not put on the hall switch, "hell, he's still working," he thought. He didn't want to let down his old Pa who had contributed so much to the sobriety and welfare of the teen-age Aides. "Nose clean,"

61

David muttered as he began to crawl up the incline, clutching at the banisters. At the top, the contents of his straining moiling gut seemed to rise up into an abrupt liquid lump and he threw up, and out, all the ingredients of the exotic celebratory supper, down the wooden stairs it flowed, and he followed shortly after. When he had picked himself up, if a little unsteadily, his belly and aching middle rumbled in relief. The loose cannon had run itself out! But what about Pa? He heard an odd, clinking noise from the landing but at first saw no signs of life. He paused a moment then set off for the top again. What a noisome mess underfoot, piles of slimy unnameable substances, the mysterious, inevitable streams of yellow mashed carrot, brown indigestible mince stew – all out of regimental control - what filth was the human body not capable of!? - but now it threatened him, at his age, right next to commissioned rank and an officers' cane, what disgrace, what humiliation! – a school-S boy toper, a juvenile sot, a stunted sicko - Ugh! As he groped across the spattered landing, his foot struck an object directly in his path. He could now make out on the floor the outline of a long-handled implement with a voluminous tangled mop on the end, a terminal cleaning device, no doubt of it, a pile of dry floor-cloths ready for use close by, and finally, a shiny metal bucket brimming with steaming hot water.

Mr Sopwith

It was twenty-nine minutes past two, time for the next lesson. As the moments ticked away, an expectant but relaxed stillness settled over the class - ten sixth formers, plus the three German students on exchange from Hanover. Headed by Hans Gruber, the senior student, the three sat uneasily in the front row as the hour of the mysterious Mr Sopwith approached. On the dot of two thirty, the door creaked open and in shuffled the bowed, hunched figure of Mr Sopwith, a file of manuscripts under one arm. The class automatically stood to attention. With hardly a nod, Mr Sopwith had them sit again. Hans was indignant, why hadn't they been informed of this procedure? He paused. Hans now sniffed the air, then stared at Mr Sopwith with some disdain. Mr Sopwith was, nominally, the history teacher although he could teach every subject up to and beyond all sixth form studies, from university trigonometry to the Celtic Languages. With a gentle groan, Mr Sopwith sank down into his chair at the head of the table. He briefly scratched his scalp. He was practically bald, with a few wisps sticking up. He never bothered to comb out these remaining shreds. "Enough is enough," he always said. He wore a threadbare hacking jacket from the days of the war, the pockets sagging with recent purchases, the lapels worn out, the elbows patched, the whole garment had the faint yellow-whiteish tinge of extreme old age. Under his trousers, he wore faded blue pyjamas, the bottoms of which hung over his holed slippers. He wore no socks. Under this jacket, he sported a faded, grey pullover covered down the front with ketchup smears and gravy splotches; the yellow egg-yoke stains came from the eggs he boiled in a kettle in the teacher's kitchen, his usual breakfast. From this highly distinctive garb, it was understood he had slept overnight in the staff-room after a piss up, and had now imbibed his usual liquid lunch on the way to his first class of the day. With a sigh, he finally looked up from the table, shook out a dirty handkerchief tucked into his sleeve, and, with an extended little finger, proceeded to pick his nose, wiping the nose-sludge or bogy off his finger onto the grimy kerchief. He then wrapped up the hanky and returned it to its sagging berth. He now put on a pair of steel-rimmed reading glasses and peered around. For some reason this elicited an instant look of respect from every student. His intensely black eyes were large as saucers and held a permanent expression of determination, warning and dismay. But Mr Sopwith was the most popular, brilliant and respected teacher in the whole school. Hans, the uninformed German, whispered loudly so his mates could hear, "Der Englander stinkt von bier." This was a reference to Mr Sopwith's 'lunch,' four pints at the local pub, The Twin Doves. Mr Sopwith heard the words and went on high alert. His eyes hardened to gimlets and bored into Hans's face. The dark orbs shone like bats in a condemned man's cell, chilling beyond redemption. Hans trembled, there was something terminal in the pitiless gaze. Hans had boobed dangerously. He shivered. It was bad enough here, he thought, but what would his professor in Hanover say about this insult to the host English school. Mr Sopwith sighed imperceptibly again. Hans seemed to disappear. Mr Sopwith's eyes finally settled on the mess in front of him. He was winding up to deliver. When he did, he enunciated each word softly but with mild bursts of passion. He leaned forward.

"The Empress Eugenie was the most ornamental and bright figure in the court of the English Queen Victoria although the loss of Eugenie's husband, Napoleon III, had plunged her into prolonged mourning, followed by flight. The imperious Queen Victoria understood, for she, too, was still lamenting the loss of her own adored husband, Prince Albert." Mr Sopwith waved his hands in a helpless gesture, "...despite the fact Eugenie was also a near champion at tennis and knew what fairplay meant, like her host the glittering Victoria." He paused, "I am now engaged in writing up Eugenie's extraordinary biography, the most definitive ever seen." All his pupils and fellow teachers knew that

Mr Sopwith had been engaged in his opus magnus for years and had never, and would never, finish it. But this did not matter, the story became more and more fascinating, illuminating and enlightening on his tongue every time he mentioned it, "The Empress suffered all the vagaries that fate could pile onto her, she was representative of the human condition over the ages and for the times to come, and her ultimate triumph over the 'slings and arrows' were assured!" he concluded emphatically, "The Empress Eugenie was simply divine!". And it was true, some pupils even wept as Mr Sopwith came to the end of the sad woman's dolorous chronicle. Mr Sopwith never married, but it was rumoured that he had been rejected by his fiancée in the middle of a tennis match. After years of solitary sorrow, he had finally found consolation in the tragic tale of the Empress Eugenie.

"A seminal event!" Sopwith went on, reviving, "and yet the tax men, the vultures of the Revenue, try to rob me. Here!" He waved an unfolded official document from his voluminous pocket. "There! A mad demand for nine hundred pounds! Too much to ask, I mean such a woman, a genius and a beauty. And the police, with my notes and books in my case here, they stopped me and searched me. They said my garments were queer and dirty, and that I was in fact a low life tramp. "And where are you going?" they asked next. "Do you mean in the existential and metaphysical sense or in the way of more mundane propositions?" I demanded back. They did not reply. They had blanked out. "Never mind," I said, "the fact is, I'm just on my way to visit the Empress Eugenie on the Isle of Wight, Osborne House, Queen Victoria's old very personal quarters. A tennis tournament, you know, in the protected inner gardens." When they heard those final damning words, they clammed up even more and turned me loose in a hurry! And thus my narrative of the wondrous Empress gathers pace from day to day!"

At the close of this most moving peroration, he shook himself like a scarecrow re-adusting his rags before leaving. His eyes seemed to glow like honeycombs, lighting up his whole face. O, Mr Sopwith, rara avis!

"Carry on now," he almost whispered.

After more prolonged studious application, including some from the abashed Teutons, Mr Sopwith made ready. The class bell would soon sound 'endgame!'- Mr Sopwith's finger was well half way up to his nose - he was a stickler for punctuality! He tugged out the speckled hanky, but finger in mid-air, he abruptly withdrew the diget and stowed away the hanky. No snot today! Why, no one knew. The bell rang. Mr Sopwith gestured to the three visitors, to come forward, "Boys," he said sotte voce to the native sixth-formers, "Our three treasured guests here must now learn that English beer does not necessarily stink of 'Englander' teachers, so I am now inviting them to The Twin Doves hostelry close by, where they will soon understand the true aroma of English beer, which does not, I assure them again, possess the slightest reek of 'Englander' teachers!" Amidst plaudits from the rest of the class, he ushered the three bewildered now pliant guests to the door. Everyone was smiling. All was well. Typical! Mr Sopwith had spoken again!

Incident in Cardiff Park

Martin F. Sweetman, B.A., Dip Ed (Hon), of the older generation, part time Director, full time tyrant, stood at his desk in his half-furnished theatre, the heart of the new over-blown show-piece Drama Department, located somewhere in the united states of North Glam. Boss Sweetman was in a sweat again, his pudgy middle-aged flesh exuded the greasy stench of his wrath. His precious Watch, it seemed, was served only by idiots and damn fools all round! Now Nicholas, his last-minute Second Assistant, making trouble as usual. First, the disappearing tea kettle, as if he, the Director himself, was responsible. He had merely detained it so the actors couldn't use it after another pointless scripted read-through. He had refused to give an explanation, but young Nick, bound by thick ears and a flannel brain, pretended not to understand, anyway. Martin F. had waived formal academic qualifications in his case, a frightful miscalculation, but he knew he'd got his 'Nicky' in the palm of his hands. He'd teach him! Half-arsed Nicky didn't know when to stop, demanding permanent status, promotion to staff rank, even a hint of blackmail there, Martin F. suspected – he could talk! and now crazily insisting on two days off so he could jump by parachute from a balloon hovering in mid-air above the University's Archeology Park, to prove something or other connected to his sick ego, no doubt. Martin F. spat into the waste paper bin in disgust. Nicky! What a freak, suffering from some unwholesome galloping eczema disease from heel to lip, and now wanting to drop from a basket of hot air in front of a gaping audience, the original 'groundlings,' for a weird self-cure, he supposed! What dementia! Nicky was there for was to be sacked when the time came, a kind of employee buffer for his own errors. The whole world would just laugh when he made his leap! A failed actor, a talentless writer, a third-rate Aide, a walking leper, did he have to show them he wasn't afraid of heights!? What a farce! Martin F. slapped the papers on his desk. Hah! All around,

67

cretins! He, Martin F. Sweetman, Dip Ed (Hon), main academic confidante and adviser to a university Principal - they certainly shared certain under-the-bed tastes – Martin F., a most assiduous licking and crawling thing, would be Professor soon, his new title up on the door in gold letters, 'Professor' Martin' F. Sweetman ,' top-class Praetorian, tried and tested, made to be on high, commander-in-Chief of this westerly satrapy, his carpeted department, newly minted, freshly blessed by the supreme being, the Prime Mover, he who had given him a free hand and an exorbitant salary - these conditions were for sure and for certain for all old chums in spare positions. Martin F. thumped the desk again. Damn, the whole thing kept coming back - his whining temporary 'gofer', the long-haired limp-wristed fairy, had challenged his authority openly in front of witnesses in the senior Staff Room, as if their affair had anything to do with it. A shouting match followed in his office, heard all over the foyer. Then what was this about his other 'bondsman,' Ben George, his 'First Assistant', hirsute troglodyte, premier arsehole! - seen but yesterday in the company of the awful arts editor of the local Daily Recorder, one Peter Davis. Martin F. cared not at all for that. He, the mighty One, infected by parochial scandal and tiny fiscal reverberations!? Never! Ben was muzzled anyway, his slippery, small-print contract saw to that. Ben was Martin F's second big mistake, he admitted it – Ben, the token native, squat like a chimp, hairy like an ape, beetle-browed, of known low cunning, a stocky Silurian stand-off, gypo boyo, given to subterfuge and wild mirages about the true role of the theatre and its place in nature. To be watched at all hours, Ugh!

Ben himself, now back in the fray, bent a ear outside the Boss's office door, his daily post, the words clear as a bell, he knew them practically by heart, they happened every day. He brushed back a lock of thick hair and concentrated. Yes, the usual: "No, I can't extend your stay here, Nicky, boy, it says so in your contract. Don't ask! No more of these silly scenes, and don't pretend you don't understand."

"It's not what you promised..."

68

"...you're not qualified for shit, and don't you ever forget it...now, come over here. On your knees..."

A bleat of protest from Nick, "...you can't do this..."

"...that's what you're here for, my Nicky."

Ben heard the usual familiar slapping slavering sounds of unrestrained buggery. After a breathless, prolonged gargantuan grunt, Martin F. came. Within seconds Ben heard the voices rise again, the same pleadings, the same rejections, the same screwings.

Ben asked himself again, with wrinkled brow, how in the hell had he, Ben George, First Admin Clerk, straight out of Reuter's International, lauded for his calm, quietness and accuracy, get landed with such a supremely nasty sadistic rutting pig? Gay, he didn't care, but cruelty...? Time to move on before he was drowned in Boss Martin F's ever-widening pools of deadly despair. Ben knew only too well that SS Obergrupenfuehrer, Martin the sodomite, held all the strings, from flawed contracts to plays, to overtime perks, excursions, lunches, and many parts, and this included the fate of those who could spell too, the writing types, like Peter Davis and himself, who Martin most despised and lived in manic jealousy of. Ben stepped back as young Nick burst out of the office, sobbing uncontrollably, tears running down his cheeks, clutching his flies. He rushed up to Ben, embraced him, burying his head in Ben's chest, "Save me, Ben, save me!" Ben didn't care about Nick's sexuality; indeed he did not give a fuck about anybody's sexuality, and besides, his wife was pregnant. Ben and Nick shared a deep loathing for their common stinking kapo camp-guard, they had been enticed into the same corner – some vestige of lingering adolescent hope perhaps - Nick with no promise for the future now, handicapped by a most unsightly affliction, his mouth and lips were bright crimson with shiny exposed flesh like a burst ulcer which would never heal. Nick had developed a crazed desire to efface this permanent devilish gash, proving himself in spite of it, while silent stalwart Ben, with a wife with a bun in the oven, also with no prospects, no reserves of cash or patience, took care of him in his darkest hour, bless him! And Ben, patting Nick's back, was beginning not to like this all at all, not one little bit. He still had, what was it?....A vision, a dream, 'pie-in the-sky', Bully F. called it - a nation brimming with more palaces of illusion, new harbours of dreams, that were ever thought of in anyone's philosophy! What was... but which was the way ahead? He had pushed the issue to critical point, with the article, his old mates at Reuter's national and international, ready to flood the market with the news...but..."

"...save me!" Nick, begged, still clinging to him, his shoulders heaving. "Come and meet me, like we said..." he whispered with a hiccup, "please, the shrink's alright... "

"...take it easy, Nick, our SS nut in there is already on the way out. And never mind the shrink. There, there," he soothed his friend.

"Thanks, Ben. You'll be proud of me one day. "

"Don't take it to heart, Nick, the great swine is wounded, I promise." Nick stood to attention, saluted with a flourish and dashed out of the foyer's swing doors. Ben knew it was time to finish it, yes, a way out had formed in his head, suicidal, he knew, but nicely matured. He'd go with the throw! He'd meet Nick later, as arranged. 'The end is a sight', he murmured as he pushed open the poor and entered the Boss's office.

"Knock next time, if you please," barked the F. Man, adjusting his waist-band.

"Sure thing, F. Man."

"F Man... he gasped - the cheek of the hooligan!

Boss F's desk was littered with unattended files, unanswered letters, unpaid bills, piles of unreturned scripts. Boss F. glanced again at the manuscripts lying in heaps behind the office door and felt more in control than ever. That was it! He knew how to deal with Ben now, the silent upstart, he just had to curb him once and for all. This one would bend for him one day too, in spite of his blond wife. He picked up a play script from the desk, screwed it up and hurled it at the door. It hit the panels with a rustling thump and joined the heap on the mat. "That's how I deal with unwanted scripts," he shrilled. The effort had jerked forward the wig he wore, and covered his eyes. He hastily pushed it back into place and glared at Ben, "I do not want to hear any of your negative clap-trap about Nicky...Nicholas. He is supernumerary here especially after that scene in the Senior Staff Room. As my trainee writer, so called, and my First Assistant, you should know better than try to excuse him. It was my fault hiring him in the first place, I admit it. Out he goes! And no! I cannot extend your contract either, we have an immense shortfall and people have to go. And if you think you can take over Press Responsibilities here, you're very much mistaken. All press releases, stories and articles to go through the Dean's office, next to the Principal's. You were seen talking to the Arts Editor of that stupid Daily Recorder, without notification, that will cease forthwith..."

"...hang on a minute..." Ben interrupted. He crossed over and picked up the poor bruised *Bard* on the floor and smoothed it out, "See, my titles always in red, on the front cover, the title, *Bard*, in red. Why look, Marty Boss, your pen must have slipped, you accidentally put your own name to it, this *Bard* is by highly respected potential professor, Martin F. Sweetman, still 'Dip Ed' I see, yourself, I do believe..."

"...I had as much to do with the writing as you!" Martin F. protested feebly. Ben took out his pen, crossed out Martin's name, and wrote in his own, "There, consider it corrected, poor bruised *Bard*, restored to its rightful owner! By the way, the actors can't get into the rehearsal room, they just left. You got the key?"

"That's your responsibility".

"The key...?"

"...for fuck's sake, can't you see, I'm snowed under!"

"OK, but seriously, young Nick is in a bad way..."

"...he's undergoing psychiatric treatment..." Martin observed disapprovingly.

"...that's what I mean, 'Professor' Sweetman, Dip Ed!"

"...sarcasm will get you nowhere. Hah! That Nicky's deranged. I shouldn't have looked at him. He wants to go up in a

71

balloon to cure his mouth. Quite unhinged. Yes, my mistake," he stuttered, "but he'll go, don't you worry..." Ben's mobile sounded. "Pardon me, Master Boss while I leave you." Ben quit the spluttering male harpy, and took the call in the foyer. He tensed at once. As he feared, Nick, a voice message, "Ten minutes. As arranged. Come now."

Ben saw most of it from the arched castle entrance. The huge, swollen, garishly coloured balloons were drawn up in a line on the Green inside, all were inflated, the largest attached to the ground by tow ropes. Ben soon spotted his friend making his way to the gondola through the throngs of spectators. Ben knew at once something was going horribly wrong. Nick was shoving his way through, grim-faced and purposeful, his mouth glistening red in the sunlight. Then in an instant, when he saw Ben, his whole expression changed, he was gentle, all smiles. Was this really how they had arranged to meet? Ben tried to shout but no sound came, as if some awful disaster had blocked out all power of speech. While the Attendants were preoccupied with the children at the front, awaiting their turn, Nick suddenly sprang forward, as if leading a cavalry charge, leapt into the canvas hamper, drew a knife and cut the tethers, to the cheers and bravos of the Attendants and spectators, who thought it all a late addition to the act. The balloon promptly shot up into the sir. When it reached five hundred feet or so, it began to drift downwards for lack of fresh intakes of gas, Nick clambered onto the side of the gondola, hanging on to the stays, waving, blowing kisses to the aghast spectators below who were now shouting frantic warnings - there was no parachute in sight! As the balloon dipped again, young Nicholas, Director Martin F's Second Assistant, apprentice writer with an inoperable facial disfigurement, stood up straight, swayed, saluted smartly in Ben's direction, then dived off like a swallow descending from the heavens.

That was the most of it. After seeing off his shattered friend in the ambulance, Ben made his way back to the theatre. He would call in on the Principal first, he had fixed an appointment, a fitting but ominous rendezvous, one way or another, for the lot of us, he thought. On the way, he bought an evening paper. He glanced quickly through the arts section, yes, Peter had included it, his article, inside front page too, he could hear the shit hitting in the fan from where he stood, still not too far from poor, bleeding NIck, his only mate in the whole Department. A copy would be by now in Martin's damp reptilian paws too, as foreseen, delivered, no doubt by one of Bully F's numerous 'honorary' actor 'allies.' The offices of Reuter International would be buzzing too.

The police car was just pulling away when Ben entered the foyer. He glanced around. The office door was open. The Boss Master stood at his desk gazing in blank confusion at the myriad papers in front of him. The sight of Ben, the most treacherous snake-in-the grass of all the simian tribes, moved him to instant fury.

"So there you are, you and ...despicable! your betrayal against me, the Department..."

" ...the police have just left, I see..."

Martin F. ignored him, scooped up the local Recorder, opened at the offending page and waved it under Ben's nose. "What does this mean!? Didn't I tell you, all Press through the Dean's office. This is the end! I warned you..."

"...have you actually read the article?"

"I know all about that! Your attack on Artistic Directors for all to see? - lies, rumours, innuendo all over the world, wherever! You call me "ego bound," by name, "ignorant, self-promoting, money-grubbing 'salary vulture' I ask you, 'unfit for purpose to the final breath,' that sums me up, does it, your duly appointed Boss, me, on staff, for people like you and Nick to piss over? He crumpled up the offending newsprint and hurled it at the door. "Your dreams of theatre are a blasted nightmare, a twisted fiction, you should leave it to the professionals, like myself, the Principal..."

"...you warned Nick too."

"Only decent thing to do. Too late now. No qualifications for the job, but I set that aside, tell that to your fucking Recorder over there! but Nick was treated with respect, as everybody knows, regular stipend, all the perks, I explained it to the investigating Inspector just here, his motivation for doing such a desperate thing to the Department, even the University. I can tell you, Inspector was very suspicious because of previous attempts, which had nothing to do with me, but he came round to the truth in the end, Nicky was unbalanced permanently, certifiable from day one. As for hack Peter Davis ...

"...Boss Martin F., I think we should have a collection for Nicky's funeral."

"...what!?...no, not as far as that, maybe private contributions, but...."

"...the Principal thinks it's a good idea..."

"...what...?!"

"...clear the air, he said."

"What are you on about now?"

He his voice faded to a halt at the bleak look in Ben's eye. A cold clammy hand seemed to grip his gut.

"...there will be no more arbitrary elevations to Professorships...." Ben went on.

Sweat began to trickle down Martin F's forehead.

"...this has nothing to do with you..." he tried to bluster on.

"...Boss Martin Sweetman, listen - the whole system of promotion to Chairs, preferments, professorships, honours, degrees, is under review by the Senate even now, including my 'Assistantship' as you call it, don't worry, I am the culprit, they had copies of all our contracts, I resigned on the spot, Principal was so sporting although it's gone public, even though the Principal's own appointment is in question. 'Old pals' net' it's called, you were both junior academics in the old university, former buddies now infiltrated into all departments down here, there won't be any new names on doors now. Even the Principal's Chair is wobbly, that's why he wanted a collection for Nick, mollify the nasty parish Press. He said you'd agree. And please to adjust your head before leaving!"

74

Boss Martin F. was struck dumb. The insolence of the man! How in the hell had he, the Director, got himself into this awful totally undeserved mess? And the rudeness, the crudeness of the indigenes! All this - the machinations of the loonies around him! And now, hell, "a collection!?" Monstrous! Boss Martin F. burst out, "You and your mad crap - that's it then!?"

"You work out the rest."

"What about your wife...?"

"...and babe - doing fine, thanks! Just this to go," he flourished the *Bard* script, "taking my poor abused offspring home. All that is left, is for you is organise the collection for our dear lost young 'Nicky.'"

"What in the fuck is this really all about...tell me!"

"The Principal requests your presence in his office, with the Dean as well 'right away'.

"For God's sake, what is going on?"

"Why, Boss Martin F., just exit the whole bloody cast! Curtains!"

Letter to The Stage June 16th 2016-06-20

Dear Sir,

Yes, do 'de-hierarchcerize' the artistic employees of all our present theatres! (The Stage 16 April) I heartily endorse the plea for mass sackings! For far too long Eton and Harrow have dominated the scene, whether as 'dramaturges' or not. There are a full 132 public schools, of which Eton and Harrow are merely a part (with Ox and Bridge thrown in.) Sack the lot I say! Let us in on an equal footing, us, the minor public schools, plain Salisbury, wuff Rugby or lovely little Framlingham, cruelly classed as 'minor' for far too long. I myself went to one such school – Latymer Upper, how could Latymer be classed as 'minor' with alumni the likes of Hugh Grant and the late Alan Rickman? What condescension! We, the old Latymerians, are in the top three!

So for the sake of fair play and decency, let the 'de-hierarcherization' commence! Play on, Latymer! Semper Phi!

Sincerely,

The Day of the Quail

P eople said it was an odd day, but for Bryn Jones it was quite
normal. He was walking down the High Street of the
dilapidated, emptied, ghost settlement of Pentre Ifan in the
glorious far West of rural Wales, Bryn's home town, a place
visitors avoided on sight. The countryside however was still
inhabited, but mainly by employees of the vast National Park,
fugitive academics searching for Arthur's Seat amid the crags and
caves above the waves down the coast, elusive native hill farmers
with their tasty sheep, and crowds of back-packing hikers and
trekkers out for an elevated environmental thrill.

Bryn reached the run-down market square, the decayed heart
of the dying town. The square was infested by hordes of bats in
the belfry of the boarded up church, which no Pest Controller
seemed to notice or care much about. Next door stood an old
Victorian library building with a prominent notice on the front
door announcing its closure and imminent destruction. Its
replacement was to be a squat Tesco store, limited by space but
perfect fodder for shrinking Pentre Ifan. The old grammar
school-house opposite was now used as an occasional hall for the
Women's Institute and Boy Scout meetings. The few shop front
windows were strewn with empty files, discarded free
newspapers, uncollected mail and broken office equipment. The
shops which were still open were laid out with sorry displays of
second-hand goods, cheap chipped pottery, cracked glassware,
garments donated from the dead and buried, smelling of washing
powder and decomposition. The goods seemed to go in circles,
from the needy to the needless, all on a summer's day. Business
was sluggish as usual.

Bryn said a prayer as he passed the stripped, rejected library.
He looked with distaste at the sole pub, the Rising Sun - more like
'setting,' Bryn muttered to himself. It dispensed stale beer, at

inflated prices, when open. Its woodwork was unpainted and peeling, old mottled brown Victorian tiles glistened on the outside walls. Close by was a nescaffé caff, with creaking chairs, stained table tops, unswept floors, the local refuge of the burgeoning body of myriad pauper oldies. Around every entrance of these sad emporiums, open or closed, were chocolate wrappers and ripped newssheets whirling in the wind. The few stalls in the open area in front were laid out with plastic bric-a-brac 'bargains,' tinny kitchen utensils all the way from Tashkent, one-pound children's book-gifts also found in the cancer and heart attack shops. The stall-holders, mostly sat vacant-eyed on their wobbly, camping stools, rubbing their empty, mittened hands from time to time, reaching for the ever-present comforting cup o'char close by. Other sellers sounded maniacally cheerful as they yelled out the virtues of their bedraggled cabbages and carrots and the supremacy of their mattresses and mesh curtains.

To the sense of helplessness of both shoppers and stall-holders, was added the seemingly universal physical deformity of obesity. In all his travels Bryn had never seen such waves of lapping fat, bulging bellies, massively drooping buttocks, of both men and women. Their ballooning clothes, he noted, were either straight out of the charity shops or going straight in to them. Their shopping baskets were never full of food, but packed with boxes of dinky donuts, cream slices, chicken nuggets, crisps - 'caviar to the general'!

Bryn looked around for greengrocer Ben, everybody's favourite. There he was, sitting among his pomegranates, setting out his Spanish grapes and English strawberries. Tall lean, bald and a grandfather, he was invariably cheerful, one of God's genuine genial souls. "How's it going?" asked Bryn. "Great," said Ben with enthusiasm, "they can't get enough of my pomegranates!".

"And your kids? "

"One boy's just passed his A's, the other got accepted at College, and my girl's going into nursing. All decided this morning, so it's good day to you." He doffed his peaked cap, and

78

laughed. It was a totally genuine sound of pure joy, one hundred per cent, and reflected his celebration of the ups and downs of life, come what may. But Bryn knew Ben's old Mam had just died in hospital, of lack of nutrition it was said; one son had just been charged with drug possession, the other with GBH, and the girl transported to hospital, with her new baby, after a suspected overdose. Bryn knew too, as everyone at the market did, that Ben was on the brink of bankruptcy and had spent the last two weeks in a tent in the woods with his sons. Today he was finally emerging. He confided to Bryn that he had now found a marvellous old period cottage in the Vale for his deserving, supportive family. Bryn bought half a dozen pomegranates, laughed along with Ben at the dolorous pedestrians who looked sick and tired of just about everything, but, they both noted, some of them wore happy expressions, "like grins on huge boiled eggs" Ben remarked, but in a very sympathetic manner. Bryn moved on with a goodbye wave, feeling better, as everyone did, after a chat with the beaming Ben. If only, he thought, the large ones of the world could laugh at their own condition like the grand old greengrocer.

Bryn bought the gardening gloves he was after and stuffed them into his pocket. The flower displays were already wilting in the dried-out display buckets. The owners would be abandoning them at the end of the day. Most of the folk knew there was little future here, a grimy fading patch on the poisonous trail left by burned-out coal tips and exhausted mines, peopled by queer and fading ghosts. The sole compensation, Bryn thought, was that the entire population seemed to be quietly going nuts, quite amiably, a condition Bryn thought both fitting and worthy of mirth. He luxuriated in these states of mild moon-madness whenever he encountered them, indeed occasionally making his own original contributions.

Bryn glanced at the library, then came to an abrupt halt. An affectionate smile spread over his face. Emerging from the doors was his father, 'the Dad', the most respected man in town, retired school head teacher, local historian and scholar. He refused to move away from the place, the area where his forbears had lived and which was full of the beloved histories he always wrote up as short stories. The family lived on the outskirts of town in Hendre, 'Home,' and it was. Bryn was taking his annual holiday from teaching.

"Hi, Dad!" he called out. 'The Dad' paused and looked his son up and down as if for the first time. "Boy," he finally said, "there is only one thing wrong with you, your legs are too short for your body."

Bryn looked down at his stunted extremities. "Well, well," he said. "I think you're right again. More books?" He gestured at the plastic shopping bag the Dad was carrying.

His father nodded, "there is no end to families in all genealogies," he said, "especially ours."

"There's an end to libraries, Dad."

"But not of books." He raised the bag.

"Then let's get a nescaffé. "

"You buy, but I won't drink," said the Dad.

"OK, then. Come on."

He ushered the Dad into the darkened hole, smelling of yesterday's re-used Brazilian grains, the counter tended by a girl scarcely out of single-figure age, but she was cheerful among the slops. Dad settled down in a rickety chair. "Your Mam wants you to stay longer," he said.

"Thanks Dad, I was just thinking of that. I'll give the College a ring. It'll be OK."

"You like it in this town?"

"The Land of my Fathers."

"You've made my day, boy," he said, "I like it too."

He had called his son 'boy' all his life and had often declared for all to hear that he wasn't going to change the term, however old and gray Bryn might become.

Bryn laughed softly. He loved his little family, so full of affection and 'funny little ways' as his Mam put it.

"How's the hip," Bryn asked.

"My replacement is a treat, don't need a cane any longer,

"said the Dad with a chuckle. "I was so lucky, you see. And I don't tire of telling you, or anyone, come to that – the luck of it - just going into the one-pound store to buy my cigarettes, slipped on the steps – crunch! I heard the old hip-bones crack, boy! When I tried to move, it sounded like twigs snapping off a branch. I was in dire straits. Lucky? That store was directly opposite the hospital. They carried me over to the A and E. They operated immediately. In two hours I was outside again, on my way home. Lucky, you see, they'd caught me while I was still warm," he added with a wink, "and I haven't smoked since! One of life's little triumphs, and for once of my own doing!"

Bryn loved the Dad's little stories, and followed him in that tendency.

"I had another funny experience too, Dad. I was walking down by the old estate where they're pulling up the cracked paving stones, and I saw our old neighbour old Mr Smith across the road, he waved to me. I couldn't cross over because of the traffic. I carried on walking. So did he. He suddenly stopped and pointed down at his feet, then at mine. I saw I was standing on the space where a paving stone had been removed. The space had been filled in with cement. I stared and froze. Someone had scrawled letters into the cement which was now solid. Those two letters were 'B J,' my initials, Dad. I was standing on myself. When I looked up, Mr Smith had disappeared. I thought he'd passed away, I think Mam said."

"He did," said the Dad, "there's many a fulfilled genealogy in these parts. It's funny, your story reminds me of when I was in the army. I was an interviewing officer on a WOSB, War Office Selection Board. Our job was to vet the officer cadets to see if they were the right type to go on to be commissioned. Well, one of my fellow officers was Tom Harris, and he asked the candidates just one question. "Describe your uniform, especially the lower garments, like trousers. Yes, say 'trousers.'" We remained straight-faced as the cadets limped through this final crazy test of their competence to become officers. I never saw Tom again for thirty years. Well, I met him at the final Regimental do last month, only time he ever came, and I asked him, "Why did you ask all those cadets to say 'trousers', Tom?" "You can always tell," he said, "'trousers' like that," he pronounced it with a slow, peculiar drawl, "officer material." He then walked out of the Mess, never to return."

"Really?" Bryn managed through the smiles.

"You see, Bryn," the Dad went on, "there are indeed a few answers to some of the pretty crazy questions in our fruitcake life, ones which wise men have found an answer to, but that certainly was not one of them – it was basically, a stray event of nil resolution. We shall never know the truth about Tom's 'trousers.'"

"Tell me, Dad, come on! You know."

"Think on it, boy."

"I will not leave this place in a state of suspended enlightenment, Dad," he declared.

"Oh, yes, you will" the Dad replied, "like the rest of us, and like it."

Bryn got the point. "Dad if I can ask you one last thing, why is that after looking at me long enough, people sometimes begin throwing stones?"

"Don't worry, boy," he replied "just the inexplicable pebbles of life." He smiled his ironic, comforting smile, a man of fun, kindness and talent. Bryn loved his old Dad.

"Thanks for the messcaffé," he said gesturing at the disgusting liquid stewing in the cups, "I'm off to the books now. Don't be late for dinner. Mam's got your special rice pudding."

Bryn embraced him. The Dad looked him up and down again, this time approvingly, and left. Bryn followed a few moments later. He stood at the worn-out denim and jeans stall in front of the old shell of a school house and watched his Dad out of sight. Everyone he passed, greeted him. The Dad was a much loved man.

He decided on a quick beer before going home and went into the public bar of the awful Rising Sun. The interior was dark, the curtains unwashed, the windows uncleaned, the shelves undusted. It stank as much of urine as yesterday's beer. 'Christ,' he thought, they really should shut this place up.' Although it was market day, there were few customers - a well-dressed, middle-aged woman, with an air of refinement, sat by the window looking out. Her red hair fluffed out, her face free of cosmetics. Bryn wondered what she was doing in this spit-pit of a place. She seemed to be waiting for someone. At a corner table sprawled a dishevelled drunk, his head resting on his arms, snoring lightly, but somehow inoffensively. Another customer, a small, restless, dark creature, simian and vocal, was pacing up and down, occasionally pausing to slap the counter with the heavy metal ring on his finger - 'crack!' There was no sign of anyone behind the bar, except an Alsatian which gave a single bark every time the man hammered on the counter. The door to the back led to some ghastly interior torture chamber no doubt. The apeman now drained his pint, looked around at the comatose, indifferent clientele, and went into a wild harangue: "There are basically only two forms of music, good and evil. The Beatles are good, the Rolling Stones, evil. Left hand, right hand. One evil, one good. Mozart good, Schubert evil. One a family man, the other a syphilitic. Like that. Left, right. I explain that at the station every time, even to the police physician. I have two mistresses, one good one evil. No one has ever seen them. Who am I to say that? Well, here is my passport! "He slapped it down on the counter. "I am privy to many secrets. Look at the last page. It is in German, is it not? This is Adolf Hitler's last testament. Cunning schweinhunt to put it in my passport. No one is aware of this. I speak five languages, so I should know. Write something in my passport. Go on, something good, something evil. 'I love Good, I love Evil,' for example. Beatles, Rolling Stones, Schubert, Mozart. Here!" He abruptly concluded his babble and shouted at the bottles, "half a bitter right now!" The dog at once leapt into life, going for the noisy one, its paws scrabbling on the wooden top, its jowls slavering. The apeman bolted for the door before the beast could get to him. As he rushed out, he nearly bowled over young Geraint, the gentle giant, the family gardener, friend of horticulturists everywhere. Geraint looks down mildly at the precipitate nutcase.

"Hi, Geraint!" Bryn said, still trying to get to grips with good and evil."

"Listen," Geraint said, joining him at the bar, "this morning I went on a quail hunt. In my garden. Cunning, knows all the escape routes that quail, you can see the track lines, holes in the hedge. Never seen one close up before. This time right in the middle, no way out. Beautiful, got a crest, a purple crest. I move forward to grab it. Suddenly it shoots straight up into the air, right up, and flies to the topmost branch and settles down so no one can see him. He sleeps there. Quail lay in their nests, very tiny eggs, very expensive. Well, next moment, I was wandering about, south-west or so of my pond at the bottom of the garden, and I spot an egg in the grass! Kind of pale blue, like a small ceramic bowl. But when I looked closer, I knew, this was not a quail egg, this was a duck egg. I tell you, that bird knows what it's doing, all to put me off its track. I tell you, I've never been so disappointed. "You can eat the egg," Bryn suggested, "No," he said, "I could never do that, I wanted those birds for my little aviary. Then we could all stare at each other and wonder what it's all about. What a disappointment!" The 'drunk' woke at this point, stared through sleepy eyes at Geraint, then focused on Bryn. He immediately leapt to his feet, rushed over and began shaking Bryn's hand vigorously, "Hello there, Fergus, lad!" exclaimed the man excitedly, "Why didn't you tell us you was coming?" He had a strong Irish brogue and was quite sober. "What you doing over here?"

"I'm sorry to disappoint you," Bryn said, "I'm not Fergus!"

"But you are Fergus, Fergus Sweeney of County Cork, everyone knows that!"

"Except me," Bryn said, "ask Geraint here. Do I look like someone else, Geraint?"

"Not that I know of," said Geraint with quiet conviction. "He's Bryn Jones of Sir Penfro. I do his Dad's garden. Honest!"

The man gaped again at Bryn, "a spitting image! You got a

doppelganger on the loose, mate. I'd better pass on the word, OK."

With a last, long astonished look, he backed out of the front door. As if on cue, the seated lady now came to life, blinked, and began, in turn, to stare at Bryn, wrinkling her brows. She appeared to be trying to remember some distant, forgotten matter. Finally, she moved purposefully across to him, still staring hard, until her face was only an inch away from his. Bryn remained stationary. Where after all, could he go? She suddenly shook her flaming curls and her puzzled expression faded for a moment.

"What in the hall has this day got in store for me now?" Bryn wondered.

"You've come for the market, haven't you?" the woman asked, her voice surprisingly gentle. Bryn nodded. It was true.

"We have many markets here. I don't think you'll be disappointed."

Bryn wondered if she had actually seen any of them.

Her reflective mood softened even more. She reached out and ran her fingers through his hair. "Your hair," she said, "so soft and silky, and falls, see here, in folds like, like the buds of a hyacinth."

"The buds of a hyacinth," repeated Geraint who had been listening intently, "I like it."

A sudden look of realization mixed with rapture spread over her face.

"My God, is it you? You are really one, aren't you?" She seized Bryn's hand," I know who you are!" She pressed his hand against her breast. "Yes, I can feel it, the electricity, like a brand in my heart, the magnetism of the songs of ancient sun-rays rising in me, and I'm not making it up. You are one of the ancient ones, from way back, the eld, come back to greet us over the ages. Can you feel that glow?" she pressed his hand to her breast again, "My God it's running right through me!" She shivered with delight. "Where do you come from? Where?!" she asked, still rapt.

"Carmarthen," he confessed,

"Carmarthen!" I knew it!" she sang out, "Merlin's town! You have come back to tell us. Feel it! I feel it. You have come back to tell us all."

"Yes, yes..." Bryn responded, his words lacking any meaning, but feeling her passion and vision, "Yes, yes, you do," she said, embracing him, holding his hand to her breast again. She finally drew apart, shuddering with pleasure, her face glowing, her eyes shining. He felt her warmth radiate his whole body. She gave him a sighing hug of farewell, kissed him on both cheeks, turned, and in a trice was gone.

Geraint blinked, "Dammo," he exclaimed, "that was a pleasant experience, that was!" and hurriedly followed her out.

Bryn leaned against the bar and thought of the ancient bards, Merlin the Enchanter, and his enigmatic Red-Haired wraiths. Going great, he thought. But when was he going to be served. The dog had now disappeared. And, yes, Geraint was right, it had been a pleasant experience. Bryn slowly moved outside. He found himself gazing at the blooms of the flower stall. The stall-holder was sitting by his dog, a massive mastiff, where do they all come from, he wondered. The hairy hulk was tethered to a lamppost, its huge head lolling from side to side as if about to fall off. For some reason, Bryn felt for his gardening gloves in his pocket. He nodded to the stall holder, who turned away and sipped his char. Quick as a whippet, without any warning, the dog darted forward. Before he could move out of the way, the hound snuffled its snout directly into Bryn's pocket, seized one of the gloves, and retreated behind the lamppost, the gardening gauntlet between its teeth. Bryn moved to retrieve it. The dog shook its hairy locks, snapped at him in warning, then settled down, the glove between its paws. It then proceeded to tear it to pieces, finger by finger, it seemed, glancing at him, as if daring him to act. Bryn stood his ground and gazed, bemused. Even the dogs were now apparently suffering from the universal dementia of the town. When all that remained was a tangled pile of chewed up fabric, the slavering beast stopped masticating and stared up at Bryn. Bryn remained resolutely still. He swore a look of disappointment came into the eyes of the hound. Bryn smiled. He had won. He had not given the dog the satisfaction of losing control and fighting back. He had lost the glove but he had won the war. The stall-holder had looked on through the whole episode with a dead-eye, fish-like expression. He had made no effort to curb the piratical mutt from its plunder or to apologise. Bryn decided he would terminate this savage canine provocation with a suitable, more subtle riposte.

"Here," he said to the stall-holder, "he seems to fancy gloves, so give him this one as well," and handed him the second glove. The stall-holder fondly ruffled the dog's great ugly head, and began feeding the mad beast its second five-fingered feast of the day, fondly watching it chomping and tearing away. Bryn nodded, and moved off. Yes, everything happily concluded, to the satisfaction of all the participants, smiles on their faces, including the dog's.

Bryn suddenly realised he had forgotten his bag of pomegranates somewhere. Should he go back for them? No, he decided - anyway, one of the unbalanced dogs of the town would have probably eaten them by now. He decided to wend his way home through the outskirts of the shrinking town, the abandoned no-man's land where few inhabitants cared to venture. He felt like some watcher of the Lees, a casual overseer of deserted scrublands. The place was dotted with varieties of industrial rot - ruined workshops, collapsed huts, a single smashed railway carriage, the rusting iron skeletons of fallen sheds. Piles of brick-bats and fallen slates and masonry made up the rubble that lay everywhere. He surveyed the seized up pulleys, the smashed security lights, the flattened gates and broken chains, all still in place, vandalized but unstolen. And to tease the mind further, a tumbledown pigeon-loft sunk in a stinking oily pool. Clinker pathways led everywhere and nowhere. Bryn picked his way through the black sacks of kitchen waste, the fat-trap dumps, the stained mattresses and sofas. The surface was spread everywhere with purple mires, troughs, lagoons of oxidising chemicals, leaching from the piles of spoil. He paused as he left the last blasted gateway of the old 'new town' and its blight-lands, and stepped onto the path, leading home. Both sides were lined with blooming clouds of Hawthorn, his and Geraint's favourite floral route to Hendre. The blood-shot alders and elderberry trees, seemed immune to chemical contagion. They were spreading happily over the whole of the toxic meadows. He sniffed the abundant buddleias crowded with cabbage whites, giving off a pervading, fragrant perfume. The ground was covered with yellow ragwort, mayweeds, creeping buttercups, and the ubiquitous cranesbills. They all merged together, all the scents, the colours and the shifting serene images, all brightness and fertility among the buds and blossoms. He stopped to listen to the grasshoppers, the chiff-chaffs, the warblers and song thrushes, especially the greater honey-guide golden oreoles, rare in these parts, friend of the buzzing bee everywhere. He felt the dreadful graveyard with its disintegrating industrial tombstones had again been overshadowed by the simple spots of sunny greenery around him. He felt a rush of pleasure. Yes, even the two-ton, gloomy, pear-shaped inhabitants, must share in it, "nature is generous as well as ubiquitous with its treasures" - the Dad's words; the Red Head happy in her dreams of Merlin; Ben laughing in his tent, canonized once more; Mr Smith back from the dead; Fergus finally laid to rest; Geraint over the moon with the hyacinth; Adolf's last testament finally exposed; all the pets in the world ever so nice; all the stall-holders sharing their cuppa, sullenness banished; even the foul Nescafe joint and the hideous 'Rising', had performed an useful social function; and no more stonings on top of it! Amazing satisfactions all round! As he approached Hendre, the hawthorn bushes seemed to swell up like clouds and burst with all the sweets of paradise. What a day!

He strode along, assured that "the subtle magic which is inevitable in the most mystifying scheme of things, has its place even in benighted Pentre Ifan," as the Dad had observed recently. Bryn increased his pace as he thought of home, his Welsh 'Hendre.' His Mam was waiting at the front gate. She hugged him and gave him a big kiss, her eyes shining, "so you're staying a few days longer, Bryn. Lovely." She took his arm and led him indoors.

"Did you have a good day?"

"Just... about normal, Mam."

"Have you decided on a name for it yet?"

"Got a bit of a choice, 'The Day of the Ancient Bard,' 'The Day of the Torn Gauntlet' or 'The Day of the Quail,' which one, Mam?"

"We've used 'bard' before, I don't know about 'gauntlet', so, - 'The Day of the Quail.'"

"So be it then!"

"Now, love, come and have some of my nice rice pudding before your Dad eats it all up."

Reflections of a Retired Hermit

In a flash at the bar, Tom's stroke, left side, face like it's sliding off, hand flapping, still a voice, "two large Courvosiers," plcks a straw from the pint pot on the marble top and sucks on it. I take deep sips too, soon sucking pissed – glasses run dry thereafter at Soho market for fresh oysters – in fine fettle at home – his beloved at the bottom of the stairs, Tom topples backwards from the top, crashes head on last step, whole corpse shudders once - dead for all time – next of kin informed – flash to lobby of neo-classical pilloried regency temple built just inside park gates – open coffin on trestles at head of hall, Tom lying there, no priests, no attendants, no altar assistants, no parsons, no cardinals, no sods, no hymns, no confessions, no tributes, just goodbyes with snuffles - rows of chairs in front – at door huge refectory table loaded with Moet et Chandon, littered with glasses, all charged, every griever a gulp at the lips as instructed – every filler a friend – all to the brim at all times till the shades fall – bare of prayer, full of love, downed by grief, cheered by wine, darkened beloved widow champers in hand, puts glass down on coffin lid, winces as hand hits glass and spills - champagne trickles down onto Tom's ex-face – friends cry out, pleasure at the measure, cheers! At the feast after I eat full bowl of spicy shrimps - develop mighty shites - "People do not die for us immediately, but remain bathed in a sort of aura of life, which bears no relation to true immortality but through which they continue to occupy our thoughts as when they were alive, as if they were just "travelling abroad." "Travelling abroad?" urn burials don't mean a thing – keep trucking, Tom, keep on never minding in the maternal moonlight or without it. Please do not ask, people, the gentleman is all ashes. The pony alpine trails hereupon lead only to one black universal spot. Huh! The articulated Green Room mannequins of Swansea's Upperlands, say they smell of lavender when you sniff them on the brink, but this is not so. These false grotesques of fake glamour lurk in the thespian Gardens of their Eden where perennial profits blossom, jobs for the gals, their souls stand like emptied, slot-machines in the dank, discarded cellars of arts and councils. You be careful, you Snotites of the Scablands, you are talking to Dai Quixote who finger-jousted with Lucifer himself and broke eggs over his head. Listen, first and last, whole generations are 'travelling abroad', the only vacation for us all, and all the others too, others always invisible to you, never you! Well, you and your infant giantisms, you dwarves of insularity all over bloody East Albion and bloodless Wales – stuff it, OK? Flash out again, Lake Leman, a vineyard, a vine plant, number 129, purchased by Gerry-full-of-life to celebrate the glad-side of Dionysus, quite right, wife not puzzled, to Mozart's 23rd piano concerto – I open the can of Speckled Hen, the dear corpse's favourite Saxon tipple, scatter the beer around the roots like a watering can. I swear I heard Gerry's living voice on high, ascending on a trellis of vine leaves, for the ashes of Gerry-full-of-life were scattered about the roots of vine 129 and still sing! I toasted Gerry, north, south east and west, holding the Speckled can above and abroad, a golden-ale goodbye. But still Scablands of earth - the Zombie product, Man, alone and around, humanity's only perfect guarantee of putrefaction - the ghouls of Silver-Sin-City in the van, diseased by mediocrity, foul interventionists by turd of mouth, cheque triumphs ubiquitous, all rich, side by suppurating side - drained of meaning, – 'who am I to speak as such?' you ask - ? 'a failed monologuist,' 'a retired herbalist?' Yes, both and many more, - you talking drains of the gracelesslands of Gwalia, you hollow champions of sterility, you very dodgy artistic directors of made-up, used-up propshops of the fainting Ordovices and Silurians, – I go all incoherent when I catch even a glimpse of myself in a mirror! - you, drop dead! - am I really called 'Dai Quixote' – or just a rumour? Well I'm not all of me! No worse than my perfidy, the truth I tell most upsets people - slimey limey Taffy! - I believe I am guilty of 'accidie', the sin of worldly sorrow, we all rot among

91

the beetroots before we are hoed out for good, so just keep 'travelling abroad', like Marcellino. Ta, boyo. Forgot to leave a note for the milkman, forgot my skiing hat on a bench, forgot to put out the filthy bins, forgot my bike on a bike-ride, my semi-colon for a colon, forgot my dental appointment twenty-four hours too early - the Green Man fucked the Carnation Woman, from right to wrong, from wrong to right I go, give me life in a grand store, like Derry and Toms any day. But never will I overlook Tom and Gerry, Eirwen 'Snowhite' and Pete and Kenneth - Ken rests by purple irises, coffin down in, with four flags, the Irish Republic, the Palestinian, the South African - Gwalia draped as over a stopped clock, bedraggled, barely visible. I want my roots back, Snotites! Gwalchmai film-maker enters by the spotless font, in torn stained Bermuda shorts, waving a coffee-spilt hanky, trainers with toes, no socks, a carrier bag for carrier bags, a half bottle of Daniels in. Sits in the only pew with one woman in, leans over, leers all over, offers her a swig, she rises like a shrew and stamps off in a huff to the still coffin of Kenneth, the only real gentleman in the shop, being dead. Disgusting familiarity, what a vagina, what a disgrace, smelly wanker, she shudders. Ugh! Gwalchmai softly weeps, he is with his best friend, the man of many flags, fighter of many causes - all these overriding paradoxa, these raptures of actualisation, these holistic tool kits, stimdross spills, nerdistan sprawls, proliferating polynucleation, all these pretentions of Man, decay guaranteed, out with you, Lady, you are no Marcellian voyageur! Why, I believe in the dancing stones of Pentre Ifan, which in motherlight whirl over singing sands, the murmuring ancestors locked up in rock as the dragon-head humps its serried back in the waves of the bay. I swear it is so! Bless Gwalchmmai and his ilk, Ken, set up by a worn, torn tombstone, like us all, what a baited wait! - if not, I shall sell my soul at a car-boot sale! Gwalchmai throws his T shirt into the ultimate clay-pit, the earth stumbles among the pebbles and stays still. If you live next door to a graveyard, you can't feel sorry for everyone. Hey ho! Wotcha Flash Pete and me, miles from his newforest cottage, jogging by the little lakeside, a small inlet, I see, I stand in the shallows, I beg Pete, my old army mucker, to have a medical. He has just climbed Everest - wears the same mountaineer's boots as when he was a gradual ingrate, they are in the hall, by the antique footwear scraper, he proudly introduces me to them, I beg him to come with me to the doc, why not? gets shirty first time ever. I paddle out of the shallows, wipe my feet on the grass, say not another word, except "not another word!" Call at two a.m. from Linda then wife now widow, Pete out for an a.m. trot, dead before he hit the ground on the very lapping spot of the day before. A vast or tiny coronary - when I get out of the car I hear the boughs of the apple tree tapping gently against the kitchen window of his little cottage. I shall not tell Linda about my doc urgings, aching with grief, on and on and on. At the funeral, Lindas' best friend is sorry:

"What a pity! This is the second time it's happened to her."

"First time for Peter," I reply, - only the truth after all before I retire from this dire overflowing dip or trough for good or ill. Flash past fuck it! What a turn up! The choir stood in the old Magistrate's Court, juristic folly in mahogany and oak, now the Hotel's Reception Chamber, used for laughs and songs, gorgings, gurglings, wakes, sleeps, the reigns of piss- artists, sentences without end, which is life - what is spoken of here signifies quietus only, and that is that! Half the new hotel skivvies and slaves, Baltic servants, Iberian waiters, Ethiopian chamber maids, crowd at the door – how about a sad song, title 'Myfanwy', all soon weeping delightedly - a glad song, 'Cader Idris,' terrific, never heard of it - a lovely Bulgar lady claws at my head, ruffling my feathers delightfully. "You are of the eld," she carols, "of the ancients, I can feel it here" grabs my hand holds it to her beast I can feel her nipple pounding, I agree and so does her husband who nods sagely, "one of the eld, very, very eld," he declares pointing at me just before the next melody soars into the firmament. Cousin 'Snowdrop' Eirwyn rises to the surface, Basso profundo, with or without a trombone, first in maths and physics, dozens of languages, from Aber Uni, 'the Ceredigion ram,' knew more about Harwell atomic station than the government, but simply wasn't interested, really, after a visit to the national Taff Opera mausoleum, sopranos and altos, 14 wenches in one night, left Nuclear blue-prints at one and only point, unknown among all the quim, Guiness and minge - SS - CIA – 007, Metropolitan Yard all in the quest for lost fission, whereas Snowdrop ends up at home in Munich's very Gotterdammerung set, an advanced ferocious beginner – with the early Teutonic blonds, Elystana, Gwenwynwyn, Goratha, Modrono the great Mother Queen of the Fair Folk, and Wedrosa all noted in the Historical Register for the year 1738, in Aber 'shagged by basso' – Snowhite died on the stairs too, at the top, dragged over the last of the steps, like Tom, head set on a pillow for life. From the final furrow to the ultimate trench, what a 'traveller abroad' passed there! And more to come, Dai Quixote never quits! And think of all the people terrified by death - all dead now; and think of all the people who died unafraid of death - all dead too; think of...?

The Archivist and his Man

The Archivist stood in his cellar before the old banks of ancient office files. They were made of solid oak with a brass frame on the front for the identification cards. Now they were all going to be digitalised and the technicians needed to know which subject they were dealing with – 'building regs,' 'comm tax,' 'education,' 'environment,'etc. The Archivist had ordered the cards to fit the slots. Today it was 'education' for the changeover. The Archivist's assistant, Emlyn Hughes, bald, fifty, shakey, anxious, always out to do his best, however badly, entered carrying a cardboard box.

"Ah," said the Archivist, "that was quick, Emlyn."

"Though I hurried, "remarked Elfin respectfully, "I been that careful with this lot, sir." Emlyn was immensely willing, which made him popular, however mistaken he might be. The Archivist had noted that Emlyn had no qualifications for working in archives, but he was at his last gasp and this was his final job at the Town Hall. His only universally acknowledged qualification was that he had been married five times, was currently going through his latest annulment and was a rich source of divorce law for his colleagues. He would shake to breaking point as he confided the details of his most recent marital disasters to his colleagues, but no one seemed to mind and listened to him to the end, regardless of his moist handkerchief as he mopped his brow.

Emlyn loved 'his' Archivist, "you can say anything to him and he never minds. No judgements. A real gentleman!" The Archivist had given him the chore that morning of preparing the education cards for the wooden cabinets, and, lo! - he had them ready, already! Emlyn picked up a few cards and passed them to his benign Master.

"Very neat," said the Archivist approvingly. The Card E-D-UC, he spelled it out - 'educ' he added, pronouncing the letters as one word. He fitted the card into its brass frame. "Perfect,' he said. Perhaps there was room in the office for Emlyn after all, he reflected as he moved along the cabinets, fitting the cards into their slots. He took up another card and began to fit it in. He came to an abrupt halt. He examined the next few cards in the box, held one up and shook it quizzically at Emyr .

"Yes, sir, very 'neat' this time, sir, as you say."

"E-D-U-C, the Archivist spelled it out, 'Educ,' here" said the Archivist, "is right, but..." he held up the next card, "look, E-D-C-U – 'edcu' is not right."

"EDCU is not right..." Emlyn echoed, his voice trailing away.

"E-D-U-C, 'educ', is right."

"E-D-U-C, 'educ' is right," Emlyn whispered.

"E-D-C-U, 'edcu,' is not.

Emlyn blanched, his hands began to wobble. Not again. His new job was flitting away already.

"Never mind" said the Archivist kindly - he would keep on Emlyn – a real treasure after all!

"...we all make mistakes, but just one thing, Emlyn, please – something you alone know in all the spacious civic offices of the world, can you explain to me, how, just how can a man get to be so wrong?"

The Last Tomato

The burly Foreman stood arms akimbo and pointed at Jurgen working away like a metronome. "Look at the Gerry, Chris, he does five plants to your one. So speed up! And turn the soil in the pots by the door, I told you, no work, no pay. You're absentees practically, see, 'cept for Jurgen. Now get on with it!" The Foreman stamped off, muttering. How he despised these "part timers, students, OAP's" – all bloody hopeless!

Chris reached up to the last tomato plants, now towering above him. He nipped the last buds at the joints at the top so the plant would grow vertically, and heaved a sigh of relief. He felt he had exhausted his patience. He knew he couldn't last here. He had been absent often enough. Getting pissed every evening was all very well, but ignoring Foreman Bill's orders was inviting retaliation. But this was a temporary job anyway before College. The only work he could find. Bloody tomatoes at 36 degrees. The plants stood in endless rows under the biggest glasshouse in the county. He wiped his brow. Like a tropical forest, inhabited only by the detested red fruit in pots about ready for picking, and three very reluctant workers, old Tom, a pensioner trying to pick up a few extra coin, himself awaiting the call of Uni, and Jurgen, from East Munich, come to learn the mysteries of Brit market gardening. Jurgen worked ferociously, his natural stance, with the heartfelt approval of Foreman and the Boss. But even Jurgen had had enough of the malignant verdure and had given in his notice. This was his last day. His fingers were already stained with the green juice of the leaves. Chris held up his own hand for inspection, and gasped. Damn! He rubbed his little finger, yes, gone! the gold ring his mother had given to him on his twenty-first, missing! - the only object of value he had left in the world. It must have slipped off during the pruning. He searched frantically for a few moments, then gave up. The ring was terminally lost somewhere in the teeming green roots, useless

97

trying to find it. He clutched his forehead. The binge with Tom and Jurgen the previous night was still getting to him, old Tom was decidedly rocky too, swaying to and fro, nearly sixty-five but on the way out though he knew the job well. Old Tom and Chris were the butt of the Foreman's wrath but Jurgen, built like a blond bullock, was the exception, he could work at speed after twenty pints during the day or night. He was way down the glasshouse with the tallest front rows behind him.

The entrance door rattled open and Foreman Billy bully entered, a chit in his hand. "Chris, Tom, Boss wants to see you - right now!" Tom and Chris, went silent. This was the end-game procedure. The Foreman nodded to Jurgen, "Pity you're going, Jurgen, Boss very pleased with you, he was going to give you a raise." Jurgen waved back cheerfully. It was too late and he was only too glad about that. Billy the bully was worse than a Prussian sergeant major. Jurgen was relishing the idea of the next binge. "Come along then!" Foreman Billy, barked. Tom removed his flat cap, always deferential, however insincere. "No room for temp workers?" had bully Billy threatened him? You bet. Ol d Tom couldn't wait to close the entrance door with its hideous work-clock chiming away his little life behind him, forever! Best to have a bit of fun in this world before moving over to the next! As if sensing Tom's insolence, Billy grabbed the shovel by the door, turned the soil in a couple of pots and flung down the implement. "There, like that! Simple. I warned you."

The interview with the Boss only took a few minutes, "Sorry, we have no room, or time, for temp workers, here's your final pay packet, goodbye and good luck, you need it." And that was that. Foreman Billy, with a malicious smile, ushered them out. No loss. No one liked the filthy green work or the bullying bosses. Chris rubbed his empty little finger, that was the only thing he felt rotten about "My ring," he murmured, "Damn!"

Jurgen greeted them with open arms, "Vee ist all frei now tho Tom says, we are broken for money tonight," he declared.

"Lost my ring," said Chris mournfully.

"Got to collect my things," announced Tom, putting on his

cap. He hurried out. Jurgen began poking about in the foliage, "No, useless looking for it, Jurgen. we're in a bloody tomato forest." Tom returned with his rucksack. He tripped as he slammed the rickety door, then paused, stooped and shouted out," "Hey, Chris," he held up his hand. Something glittered between forefinger and thumb. "Christ!" Chris yelled, "my ring." Old Tom sang out, "bloody Billy turned the soil there, right in front of me left foot!" Chris gently received the precious object and kissed it." Ma, knew you wouldn't let me down! Know exactly what to do now! The Pawn Shop in town, only temporary, mind, Mam, and for the rest of the day and night a monumental binge at the old Five Hoops. What say we three!?" Their cheers echoed from the glass house and could be heard in the town centre!

The Moonbaker

It was Monday night and closing time at the Duke of York's, the only local in the entire area. Gareth, a new boy in the village, was resting between supply teaching work. He was on his fourth pint, for free, which the landlady, Gladys, did not begrudge him. She was a divorcee, in her early forties, a well preserved, fleshy sensual figure. She alone presided over the Duke's bars. Gareth gazed around the room, its shoddy curtains drawn against the hoi-polloi, the stained small round iron-wrought tables and scuffed carpets. He wondered idly if she would be available that night. Gareth was slender, good looking and free. Gladys had had a thing about him from the moment he entered her watering hole. He now heard her firmly ejecting the last of the drinkers in the public bar, "time gentlemen please!" a hangover from the old days. The door to the bar gently swung open and Tommy the town baker entered. Gareth had only met him once, a reserved deliberate sort of man, highly organised, especially among his ovens, Gareth had been informed, and middle-aged if he was a day. Tommy glanced around the room, closed the curtains tighter, came over and leaned on the counter. He fiddled all the while with the strap of the old luminous military stopwatch on his wrist, as if observing some invisible timetable. He gave Gareth an abrupt snappy salute. He was affable although short on words. But tonight, he seemed different. Without ado, he began talking in a low steady monotone. "Been busy have you? I've been very busy. Yesterday, Egypt, Cairo again. Invited as 'Prime Conciliator' as they term it, tho' MI6 is my metier. The Israeli reps were there, as usual, all members of Mossad, even more standoffish than the Syrian officials, armed to the teeth, you could tell by the bulges – shoulder holsters. But I was leading the Conciliator Mission nominated by the warring parties, so no one dared to draw a weapon in my presence - it was cessation of hostilities on all fronts, don't you see." He paused and took out an official looking document covered with red seals and stamps. "This is the acknowledged peace Treaty formulated by myself in my secret ovens, 'bureaus,' I mean. They all know that, and their signatures are affixed to the bottom of this document. The Arab nabobs were dying for peace and my conciliation did just that for them! See!" He dipped into his pocket, pulled out a silver cigarette case and snapped it open, "Look," he exclaimed, "the inscription 'for Billy Moonbaker, Chief Conciliator, our thanks!' "See," he finished triumphantly, "I do bring peace as well as simple bread into this world." He thrust the papers and case back into his pocket. "But I am so busy, my services are called on even late unto the night - Baghdad, Damascus, Rhiad, the Tigris, Euphrates, the Sea of Galilee, the Afghan peaks, I've seen them all and will see them all again, when peace comes back to these tragic war-torn graveyards. Now, sorry to depart, but I have to check my ovens for messages!" He tapped his watch. "Nice to see you again, 'Gareth' isn't it? So friendly here. But have to go." He gave Gareth another sharp military salute and let himself out as quietly as he had let himself in. Gladys who had got rid of the last drinkers, hurried in. "Did you hear that?" asked Gareth. Without a word, she marched over to the window, flung open the curtains and pointed upwards as a bright shaft of light illuminated her whole body. "There, you see," she said, "full bloody moon again. Don't take any notice of the mad 'Moonbaker' high tide just once a month, quite harmless – old fool! Come on, we're wasting time, let's get to bed."

Never Wrong

My Pa settled into his chair and puffed on his pipe. He had a peculiar whimsical grin on his face. "Just bumped into an old comrade of mine, twenty years back, quite by chance, the remarkable Brigadier General Huw Francis," he said with a chuckle."

"I didn't know if he was alive or dead, I've told you about him, - the man with a long, long secret. He was C.I.C., Commander in Chief of the War Office Selection Board, the one which decides who does and who does not become an officer. There we were, all assembled at the W.D. table in the barracks as per usual, taking our turns with clever penetrating questions. When it came to Huw's interrogation and all of us wondering what he'd come up with next, he never did, he would always ask the same things. He'd stare at the cadet, look him up and down like a battalion on parade and give orders in such noisy tones you could hear him from the cookhouse, "Stand to attention, Officer Cadet. Now describe the uniform you are currently wearing. Start with the shoes, something simple, go on!" The Cadet would begin and Huw would interrupt, "never mind those. The Sam Brown, describe the Sam Brown. "The Cadet - usually with a look of bewilderment, "Sir, the Sam Brown is a kind of belt that goes over the shoulder...", the Brigadier would interrupt impatiently, "and what is the article with a seam down the side you had to line up your thumb with while in the act of saluting?"

"The battle dress...?" the Cadet would whisper tentatively.

"Never!" would roar Presiding Officer Huw!

"Now remember, my boy" my Dad gently advised me, "this is the General i.c. who is always right about officer material - every time his weird protocol proved perfect, all excellent future officers, however odd the queries and responses. Now, listen, when I mentioned to the egregious Huw that pronunciation was a pretty meagre qualification for officer status, he shouted back, "have I ever been wrong?!" He hadn't, it was well known. My father went on, "but just a few moments later, the Mystery of the Brigadier's Uniform was solved." I leaned forward, this was going to be interesting, it always was at this point in one of my Pa's pointless stories, he concluded with shining eyes, "The Cadet just had to pronounce the word correctly according to the accent of the Commanding General, all of twenty years ago..." "...I get the message, Dad. Like - "Trawsurs, sir,"" I suggested, I'd know the Brigadier's accent anywhere, he'd been the one who'd interrogated me! "Never," shouted my Dad, "nothing like that. Not 'trawsurs, sir,' like any bloody tradesman," he sprang to his feet, lined his thumb up with the crease in his trousers, saluted and yelled, "like this," He spelled out the once enigmatic word at the top of his voice. "T-R-A--Z-A-A-H-Z-Z!! T-R-A-Z-A-A-H-Z-Z! – Never wrong!" then fell back in his chair, laughing uproariously.

Vlasta and the Penny Farthing

Dave was driving towards the metropolis of Saffron Walden in his ancient rattle-trap Volkswagen. His beloved jalopy could boast unique lines of rust around every window and he didn't mind. As a casual teacher of English, he could afford little else. In the worn passenger seat was the glorious Vlasta, a Croat student from Zagreb University. She was here in the City of Cambridge on a four-week course in English grammar, at which she was already adept. Dave had singled her out at the induction course and managed to get her to accept his invitation to view the beauties of the English countryside on that very summer afternoon. He was hoping the glamorous Vlasta would be his next inomarata, or fuck, take it as you will. Her golden tresses, as they say, lay in confusion over her shoulders, a fine ash blond colour. She had a broad face, high cheek bones and a perfectly oval face. Her figure was just as striking, strongly built, trim at the waist, wide across the chest, ample breasts, as they say again, but her most striking feature was her laughter, a peal of mini-fairy bells, tinkling and musical, a sound which everybody turned to listen wherever she was.

Dave had decided first to call in on his old boss, Phillip, the local forester, in charge of the largest remaining wild woodland in town, over forty acres and all Philip's pleasurable responsibility. He loved those darling birches, oaks and ash as if they were his own offspring. He had employed Dave as a day labourer for months when he was down and nearly out. Phillip lived alone in a spacious, well-kept thatched cottage in a deserted copse among the trees, it was just reachable along the rutted track up to the front yard. He took more delight in the leaves, boughs and berries than of any noisome human who might be lurking beneath. But he had actually taken a liking to the penniless Dave and on hearing his voice again had invited him for another of his 'woodman's lunches' - the ingredients of which were always a mystery and sometimes not so tasty. Dave didn't mention the presence of the divine Vlasta. She would be a surprise, and anyway, Vlasta, he judged, could give a good account of herself wherever she was. Beside Phillip's house was a large barn, with two wide doors, nearly always locked, and a mounting block of four steps close by for the use of undersized horsemen. Inside were Phillip's second treasure, a highly polished collection of antique bikes. He specialised in the ungainly Victorian penny-farthing and rode his favourite one, the 'Red Flyer,' every day. From spoke to saddle, he had painted this one a fearsome, bright red. Phillip believed the human being had done only one thing of real worth along the ages, and that was the penny farthing, the sole achievement the human could really be proud of. His particular pleasure was to ride the 'Red Flyer' in circles around the yard, talking and singing to it. Phillip had heard Dave's sputtering arrival and the brakes squeeking. At once, the barn doors burst open revealing the Woodman in all his glory, mounted on his number one 'Red- Flyer' pedal steed. Phil was no upper class MFH, Master of Fox Hounds, but a man with the sacred mission of freeing trees, which covered every eventually. He was short, rotund, with a receding hairline covered by a flat cap, and a Northen accent. In his cap was a cock pheasant's longest tail feather which quivered as he walked. He possessed a rich baritone voice of which he was very proud. He sported a Van Dyke goatee beard like the original musketeers. Phil urged on his large and small, steel and rubber mount, slapping it with a hunting crop and singing 'D'ye ken John Peel' at the top of his voice. But the fiery machine, in spite of his thrustings, moved only in jerks and starts. Something was seriously out of balance with its working parts. On seeing this colourful bucolic spectacle from another age, the change in Vlasta was instantaneous and total. From a rather sedate young lady, she went into wild amazonic applause, waving her fists and cheering, "Charge!" Charge!" running after Phillip, skipping and bouncing in his wake, shaking her locks and blowing kisses every time Phil urged on his reluctant rainbow mount. At that point, it was obvious to everyone – except Dave, that something akin to the romantic was going on. Between Slav and Saxon, something was becoming highly mutual. Whenever Phil flourished his crop, she blew a kiss and he threw the kiss back. Every time she gave her heady trilling laugher, he added, in bursts of ecstatic mirth, his rich, expansive baritone. As he rode on, with some difficulty, the bike suddenly veered. The solid antique rubber tyre he had just installed on the big front wheel, loosened on the frame and flopped loose. It unwound its grip, and peeled off like a snake leaving its serpentine skin behind in the dust. Entirely undamaged, Phil slipped off the leather seat and slid to the ground, this time doing the post horn gallop. This drove Vlasta into fits of uncontrollable laugher, joined in by the bearded unhorsed baritone. An alarm clock sounded from the house. Phillip pointed towards the kitchen, "The bell is rung, Lunch is done!" he declared and motioned his guests to follow. Arm in arm with Vlasta, he conducted them to the promised feast. The wooden dinner table was already laid, the saucepans bubbling away on the solid inextinguishable Aga, the roast spitting nicely in the oven. Phillip settled them into their sets, Vlasta next to him. He laid out ordinary tooth-paste tumblers for drinks, then took out the roast in its tray. It's now pinkish and slightly browned body, was a bit like a miniature rabbit's, but the odour was quite different. Phillip sliced up the carcase and dished it out next to the watery vegetables. Phillip did a quick 'do re mi' stroked his goatee and wiped the saliva away. He could have eaten a horse, as they say, again and again. Then his next move - a total surprise - he reached under the table and brought out a full bottle of Green Chartreuse. He filled each tumbler to the brim and shouted 'Prosit!' to his new love – no use pretending. Vlasta kissed him on the cheek as if he had just sung the national anthem. They toasted again, knocking back the green concoction as if it had just been freshly fished from the pond in the wood. They then tucked one hundred per cent into the malodorous feast. After prolonged mastication, Phillip put in, "I bet you don't know what we're eating."

106

"Well, my Champion jockey, what?" gushed Vlasta. "Grey squirrel!" he chortled. "Wonderful,' Vlasta gasped, "so original!" 'Jesus, grey squirrel,' thought Dave, "a tree rat, and I've just eaten of one, slippery as extreme unction." He felt his gorge rising. The host and the host's most vociferous fan chortled in chorus and gobbled onwards, emptying their glasses as if Chartreuse was the original ambrosia, the booze of the gods. Dave managed to down half a glass, then came to a shuddering halt. "How did you find such a passion for old cycles," asked Vlasta, "I just fell into it," Phillip riposted. More tinkling and rich baritone hymnals. Dave now gagged at each niff of the banquet. Soon his stomach followed, roiling and heaving. Without a word, he rose and rushed to the bathroom. Vlasta and her partner, mouths full, took no notice. Dave arrived just in time. He flung back the lid and emptied his bowels in three or four or more giant heaves. The bowl filled with gutsy detritus coloured green and yellow, covered with an oily sheen. He paused, panting, making sure he had voided himself terminally, then washed his face, swilled out his mouth, and took a brief pause. What a brunch, he thought, worse that the overhung pheasant of last time. And what was going on between Vlasta and Phillip?' He returned downstairs to the kitchen. It was empty. He suddenly heard Vlasta's Queen of the Fairies laughter from the yard. He listened, entranced and went outside. The song thrushes in the silver birches in the glade, the blackbirds in the hawthorn hedges seemed to join in with the choral lovers. A sort of melodious low trilling filled the yard and finally faded in the higher branches, while Vlasta and Phillip gurgled on melodiously, preparing themselves for the race below. Dave couldn't help wondering about the green stuff sloshing about inside them. They must have stomachs like iron, he thought. More unusual developments! Dave could hardly believe his eyes. Vlasta was now in the process of climbing onto the seat of the monstrous red Penny via the mounting block, helped by Phillip who had evidently mended the elongated puncture. To more thumping hurrahs from Vlasta, Phillip pushed off the conveyance. It shot forward, hit a few bumps, then capsized in slow motion, tipping Vlasta into the dirt, the revenge of the 'Red Flyer,' David supposed. Oddly, the farthing part of the contraption remained on its feet. Without warning, an ecstatic stillness enveloped the whole scene. Undeterred, Phillip reached down and gathered the fallen Vlasta in his arms. Breathing heavily, they gazed into each other's eyes. Dave got the message loud and clear, bit slow but there you are, retreated into his dilapidated Volks and started it up. He was not surprised any longer that this was not noticed. He drove out of the yard, and before disappearing from view, thrust his arm through the driver's front window, and waved – just to show there was no ill feeling, but this was not noticed either. And from that moment to this, would you believe it, Dave did not see anything of either of them ever again!

Demetrius (and his brother) to the Round Tower came

It's quite nice living in a castle, especially when young, as I was, Demetrius by name, aka 'Dem' for short, with his brother Huw. The castle in question was perched on an old Keep situated on a huge outcrop of rocks and boulders four storeys high, hence its name 'Roch Castle.' The structure was built entirely of dressed stones, a rotund main tower with a massive crenelated Victorian wing added to one side. The castle surveyed the whole countryside, from the gorse bushes of the cliff slopes down to the wide beaches of the seas and shifting sands. The Castle was surrounded by deserted vegetable gardens, a relic of the necessities of wartime. My room was the topmost in the tower itself. The bedroom of my brother was directly below mine. From his door, a steep stone staircase stretched downwards to the bottom where it merged with the shadows. My dear old Dad, obsessive local historian that he was, had bought the whole folly with his Major's pay, accumulated in North Africa during his years against the killjoy German, Field Marshall Erwin Rommel. He was still wondering what to do with the property. First, he intended to make his mark - he had made a good start – the Castle was visible for a radius of twenty miles. He hadn't yet decided what the next step was but was first determined to make me and Huw into skilled hunters. We learned how to shoot quail, wild duck, pheasants, moorhens, widgeon, pigeon, rabbits, hares, "No don't shake it, the bowels will burst!" then hung the little corpse from the bough of a hawthorn tree and showed us how to skin it, and most important of all how to eat it. We were soon competent shots with the forty -five shotgun and the more hefty twelve-bore.

The 'chambers' of the place were vast, especially the main hall but very poorly lit, the narrow arrow-slits were often the only source of illumination. We regularly had recourse to Xmas candles. Here, electricity was in its infancy, and a pretty unreliable one at that. Huw and I would clamber through the single trap door, onto the flat roof of the tower and draw maps of the entire area – much to the delight of my father, tho' he warned us of the loose chimney pots and the heavy slate roofing. The outside was blue heaven but inside, dark as an attic.

I admit I was the timorous one. I jumped at every hooting owl. Things that went 'bump!' in the night petrified me. I would often hurry downstairs from my 'chamber' and spend the night with my unafraid brother, sometimes to his irritation, a school boxing champion already. Yes, I have to say, Huw was the intrepid one. Dad would call "Lights out" every night at 10 thirty on the dot and would then leave us to our own devices. On that particular night, there was a moon, but the light from the arrow slits eliminated not a single shadow; a safe passage to our beds was never guaranteed, it seemed to me.

I got into bed and shivered. It was pitch black. Sleep eventually overtook me.

I awoke with a start and sat up in bed, listening intently. My brother's voice came from below, "Dem! Dem!" more in irritation than anything. I heard a faint rattling sound, the old Victorian antique door fitments were quite distinctive. "Dem, Dem!" the tone getting angrier. Again, the rattling. There now a fearful urgency in Huw's shouts, "Come on in then. Come on, or I'll bash you!" I was beginning to tremble too, I gathered up the little courage I had at two in the morning and made a dash for downstairs. As I stepped onto the landing outside my brother's door, my attention was drawn sideways, down onto the steep stone steps. I saw quite clearly the figure of a man in a hurry. He was dressed in a brocaded overcoat, which proclaimed the gentleman, an elegant cravat, with a heavy cloak over one arm, a short sword grasped with it, shiny leather boots going 'clip clop, clip clop' like a woman's. As soon as I looked straight at the figure, it faded into the shades at the bottom of the flight of steps. Huw now wrenched open his door holding a guttering candle. He was about to yell something at me, but checked himself when he saw my face. It must have been as white as his. He pointed shakily at the stairway, I dumbly nodded. He was as momentarily paralysed as I. We clung to each other for the rest of the night, not even trying to work out what we had so terrifyingly beheld.

Next day, our Pa settled the whole business in five minutes. After a super lunch of rabbit stew and onions, he leaned back puffing on his pipe.

"Now, the apparition you saw was the eccentric Honourable Algernon Arbuthnot, Marcher Warden of the Castle Demesne. He had brought these lands under his control simply because he had fallen in love with the view. Like you boys, he was often seen on the roof enjoying the sight of the marvellous countryside and distant seas. But he committed one unnecessary act of cruelty – he had turned out an old crone who had harmlessly inhabited the dilapidated stables in the orchard all her life, and tore it down. On her last day outside her shattered home, she cast a curse on him, "On July the 21st, you will die in dismal circumstances..." her very words. Algernon was highly superstitious and as the fatal day approached, he put his plan into effect. He barricaded himself onto the flat roof, locking up the only door. He laid out food and water and, most important, he rigged up a grate against one of the chimney stacks and lit a modest fire to warm the clammy night air during his vigil. He piled up coils of rope, for use in case of emergencies. This plan Algernon was sure would ward off any dreaded curse. He wrapped himself up in his overcoat and after one last look at his glorious lands on the far side of the parapets, settled down and managed to fall asleep. He was awakened after a few hours, shivering with cold. The fire was all embers. He shouted down to his servant to send up a basket of kindling and lowered the emergency rope. He soon had the fire going merrily again. As he reached for the last length of kindling, he gasped in pain and jumped back. Too late. By all accounts, he collapsed and died in five minutes. The Warden of Roche himself, with the power of life and death, was gone. They found a double puncture wound between his forefinger and thumb, oozing blood as if pierced by needles. It turned out to be the bite of one of the oldest inhabitants of the place, an ancient asp also chilled by the night air searching for warmth. The reptile had found finally comfort among the twigs of the kindling. How such a beast had got there in the first place was never explained. They couldn't even locate its deadly lair among the heated boulders. Now," Pa went, on waving his pipe, "The cloak over his arm was his best, sent up by his servants, the 'sword' was the last length of kindling; before the deadly strike; the clip-clop noise was his shoes, high heeled for males too, the style of gentleman of the day, as he rushed downstairs to escape his hissing, spitting antagonist; to no avail, he could not elude his ordained fate. So, boys, don't be afraid to come to the Round Tower, Algernon's ghost only appears once every generation, so he has used up his turn with both of you. So, yes, Dem, Huw, it is nice to live in a castle – sometimes! And now I am off through the old orchard, around the buried stables – watch it! - there we all go! And what a view!"

THE SACKING OF CLOVIS (A ONE ACT PLAY)

CAST

MADAME GORRINGE, 40: Head of English Dept at an English public school.

CLOVIS (30): Part time teacher in same dept.

(Empty corridor, Office close by. Madame GORRINGE, Head of English Department, steps out. Spots Clovis as he passes, grasps him by arm)

MME GORRINGE: A word if you please, Clovis.

CLOVIS: As you see fit, Madame Gorringe, boss.

MME GORRINGE: In my office.

(*Clovis enters 'office' MADAME GORRINGE motions him to sit*)

And please, just 'Head of Department,' will do.

CLOVIS: Yes, of course, Madame Gorringe, 'Head of Department,' - at this highly expensive public school of ours.

MADAME GORRINGE: Don't be such a fart, Clovis. You're only part time here, short term, remember.

CLOVIS: Never have I ever taken liberties, Madame.

MADAME GORRINGE: Now, I want you to listen, off the record, as they say...you see...listen...not a problem really...I can handle it...but, you see, I have no friends here, no real friends I mean. Even after fourteen years. I try, say 'hello', pass the time of day. Smile all the time in the staff room. For years and years and years. What is the matter with the lot of them? You see, Clovis, there is no one here, in the department, in the Staff Room or even at home, you hear me, that I can really confide in...

CLOVIS: ...feel free, Madame Gorringe...

MADAME GORRINGE: ...my husband...hell, Clovis, hell!

CLOVIS: If you say so Boss. Ha, ha!

MADAME GORRINGE: Shut up, you idiot!

CLOVIS: Yes please, Boss.

MADAME GORRINGE: Listen, it's my man, my bloody husband...

CLOVIS: ...go on, Boss...

MADAME GORRINGE: I will, don't you worry.

CLOVIS: Well, Madame Head of Department of English...?

MADAME GORRINGE: ...sarcasm, is it now?

CLOVIS: Just my sense of fun, a passing note, I assure you.

114

MADAME GORRINGE: My bloody husband had the gall to confess to me...

CLOVIS: ...he did, Madame Gorringe?

MADAME GORRINGE: Yes!

CLOVIS: About what, may I ask?

MADAME GORRINGE: Well, he said... he'd gone to bed... with a woman, a Slovene.

CLOVIS: What? A woman Slovene! In bed! Fancy that!

MADAME GORRINGE: At that damn International Teachers' Conference...

CLOVIS: ...the one in Prague?

MADAME GORRINGE: Where else? And for God's sake stop interrupting me!

CLOVIS: To bed. Just like that, you said?

MADAME GORRINGE: Not quite like that, you fool. They had borsch first, he said, with a mild Tokay, and then... (pause)

CLOVIS: ...and now?

MADAME GORRINGE: He swears it was just a one-night stand, he doesn't want her over here, or there, or any time......

CLOVIS: ...she 'made me feel so young...'

MADAME GORRINGE: ...if you go on like that...

CLOVIS: ...cancel it, svp, Boss, I didn't mean it.

MADAME GORRINGE: He telephones her, twice a week, only on Mondays...

CLOVIS: ...I see! You listen on the extension...

MADAME GORRINGE: ...and just what are you implying?

CLOVIS: Nothing. Nothing at all.

MADAME GORRINGE: Yes you are! You men, always stick together, especially when lying. I know you, Clovis, like the rest of them here, for years and years, can't confide in anyone, can I? Well?

CLOVIS: Well, sounds like an ordinary one-night stand to me, like he said.

MADAME GORRINGE: 'Ordinary'? Did you say 'ordinary'?

CLOVIS: Of course I didn't, Boss. Didn't mean it, I meant.

MADAME GORRINGE: I could skin him alive while he's lying in bed over there!

CLOVIS: You have absolutely no doubt about that, Boss?

MADAME GORRINGE: Would you like a one-night stand?

CLOVIS: '...I just wanna hold your hand...'

MADAME GORRINGE: I mean, right now.

CLOVIS: Take it easy, Madame, please.

MADAME GORRINGE: I could stick thorn needles into his eyes when he's half asleep.

CLOVIS: No, you couldn't do that, Madame.

MADAME GORRINGE: I bloody well could!

CLOVIS: No, I mean, you and him, a team, think of your joint pensions. Top jobs. Golden handshakes. What grand maturities! The future comes quickly enough. In fact it's here right now! And your sweet kiddies, dark, rescued Ethiopians, they owe you everything...

MADAME GORRINGE: ...all bloody adopted.

CLOVIS: Admirable, Madame Gorringe.

MADAME GORRINGE: Not my fault. Hell, my man, his sperm count was paltry – from the very beginning. As for your own kid, hah! My daughter got ten 'O' levels, first time! Yours broke down. Mine got awards and prizes. Yours got a pothead! My daughter was brought up to be sane. Yours was brought up to be a...raver!

CLOVIS: I am happy indeed that your own daughter herself is at this very expensive public school, and enjoys scholastic life on an even keel...

MADAME GORRINGE: ...and yours is at the Clinic, West Loony Wing!

CLOVIS: Nevertheless she is my darling, my angel, my heart's delight.

MADAME GORRINGE: Hell, she wasn't right in the head even when I met her first time in the playground. And you think this piddling little teaching job here is going to pay

117

for her medicaments and psychotherapies. We'll see about that! Hell, I should get a bonus for all the extra work I've done here, building up the department, making it popular, raking in fees. From nothing! Let me tell you, my father was an itinerant Spanish tile and brick layer, just passing through, the bastard. Slept with silly old Mum just that once. And got pregnant, so why can't I?

CLOVIS: Afraid all this is a bit beyond my ken, Madame Gorringe..

MADAME GORRINGE: I'd say so! Never even saw him, never got in touch, the utter swine.

CLOVIS: Madame Boss, Gorringe, your kids look up to you. Yes, I've seen them.

THE TRAGEDY OF TRAGEDIES (A PLAY)

or
The Life and Death of the Great Tom Thumb

A burlesque by Henry Fielding
as re-told by
Dedwydd Jones

FOREWORD

by
Henry Fielding

This city has seldom been so divided in its opinion concerning the merit of the following acts and scenes of my piece *The Great Sir Tom Thumb*. While some publically affirmed that no author could have produced so fine a piece as Mr Henry Fielding; others have vehemently insisted that no one could have written anything as bad as Mr Fielding. Nor can we wonder about this dissension about its merit while the learned world has not even decided on the nature of Tragedy itself. For though most of the universities in Europe have honoured it, praising it as the highest and most outstanding work and the famous Professor Burman has styled *Sir Tom Thumb* as 'possessing the most heroic qualities of Tragedy.' Among other languages, it has been translated into Dutch and celebrated with great applause at Amsterdam – where burlesque itself had never actually reached. Under the title of *Mynheer Vander Thumb*, the worthy burgomasters received it with that reverent and silent attention which so becomes all audiences of tragedy. Yet notwithstanding all this, there have not beenwanting some who have represented these marvellous Tom Thumb's scenes in a ludicrous light. The Poet Laureate himself was heard to say, with some concern, that he wondered that such a tragical and Christian nation as ours would permit the representation on its stages a version so visibly designed to ridicule and extirpate everything that is great and solemn among us. And why? This learned critic and his followers were led into so great an error by that surreptitious and piratical copy which stole into the world last year, with such injustice and prejudice to our author. I hope this will be acknowledges by everyone who shall now happily peruse the genuine and original copy presented here. Nor can I help remarking to the great praise of our author, that however imperfect the former copy was, it still reflected the resemblance of the true *Tom Thumb* and contained sufficient beauties to give it a run of two hundred and forty performances to the politest of audiences. But in spite of the applause which it received from the best judges, it was severely censured by some few bad ones, and I believe rather maliciously than ignorantly, and reported to have been intended as a 'burlesque' on the loftiest parts of tragedy and designed to banish what we generally call 'fine things' from our stage. Now, if I can set my country right in an affair of this importance, I shall lightly esteem any labour which it may cost. And I undertake this, firstly, as it is indeed in some measure incumbent on me to vindicate myself from that afore mentioned surreptitious copy, published by some ill-meaning people under my name! Secondly, knowing myself more capable of doing justice to our author than any other man, as I have given myself more pains to arrive at a thorough understanding of this little piece, Tom Thumb, having for ten years read nothing else! - in which time I think I may modestly presume, with the help of my English dictionary, to comprehend all the meanings of every word in it.

But should any error of my pen awaken any critic to enlighten the world with his annotations on our author, I shall not consider it the least reward or happiness arising to me from these, my endeavours. I shall avoid at present those things which have caused such feuds in the world of learning – whether this play was originally written by Shakespeare – which certainly, if it were true, would certainly add a considerable share to its merit, especially with such who are so generous as to buy and to commend what they never read, from an implicit faith in the Author only – a faith which our age abounds in, as much as it can be called 'deficient' in any other. Let it suffice that the Tragedy of Tragedies or The Life and Death of Tom Thumb was written in the reign of Queen Elizabeth I. Nor can the objection made by the academic Mr Wright, that the tragedy must then have been antecedent to the official history, have any weight, when we consider, that tho' the history of Tom Thumb, printed by and for

Edward Meek at the *Looking Glass* on London Bridge, be of a later date, we must still suppose this version to have been transcribed from some other source, unless we suppose the writer thereof to be inspired the beauty of the matter. But this is a gift very faintly contended by the writers of our age. As to this history not bearing the stamp of second, third or fourth edition, I see but little in this objection, for editions are very uncertain lights to judge books by. Perhaps Mr Meek may have joined twenty editions into one, as Mr Wright has now divided one into twenty. Nor does the other argument, drawn from the little care our author has taken to keep to the letter of his history, carry any greater force. Aren't there instances of plays wherein the histories are so perverted that we can know the heroes whom they celebrate by no other marks than their names? No, we do not find the same character placed by different poets in such different lights that we can discover not the least sameness, or even likeness in the features? The *Sophonisba* of Mairet and of Lee, is a tender, amorous, passionate mistress of Massinissa; Corneille and Mr Thomson give her no other passion but love of her country and make her as cool in her affection to Massinissa, as to Syphax. In the two latter, she resembles the character of Queen Elizabeth; in the two former she is the picture of Mary Queen of Scots. In short, the one Sophinisba is as different from the other as the Brutus of Voltaire is from the Marius Junior of Otway, or as the Minerva is from the Venus of the ancients – just a little aside for academic clarity's sake. Let us now proceed to a regular examination of the tragedy before us. I shall treat separately of the fable or plot, the moral, the characters, the sentiments and of the diction. First, the fable or plot- which I take to be the most simple imaginable. To use the words of an eminent author, 'one regular and uniform fable, not charged with a multiplicity of incidents and yet affording several revolutions of fortune by which the passions may be excited, varied and driven to the full tumult of emotion.' Nor is the action of this tragedy less great than uniform. The spring of all is the love of Tom Thumb for Princess Honeycombe Awena, which caused the quarrel between their Majesties in the first Act, the passion of Colonel Farr-Parr Grizzle, in the second; the rebellion and fall of Colonel Grizzle and the giantess Corporanda, and that bloody catastrophe in the third, the bloody devouring of Tom Thumb. Nor is the moral of this excellent tragedy less noble than the plot. It teaches two instructive lessons, ie, that human happiness is extremely transient and that death is the certain end of all men - the former fate illustrated by the fatal end of Tom Thumb and the latter, by that of all other personages on stage. The characters are I think sufficiently described in the Dramatis Personae. You will find few plays where greater care is taken to maintain that punctiliousness throughout and to preserve in every speech that characteristical mark which distinguishes them from each other. And says our wise critic, Mr C, 'how well does the character of Tom Thumb, whom we must call the hero of this tragedy, if there is one, agrees with Aristotle's Precepts, in which tragedy is defined as being 'the imitation of a short but perfect action, containing a just greatness in itself.' What greatness then can be in a fellow, which History tells us is no higher than an ape. This gentleman seems to think that the greatness of a man's soul is in proportion to his body, but this I assure you is disputed by our English physognominical writers. Besides, if I understand Aristotle right, he is speaking only of greatness of action and not of the person. As for the sentiments and the diction, which now only remain to be mentioned, I thought I could afford them no stronger justification than by producing parallel passages out of the best of our English writers. Whether this sameness of thought and expression which I have quoted from them, proceeded from an agreement to their way of thinking, or whether I have borrowed from our author, I leave the observer to determine. I shall venture to affirm this of the sentiments of our author – that they are generally the most familiar which I have ever met with, and at the same time delivered with the highest dignity of phrase! - this leads me on to speak of his diction and here I shall make but one postulate – that the greatest perfection of the language of a tragedy is that it is not understood, which granted, as I think it must be, it will necessarily follow that the only ways to avoid this is by being too high or too low for the understanding, which will include every thing within its reach. These two extremities of style, the Poet Laureate illustrates with his familar image of two Inns, which I shall term the 'Aerial' and the 'Subterrestrial.' Horace goes farther and shows when it is proper to call in at one of these Inns and when at the other. He clearly approves of what he calls the 'Sesquipedalia' style because some authirs used this diction in prosperity and could hardly have dropped it in adversity. The 'Aerial' Inn therefore is only to be visited by Princes and other great men of the highest affluence of fortune; the 'subterrestrial' is appointed for the entertainment of th poorer sort of people, the proles, as in Roman times, Horace again observes. The true meanings of these Horatian quotes is that bombast is the proper language for Joy, and doggerel for grief. Cicero highly recommends this Aerial diction, for he asks what can be so proper for Tragedy as a set of big-sounding words so mixed up together as to convey no meaning at all - which as Ovid himself agrees, declaring he would show one day the divine presence in the 'Aerial.' Moreover, Tragedy of all writings has the greatest share in Bathos, so say the scribblers, but I shall not presume to determine which of these two styles be right for Tragedy , suffice it to say that our author excels in both. He very rarely intrudes himself throughout the whole play, either rising higher than the eye of your understanding can soar, or sinking lower than it can stoop. But here it might be said, that I have given more frequent instances of Authors who have imitated our author in the sublime, than in the opposite - to which I answer something like this - first, bombast being properly a redundancy of genius, instances of nature occur in poets whose names do more honour to our author than the writers in doggerel, for his chosen style proceeds from a cool, calm, weighty way of thinking. The opposite of this are most frequently noted in Authors of the lower class, the untutored proles - if the works of such low types can be found at all. Furthermore, it is a very hard task to read them in order to attempt to extract some blossoms of beauty from them, and finally, it is very difficult to transplant them, because like some flowers, they are so delicate in nature they can flourish in no soil but their own. For it is easy enough to transcribe a thought but not the want of one. The good Earl of Essex, for example, has a little garden of choice rarities, from which you can barely transplant one line so as to preserve its original beauty. This must account to the Reader for his missing the names of several of his literary acquaintances which he would certainly found here if I had read their works. However, the reader may meet with due satisfaction on this point for I have a young undergraduate and commentator, who is currently reading over all the modern tragedies, at five shillings a dozen, and recovering all they have stolen from our author, which we shall shortly be adding as an Appendix to this Preface.

(ENTER SPY, in 18th century costume, with cane and surveys the scene with hostility. The 'SPY' in fact is SIR ROBERT WALPOLE, PRIME MINISTER, unrecognised by AUDIENCE until the final curtain!)

SPY: Now let us leap straight into the Dramatis Personae! *(Reads out cast list)* The men first: ARTHUR II, KING of the Brythons, a passionate sort of man, husband of QUEEN DOLLALLOLLA; ARTHUR II stands a little in fear of his QUEEN; KING and QUEEN are parents of PRINCESS HONEYCOMBE HUNCAMUNCA , of whom KING ARTHUR is very fond; ARTHUR II is in love with GLUMDALCA, captive QUEEN OF A TRIBE Of GIANTS, a giantess herself; 'the name of the game' GENERAL TOM THUMB THE GREAT, a little hero with a great soul, a bit violent in his temper, which is soothed somewhat by his love for his adored PRINCESS HONEYCOMBE HUNCAMNCA; GHOST of KING ARTHUR's ancestors, a whimsical kind of family apparition; GHOST is also TOM THUMB's magical mentor, the Taff wizard MERLIN; the two-faced, rebel leader, COLONEL FARR-PARR GRIZZLE, extremely zealous for the liberty of the subject, especially if under his control, very bad-tempered and in love with PRINCESS HONEYCOMBE; GRIZZLE is a traitor to the end; COURTIERS and PLACEMEN, NOODLE and DOODLE; DOODLE in love with MUSTACHA, CHIEF LADY-IN -WAVING; 1st and 2nd PHYSICIANS, DOCTORS FILLGRAVE and GRAVEYARD; 1st, 2nd BAILIFFS; the SPY, SIR ROBERT WALPOLE; various COURTIERS, PETITIONERS, SOLDIERS, SERVANTS.

And now to the Ladies:

QUEEN DOLLALLOLLA , wife of KING ARTHUR II, mother of PRINCESS HONEYCOMBE HUNCAMUNCA; QUEEN DOLLALLOLLA is an entirely faultless woman except she is a bit given to drink and is a little too much of a virago towards her husband; she is also in love with GENERAL TOM THUMB the GREAT; the PRINCESS HONEYCOMBE HUNCAMUNCA, who is of a very generous, and amorous disposition, equally in love with TOM THUMB and COLONEL FARR-PARR GRIZZLE, rebel pretender; the PRINCESS desperately wants to marry both; GLUMDALCA , OF A NEARBY TRIBE of giants, now captive, QUEEN GLUMDALCA beloved of the KING, but GLUMDALCA is also in love with the mighty TOM THUMB; MUSTACHA, MAID OF HONOUR, CHIEF LADY-IN-WAVING, in love with DOODLE, waves royally in every scene.

To the Plot, Fable or Action now! Enjoy!

(EXIT SPY)

ACT 1 SCENE I

(Court of KING ARTHUR II, throne room of the Palace of Buckingham, set on a spreading green plain. Sound of trumpets, drums, cheering off stage; ENTER fawning COURTIERS, DOODLE and NOODLE. They look in the direction of the cheering)

DOODLE: I tell you, such a time as this was never seen!

NOODLE: The sun himself on this divine appointed day,

Shines on a real General in his new armoured suit,

Dressed to the nines, decorated for the masses,

Praised to the skies, the silly bloody asses...

DOODLE: ...so Nature wears one universal grin for him!

DOODLE, NOODLE: Hip, Hip Hooray!

This day, Master Doodle, is a day indeed...

DOODLE: ...a day we never saw before ...

NOODLE: ...a day of royal pageantry and awe!

DOODLE: ...look! The mighty Thomas Thumb victorious comes.

See, millions of giants crowd beneath his chariot wheels. The true Gigantics! to whom the giants of Whitehall are infant dwarfs! As when some cock-sparrow in a farmer's yard

Hops at the head of this huge flock of turkeys,

Which frown and foam and roar like the pretender Grizzle

While Tom regardless of their noise rides on.

DOODLE: When good Father Thumb first brought this Thomas forth,

The genius of our land triumphant reigned;

O, yes, our Arthur II, was all for me and you!

NOODLE: They tell me it is whispered in the books

Of all our advisers, that this mighty hero

By Taff Merlin's spells begot,

Does not have a single bone beneath his skin,

Just a bunch of useless gristle stuck within.

DOODLE: Then it is gristle of no mortal kind,

Some god, my Noodle, stepped into the place

Of gaffer Thumb who only half-begot

This mighty Tom.

NOODLE: I am convinced he was sent express from heaven

To be a pillar of our state, by divine right, alright.

Although Tom's body is so very small

The leg of a chair is more than twice as large as his,

Yet is his soul like any mountain - big,

And as a mountain once brought forth a mouse,

So does this mouse a mighty mountain now contains.

DOODLE: Mountain indeed! So terrible is Tom's name,

Gentle nurses and nannies frighten babies with it

And cry 'you naughty one, Tom Thumb is come

And if you re naughty once again,

You'll go to bed in dire and bloody pain!'

NOODLE: Listen to those marvellous bugles,

Fanfares of the King's approaches.

DOODLE: He's in time for my petition,

The Chamberlain's job is my position.

NOODLE: No, it's mine.

DOODLE: Mine I say...look at it from all sides then, Doodle,

Palaces and mansions, like stables and sties

Can still be the haunt of asses and flies.

And don' forget, MP's and Premiers, too,

All have their price, like me, like you, banked in a trice!

NOODLE: With you there, bro. Gimme five!

DOODLE: The Marshall of the Fleshpots now arrives,

Job Dispenser number one,

Be kindly to his Highness as to no other.

ACT I SCENE II

(ENTER KING ARTHUR II, QUEEN DOLLALLOLLA, in fab ermine and crowns, COLONEL FARR-PARR GRIZZLE, and COURTIERS. All drunk, slur words, hiccup, some with glasses, gulp booze, wave bottles, fawn and bow to the royals as they sit on the throne. MUSTACHA, CHIEF LADY- -IN-WAVING waves to audience, royally throughout)

KING ARTHUR: (on throne) Let nothing but a face of joy appear today,

The man who frowns in this happy hour

Will lose his head, not to say his tongue,

So he'll have no face with which to frown at all

And no speech to grace the honour of Tom Thumb.

Smile Dollallolla, dear! Hey, what wrinkled sorrow hangs,

Sits, lies, frowns upon your knitted brows?

And why these tears all down your blubbery cheek

Like swollen gutters gushing in the streets?

QUEEN DOLLALLOLLA: I've heard folks say, my Lord,

That excess of joy makes tears

As much as excess of grief.

KING ARTHUR: If that is so, let all men cry for joy,

Until my whole court is drowned in tears!

Yes, until they overflow my farthest lands

And leave me nothing but the sea to rule!

DOODLE: I have here an eloquent petition, Sire.

KING ARTHUR: You don't say!

DOODLE: Have I got the Chamberlain's boss's job at last?

KING ARTHUR: Petition me no petitions today, sir,

Let other hours be set aside for business.

Today it is our pleasure to be drunk

And here our Queen shall be as pissed as we.

DOLLALLOLLA: *(Aside)* I'm half three sheets to the wind already.

But if the next capacious goblet overflows

With punch, by George, I'll swig it down!

Rum and brandy I won't touch a drop,

Why Punch is two shillings a quart,

And rum and brandy up to six,

New gin leaves you half dead, one tot

Is the cheapest and the deadliest of the lot...

KING ARTHUR: *(Aside)* ... how the cringing hypocrites fawn on me.

The sunshine of a court can in a day,

Ripen the vilest insect to an eagle,

And every little wretch who but an hour

Ago had scorned and trod me under foot,

Shall lift his eyes aloft and gazing at the throne,

Flatter what they scorned a short hour before.

FARR-PARR GRIZZLE: *(aside)* I don't mind bowing to the ground

And welcome treason when it's sound,

My Regiments are still my bestest friends,

True sons of Liberty! - swords and daggers all,

The lair is laid, I'm off, with them, to final victory!

(EXIT FARR-PARR GRIZZLE. DOODLE EXITS after FARR-PARR, has a word with him and immediately RE-ENTERS, nodding thoughtfully)

DOODLE: I've had a further order from clever Grizzle, there,

He'd already set up bailiffs, two or more,

Who'll leave Tom Thumb both bruised and sore;

Just as Dollallolla wishes, tho' she keeps silent as a nun,

She also dotes on various aspects of the Great Tom Thumb,

But just to teach the lesson - royalty is always served!

But I did not like having my petition cast aside,

Like an empty lobster's claw at a forbidden feast, either.

NOODLE: Neither did I.

DOODLE: I'm off, like the man called Farr-Parr, with huge preferment on my mind.

NOODLE: Ditto and likewise.

KING ARTHUR: Doodle and Noodle, honey locusts both,

Like two snakes in the grass you are,

Worse than bloody gnats, so bugger off!

(EXIT DOODLE, NOODLE fawning. MUSTASHA waves)

KING ARTHUR: ...but rather than quarrel about the price of pots,

My Queen, you will have your way,

Roll out the barrel! *(ALL cheer)* But look who's coming now,

The great Tom Thumb at last!

You mini-hero, you giant-killing boy,

The saviour of my Kingdom, has arrived!

(ALL cheer, toast)

ACT 1 SCENE III

(ENTER TOM THUMB flourishing a bottle and a battle-axe, with OFFICERS; GLUMDALCA captive GIANT QUEEN, in chains)

KING ARTHUR: O, welcome, Tom, welcome to my arms!

What rewards of gratitude can thank away

All the debt your valour lays on me.

DOLLALLOLLA *(aside, of TOM)*: O God, he's gorgeous.

TOM THUMB: When I am not thanked at all, I am thanked enough,

I've done my duty and I've done no more.

DOLLALLOLLA: *(Aside)* I've never heard such a godlike idol speak!

KING ARTHUR: Your modesty is like a candle, boy,

It illuminates itself and shows your virtues too.

But tell me, boy, where did you leave the giants?

TOM THUMB: Outside the arches of the castle gates, my Liege,

Which are too low for them to pass through.

KING ARTHUR: What do these foreigners look like?

TOM THUMB: Like nothing but themselves.

DOLLOLALLA: *(Aside)* And you certainly are nothing like anybody else, lovely boy!

KING ARTHUR : Enough of this chatter! *(Aside)* A vast vision now fills my soul,

> I see them, yes, the giants, now before me,

> The monstrous, ugly, barbarous, sons of whores!

(GLUMDALCA comes forward)

> But what's this majestic form that rises up before our eyes?

> So perfect it seems the gods on Mount Olympus were present

> At her birth; and when delivered all cried out "This is a woman!"

(GLUMDALCA's chains fall off. ALL cheer)

TOM THUMB: Then the gods were mistaken - she is not a woman

> But a giantess, Glumdalca by name, who we strained to drag inside the town,

> For she is a foot taller than all her subject hairy mammoths.

GLUMDALCA: Alas, yesterday we were both Queen and wife,

> With one hundred thousand giants at our finger tips,

> Twenty of which I was happily married to ourself.

DOLLALLOLLA: What a happy state of giantism – where husbands

138

Like mushroom grow, while, awful fate, we are forced to take

But one - unless it be the lovely boy, Tom Thumb, for me.

GLUMDALCA: But to lose them all in one black day!

The sun that rose saw me wife to twenty giants,

And when setting saw me widowed of them all,

My heart is worn-out and like a leaking ship

One more drop of water, we will quickly sink.

DOLLALLOLLA: Madame, believe me,

I look upon your sorrows with a woman's eye.

But now learn to act with all the strength you have,

For tomorrow we will have all our Grenadiers drawn up in line,

And choose as many husbands as you like, absolutely fine, believe me.

GLUMDALCA: Madame, it will be done! I am still your most humble and obedient servant!

DOLLALLOLLA: Wave, Mustacha, wave, you are not Chief Lady-in-Waving for nothing!

KING ARTHUR: My alien and curvaceous Queen Glumdalca,

Go now, but regard this court as your own,

Do not do not look on me as a tyrant Landlord of a royal Inn,

Order freely any drink, there'll be nothing to pay – go now.

(EXIT QUEEN GLUMDALCA)

KING ARTHUR: Jesus Christ, I feel a sudden pain inside my chest,

Ah! I do not know whether it comes from love,

Or if it's just a burping-fit - time alone will tell.

O Thumb, now tell us, what do we owe to your valour,

Ask for such a huge reward, no monarch can deny!

TOM THUMB: I don't want Kingdoms, I can conquer those,

I don't want money, I've got plenty of that,

But for what I've done, and what I mean to do,

For giants killed, and giants yet unborn,

Which I will slaughter, and If this is Debt,

Reward my request in full – I ask but this –

To sun myself in Huncamunca's limpid eyes!

KING ARTHUR: What a prodigious bold request!

DOLLALLOLLA: *(Aside)* Be still, my beating breast!

TOM THUMB: My heart is at the threshold of your mouth

And waits for its answer there. O, don't frown,

I've tried to tune my breast with reason, but broke the strings,

But I say to you, even if Jove himself had shouted out, 'you shan't have her,'

I would have loved her all the more!

What a strange fate, that when I loved her least,

I loved her most, another bloody paradox!

KING ARTHUR: It is decided – the Princess is your own!

TOM THUMB: Oh, happy, happy, happy, happy Thumb!!

DOLLALLOLLA: But my Leige, consider - reward your Grenadiers,

Yes, but do not give sweet Huncamunca to Tom Thumb!

KING ARTHUR: 'Tom Thumb!' my wide and ever growing realm,

Does not know a name so glorious as 'Tom Thumb!'

Macedonia had Alexander, Rome her Caesar,

France her sun-king, Holland her Mynheers, Ireland her 'O's',

Scotland her 'Mac's,' Wales her Taffs,

But let England boast no other name but 'Tom Thumb!'

DOLLALLOLLA: *(ASIDE)* However swollen with virtue his character is,

He shall not have my darling daughter!

KING ARTHUR: You talkin' about our dear Huncamunca?

DOLLALOLLA: I say you shall not have her, that's for sure.

KING ARTHUR: Then by our royal self, we swear you lie.

DOLLALLOLLA: Who but a dog would treat me as you do,

    Me, who laid so randy by your side these twenty years or so.

    But I will be revenged, I will see you hanged!

    So now tremble all of you who were for this match,

    For like a cat in the topmost boughs,

    I'll squat and squirt down royal vengeance on you all,

    Piss on the lot of you!

(EXIT in fury)

KING ARTHUR: *(Aside)* My god, the Queen is in a passion,

    And without benefit of toilet. But whether she is or not,

    I'll see my daughter now, and pave the way for Thumb.

    Yes, I'd look a pretty ripe wimp to give in to her will,

    When by force or art, the wife overeach the man,

    Then let him wear the petticoat and her, the trousers on!

(ENTER TOM THUMB)

142

(Aside) O ye winds above,

Now whisper dear Huncamunca's mine!

The dreadful business of war is done

And beauty, heavenly beauty, crowns my toils.

I've thrown aside the bloody swords and spoils,

And to pretty dances on the village green invite my bride.

(Still aside) As when some chimney-sweeper sweeps all day

In dark and dusty tunnels, at night he flies away,

His hands and face to wash, and in a fresh shirt

Lies down with his love to splash and splash.

C'st moi *(bows)* le plongeur!

(EXIT TOM THUMB. FARR-PARR GRIZZLE ENTERS LEFT STAGE FRONT)

KING ARTHUR: *(Aside)* Some laughter there I do declare

But here they come again, *(sniffs)* accursed similes on the air -

God smite the poet who first wrote one,

The devil punish every bard who uses them,

Tho' I have seen some comparisons both just and true,

Familiar names well known to you and I,

While other wordy fools, who liken all

To a block of rotten wood or cheese.

I tell you the devil's happy here, for the whole of creation,

Cannot furnish an apt metaphor for his situation.

(ENTER DOLLALLOLLA. EXIT KING ARTHUR)

DOLALLOLLA: So there you are at last.

Has it come to this, then, Colonel Farr-Parr Grizzle,

That you have thus come to my aid?

FARR-PARR GRIZZLE: You have something to tell me, my gracious Queen?

DOLALLOLLA: You, a spiteful mountain of greed and treason, as ugly as Beelzebub,

Must I ask you teach me to scold, instruct this bloody mouth of mine

To spout out words as malicious as your own, you nasty-minded man,

Words which would shame the brawling fishwives of the town.

FARR-PARR GRIZZLE: I'll say you never said a word of that,

We are allies natural and courteous

To the outside world, there is no conspiracy

Between you and me or any

Of my paid informer-patriots out there.

O please, my Queen, far from my pride it is,

To think my humble tongue, your royal lips could

Instruct in that art where you so excel,

But may I ask, without appearing forward,

Why and where you would wish to grab, and blab and stab?

DOLLALLOLLA: 'Why and where!?' By Jove, haven't you heard

What every corner of the court resounds with?

That weeny Thumb will be made into a great, great man!

FARR-PARR GRIZZLE : I confess I did hear something about it,

I could easily have stopped my ears, as usual,

But the grinding sounds of treachery and deceit,

Set my teeth on edge and I did, perforce, listen once or twice.

DOLLALLOLLA: I would have preferred to hear at the still noon of night

Warning cries of 'Rebellion!' in every street.

Hells' bells, I believe I'd hang myself like a piece of juicy meat

To think I would be made a grandma by such a freak!

Oh, the King forgets that when she was with pudding,

The bastard by a tinker on a stile was dropped!

O good brave Grizzle, saviour of the nation,

In every bloody station, I can't bear to see this Thumb

From a blancmange swell into a king, O protuberance vile,

Could my sweet honeycombe Huncamunca,

Ever take this filling from between the sheets?

FARR-PARR GRIZZLE: O horror, horror, horror, horror! Don't go on my Queen,

Your voice like twenty screech-owls makes me cringe.

DOLLALLOLLA: Then rouse yourself, we may yet prevent this hated match.

FARR-PARR GRIZZLE: We will! And if fate itself should conspire

With us to cause it, I'd swim through the seas,

Ride upon the clouds, dig up the earth, blow out every fire,

I'd rave, I'd rant, I'd rip, I'd roar,
Fierce as the hero who overcame the singing sirens,

And from poetic dangers swam to prosaic shores,

I swear I'd tear the scoundrel Thumb into one and twenty pieces,

Meaning 'Totals krieg!' before the peace is.

146

DOLLALLOLLA: Oh, yes and no! prevent the match but do not hurt him much.

For although I do not want my daughter to bend the knee,

Yet can we kill the man who killed the giants?

FARR-PARR GRIZZLE: I tell you, Madame, it was all a trick.

He made the giants first, then killed them -

As fox-hunters bring foxes to the wood,

And set the hounds again to drink their blood.

DOLLALLOLLA: Nonsense and stuff!

Rumour and insinuation to discredit

Thumb before the nation and before me!

FARR-PARR GRIZZLE: How's that?

DOLLALLOLLA: Haven't you seen the giants?

Aren't they now in the yard below, ten thousand proper ones?

FARR-PARR GRIZZLE: Indeed I can't positively tell but I firmly

Believe there is not a single real one.

DOLLALLOLLA: What!? Get out of my sight, you traitor, bugger off!

By all the stars, I swear you are jealous of Tom Thumb.

Go, now go! you sniffing, shitty dog,

Go cock your leg against some... nettles...or something!

FARR-PARR GRIZZLE: Madame, don't worry, I'm withdrawing now,

> I have removed every fiery sting from him. But I promise,
>
> Tom Thumb will feel the anger he has roused,
>
> Like two dogs fighting in the streets,
>
> When a third dog the two dogs meet,
>
> With savage teeth, they bite him to the bone,
>
> And this dog smarts for what the two nasty dogs have done.
>
> I'll keep in touch, hypocrisy has pretty savage bites as well
>
> And well protected against the sharpest
>
> Hedges of all third-rate, ill-born similes, I go.
>
> I can fool anyone with *my* honey tongue!

(EXIT FARR-PARR GRIZZLE. QUEEN alone, paces)

DOLLALLOLLA: And which direction shall I move in now?

> Where can I go? Blast and damn,
>
> I love Tom Thumb, but must not tell him,
>
> For what is a woman when her virginity's gone? -
>
> A coat without a lapel, a wig without its curls,

148

A stocking with a gaping hole. I can't live without my virginity

Or without Tom Thumb. Then let me weigh them

In two equal scales, in this scale put my virginity,

In that one, Tom Thumb. Oh, shit, Tom Thumb

Is heavier than my virginity - but hang on a bit,

Perhaps I may be left a widow,

If this match is prevented, then Tom Thumb is mine,

In that dear hope I will forget the strain.

And Farr-Parr Grizzle still wants my rapport,

He'll set the Bailiffs one or two upon their camp,

As even if, like some tart to Bridewell sent, to wind hemp

And endure floggings by the score, I am still content -

Because I know in time I'll ease my present pain

And freely walk the streets, an honest, drunken royalwhore again!

(EXIT DOLLALLOLLA)

ACT 2 SCENE 1

(1st BAILIFF, 2nd BAILIFF armed, hiding in street)

1st BAILIFF: Come on, faithful friend, Bailiff to the end,

Do your duty tonight and triple mugs of beer

Will welcome you at home. Stay before me now,

This is the way the bastard Doodle always goes,

Such a 'friend' to Dollallolla, and even more her man,

Plotting and planning like a fiend,

Suspected by all third persons in the land.

2nd BAILIFF: Say no more, friend and fellow Bailiff,

Every word inspires my soul with virtue,

How I long to meet the enemy in the street

And lay these honest hands upon his back, nab him,

And drag the trembling wretch to the Debtor's dreary cell!

2nd BAILIFF: Then when I have him there, I will squeeze him dry,

Oh, glorious thought. By the sun, moon and stars

I enjoy it even now, though in thought at first,

But in plain sight, it will lighten up the view!

(THEY hide in the shadows)

ACT 2 SCENE 2

(PRINCESS HUNCAMUNCA'S chambers, with Chief Lady-in-Waving MUSTACHA, waving)

HUNCAMUNCA: Give me some music to ease my heart – no, enough!

O Tom, why weren't you born of royal blood?

Why wasn't colossal Caesar your very own grandpa,

And you, saintly Prince of Bradford, old and new?

O Tom Thumb, Tom Thumb!

Wherefore art thou Tom Thumb?!

(ECHO OF HUNCAMUNCA'S words off stage as GHOST imitates her)

GHOST: Wherefore art thou, huh!

HUNCAMUNCA: Come out whoever you are, I'm not afraid of you.

GHOST: You have no reason to be afraid of me. I am your friend.

(GHOST appears back stage)

GHOST: Merlin's the name, conjuror by trade,

Kin to kings and Enchanters alike,

And to my art, Tom owes his very being.

HUNCAMUNCA: What? How's that?

151

GHOST: Have you never read my epic poem, 'The Getting of Tom Thumb?'

Listen! 'His father was a ploughman plain,

His mother milked the cow,

And yet the way to get a son

This couple knew not how,

Until such time the good old man

To learned Merlin went, myself,

And there to me in great distress

And in great secrecy showed

How in his heart he wished

To have child so much, in time to come

To be his heir, tho' it might be

No bigger than a thumb

Of whom old Merlin here did foretell

That his wish he would have.

And so a son of stature small,

The Enchanter gave to him

And so his family moved from two to three

And all lived happily. But...

MUSTACHA: ...Huncamunca, you're talking to yourself again, which must be very boring for you.

HUNCAMUNCA: Farewell, sweet, delirious shade.

(GHOST vanishes)

MUSTACHA: What on earth was that?

HUNCAMUNCA: Just Tom Thumb's wrinkled guide and mentor.

MUSTACHA: From where?

HUNCAMUNCA: Carmarthen, near Camelot.

MUSTACHA: I am surprised that your Highness can give yourself a moment's uneasiness

about that insignificant little fellow. He's no better than a toy-boy for a husband, if

he was my man, his horn should be as long as his tibula. If you had fallen in love with

a grenadier, I should not have been surprised - if you had fallen in love with

something, but to fall in love with nothing...!?

HUNCAMUNCA: ...now shut up your stupid point of view, it's done. Listen,

The gentle winds of heaven when they blow in flowery meads ,

Are not so soft, so sweet, as my Thummy wummy's breath,

And sometimes, even so, the dove is not so gentle to its mate.

MUSTACHA: But the dove is every bit as proper for a husband,

But sad to say, there's not a Beau about the court

Looks so little like a man. Thumb is a perfect butterfly,

A thing without substance, almost without a shadow too.

HUNCAMUNCA: This rudeness is most undesirable, shut up your lies, I said, or I shall think

this railing comes from love of the tiny man. Tom Thumb is such a creature that no

one can abuse unless they love him. And I can't help my passion either, if I am also in

love with Colonel Farr-Parr Grizzle, our highly principled rebel leader.

MUSTACHA: Watch out! Princess, the King's coming back!

HUNCAMUNCA: Then be off with you, I have affairs of the heart to manage,

Which are infinitely harder than affairs of state.

(EXIT MUSTACHA, waving. ENTER KING ARTHUR)

ACT 2 SCENE 3

KING ARTHUR: Let all but sweet Huncamunca leave the room.

My dear daughter, I've been noticing

Every day more sadness in your expression.

Your eyes, like two open windows,

Used to show the beauty of the room within,

Now have Venetian blinds dropped over them,

What's the matter, dear daughter, what is the cause of this?

Don't you have enough to eat and drink,

We've given strict orders not to stint you anything.

HUNCAMUNCA: Alas, my Lord, a tender maid like me may want

What she can neither eat nor drink.

KING ARTHUR: What is that then? Tell me.

HUNCAMUNCA: Oh, spare my blushes, I mean, a husband.

KING ARTHUR: If that is all, then I have already provided one,

A husband great in arms, whose bloody sword streams

With the yellow blood of slaughtered giants,

Whose name is even known in Matilda's wild billabongs,

Whose valour, wisdom, virtue, fame make a noise

Greater than the kettle-drums of one and twenty regiments.

HUNCAMUNCA: Who is my royal father talking about?

KING ARTHUR: The great Tom Thumb.

HUNCAMUNCA: Is this really possible?

KING ARTHUR: The Venetian-blinds are gone, I see instead

A village dance of joys and jigs, right now, in your face,

Your eyes spit joy, your cheeks glow red as beef,

For desire of mighty Tom.

HUNCAMUNCA: 'Tom!' Oh, there's magic-music in that name,

Enough to turn me inside out.

Yes, I'll admit Tom Thumb is the cause of all my grief,

For him I've sighed, I've wept I've gnawed my sheets.

KING ARTHUR: Oh, you won't have to gnaw your tender linen no more,babee,

A husband you shall have to mumble to, instead.

HUNCAMUNCA: Oh, what happy sounds.

Let no one say my virtue's done. I am overjoyed.

KING ARTHUR: I can see you really are.

Delight lights up your eyes,

156

And the dark frowns of your brows

Fizzle out like lightning in the night,

And leave your soul intact, your sorrows

Blasted like small-shot through a hedge.

HUNCAMUNCA: Oh, don't say 'small.'

KING ARTHUR: This loyal news will ride post on this royal tongue,

Ourself will bear the glad tidings to Tom Thumb,

But don't think, dear daughter, that your powerful charms

Will detain the hero from his arms,

His duties are as varied as his delights,

Now it is his turn to kiss, then it is to fight,

And then to kiss again. Like Mighty Jove

When tired of excessive thunderings above,

Comes down to earth and has a quiet bit,

Then flies back to his trade of reigning us again.

(EXIT HUNCAMUNCA, KING ARTHUR. Street in town, ENTER TOM THUMB, DOODLE, MUSTACHA, waving back stage)

ACT 2 SCENE 4

TOM THUMB: I'm glad we met again,

    My Doodle, I am sickening very strange,

    For tho' I love sweet Huncamunca and her honeycombes,

    Yet at the thought of marriage I grow pale;

    For, Oh, but swear to keep it ever secret,

    And I'll tell you a story that will make you stare.

DOODLE: I swear by sweet Huncamunca's charms,

    I'll keep it under my tongue for life,

    Like you, triumphant Tom, I love all salaries,

    Especially when discretely in my pocket.

TOM THUMB: Then know, friend Doodle, my old grandma often warned me,

    'beware of marriage!'

DOODLE: Sir, I blush to think a warrior great as you,

    Should be frightened by his dead grandma,

    Can an old woman's empty fears

    Deter the blooming hero from the virgin's arms?

Think of the joy that will your soul embrace

When in her fond embraces gripped you lie,

While on her panting breast dissolved in bliss,

You pour out Tom Thumb, with such an endless kiss.

TOM THUMB: O, Doodle you have fired my eager soul again,

Although I know your interest dwells in one moustache as well.

In spite of my Grandma, the Princess will be mine,

I'll hug, I'll caress, I'll eat her up with all my love.

Whole days and nights and years shall be too short

For our enjoyment; every sun shall rise

Blushing to see what antics we get up to in bed.

DOODLE: O, mon general, I will pursue this plot to the utmost, too,

For dear Mustacha's sake,

For St George and merry England,

For Freedom, for slaves, for women, for adolescents

Human rights for all of them, the twats, that's what!

TOM THUMB: Bravely said, my Doodle.

MUSTACHA: I agree with His Highness, King Arthur Number II

And with my Doodle. Like anything!!

TOM THUMB: Bravely said again.

DOODLE: I am for the victorious side in every war!

KING ARTHUR: Yes, there are never too many ' bravely saids'

In our heroic kingdom! Farewell, baby!

MUSTACHA: Dig ya, man.

(MUSTACHA EXITS WAVING)

ACT 2 SCENE 5

(ENTER 1st, 2nd BAILIFF, right. They spot TOM THUMB, DOODLE)

2nd BAILIFF: You are Mr Doodle? Well, stand and deliver for the law's own sake!

1st BAILIFF: We have here an action taken out against you and him,

A neighbour put this warrant in our hands

For uttering foul calumnies against the King

Drink, fornication and all kinda sin,

Off to Bow Street now!

TOM THUMB: What, you dogs, arrest my friend in front of my very face?

Do you really think Tom Thumb would suffer this disgrace?

But let you vain cowards threaten with an empty word,

Tom Thumb will show his indignation with his sword.

(TOM THUMB kills 1st and 2nd BAILIFFS with sword thrusts)

1st BAILIFF: Ah, I am hit, I'm bleeding. Look.

2nd BAILIFF: I'm wounded as well! See me!

To the dismal shades below

This Bailiff's life must also go.

DOODLE: Go then both to Lucifer, like the villains of Hades that you are!

1st BAILIFF: But we'll serve well the topmost Bailiffs down in hell.

TOM THUMB: Thus perish all bailiffs in the land! Forever onwards,

Till all debtors at midday can walk the streets

And have no fear of one Bailiff and his lousy treats!

(1st, 2nd BAILLIF die)

DOODLE: Bravo, Tom Thumb another victory on your hands!

(EXIT TOM and NOODLE)

ACT 2 SCENE 6

(HUNCAMUNCA'S chamber, with CONSPIRATOR FARR-PARR GRIZZLE, would be suitor, of HUNCAMUNCA)

FARR-PARR GRIZZLE: Oh, sweet Huncamunca, your pouting breasts,

Like cymbals of gold, give everlasting beats of joy,

As bright as brass they are and just as hard,

Let me caress them, O Huncamunca bright!

HUNCAMUNCA: What? You dare!? Don't you know me,

Princess that I am, you dare play games with me?!

FARR-PARR GRIZZLE: O Huncamunca, I know you are a royal Princess,

And daughter of a King, but love does not scorn

The meanest of the tribe, nor is afraid of power,

Love often takes Lords and Ladies to the cells,

And commands the Guard to throw away the bells.

Nothing is too high, or low where true love dwells.

HUNCAMUNCA: But if what you said was true, my love now, I am,

To another due. It's quite useless to press your suit on me,

I've been promised to Tom Thumb, by order of dear daddee.

163

FARR PARR-GRIZZLE: Can my Princess really marry such a tiddler –

>He's fitter for your pocket than your bed.

>Listen, sweet Huncamunca, shun this worthless embryo,

>Never be taken between the sheets by such a titch.

>Oh, let me fall into your arms and never flinch,

>I am a man of Thor, every straining inch

>And while we are in pleasure both together

>I'll press your soul and it will breathless music make

>While the whole world stands approving of your mate.

HUNCAMUNCA: If you are suggesting you can remove all official promises and engagements, just like that, your manhood is not proved at all.

FARR-PARR GRIZZLE: Let tiny Tom find some attractive dwarf, some fairy miss,

>Where no stool is needed to rise up to her breasts,

>For just a simple suck. By all the stars of fame and glory,

>You appear to be far more fitting for a Prussian Grenadier,

>And look at Atlas, one single globe upon his shoulders,

>But two dozen would not equal Awena's wonders.

>The mountains of the moon are never flat

Your Milky Ways are ever close to that.

HUNCAMUNCA: I find your words so heaven sent,

I'm truly moved by all your eloquence.

FARR-PARR GRIZZLE: Oh, say that again,

And let the sound echo from one pole to another;

Let earth and sky be a kind of sacred locker,

With battle-doors shut, the echoes all within, just for one hour,

Lest we meet life's hangman at the door

And be chained in Fleet prison, a tragic blow,

So I will like an arrow fly from Cupid's bow,

And get a marriage licence, directly from the Commons,

And tie the knot upon a stage far from that chartered chamber,

As all the powers forbid a Princess should do it on her own,

For that ungodly act, breaks the right of holy kings,

And poisons all their sacred veins. My quick return,

Shall to you prove I travel by the post-horses

Of passion, steeds some twenty hands or more in height, you'll see.

But they will seem too slow for me in flight, give me Mercury,

The swiftest of the gods, whose messages, like mine, are for posterity!

We will ride together in the chariot called - 'destiny'!

(FARR–PARR GRIZZLE RUSHES OFF)

ACT 2 SCENE 7

(HUNCAMUNCA paces. ENTER TOM THUMB, looking around. HUNCAMUNCA hides behind bush)

TOM THUMB: Where is my Honeycombe Princess, where is my Huncamunca fair?

Where are those eyes, those trump-cards of adoration

That lighten up my waxen soul with love? Where is that face,

Made by nature in the same mould as radiant Venus?

HUNCAMUNCA: Oh, what is music to the ear that's deaf?

Or venison pie, to him who's who has no taste?

(Approaches TOM THUMB)

What do these praises now mean to me? For I am tempted by another.

TOM THUMB: 'Tempted'? - a word of many meanings - in your vocabulary, changed as soon as spoken.

HUNCAMUNCA: It is all written in the book of fate.

TOM THUMB: Then I will tear up the leaf on which it's written, and if fate doesn't like

that, or won't allow so large a gap in her very scary diary, I'll blot out the ink of it, at

the very least.

(TOM THUMB DEPARTS. Aside, as he exits)

And the King's dead right about these interminable bloody metaphors, like man, I don't know what!

ACT 2 SCENE 8

(HUNCAMUNCA paces. ENTER QUEEN GLUMDALCA)

GLUMDALCA: I need not ask just who you are, your brandy nose declares you ....

HUNCAMUNCA: ... a most noble Princess of the blood royal, have a care, and I don't need to

ask who you are either, a jenny wren could spot your lardy wobbles a mile off.

GLUMDALCA: A sad tale there, don't be bitchy, dear, a giantess I was, alas, who once made and unmade queens.

HUNCAMUNCA: The man whose chief ambition is to be my Lord and Master, destroyed those mighty giants of yours.

GLUMDALCA: Your 'Lord and Master?' Do you think that a man who once wore me as a portion of the spoils, will ever wear you for a moment?

HUNCAMUNCA: Well, may your chains be light as feathers,

As my royal father did for you,

For if what fate tells be true,

You have dropped those fetters twenty

Times a night, pulled on and off like easy boots,

Your under garments in the basket, soiled as soot.

GLUMDALCA: I still glory in the number twenty-one, and when I settle down, like you,

> Content with only one, never ye heavens, I pray, never

> Change this face of mine for one as red as yours,

> I remain at twenty-one, pale as a silent swan!

HUNCAMUNCA: *(Seizes candle, hold it over GLUMDALCA's face)* Now let me be nearer to

> this enormous beauty, which captivated men and grenadiers in showers. Oh,

> Jesus Christ, now I look, you're as ugly as the very gargoyle itself! Ugh!

GLUMDALCA: Hell, you'd give the best piss-pots in your boudoir to be half as lovely.

HUNCAMUNCA: Since you're still going on and on about that, I'll put my beauty to the test!

> See, here comes Tom Thumb. *(ENTER TOM THUMB)* Tom, I am yours if you go with me right now!

GLUMDALCA: Oh, stay with me, Tom Thumb, and you alone will fill that bed where twenty giants a night were fed.

TOM THUMB: In the back alley I saw a whore shag two apprentices,

> One had a half crown in his hand,

> The other held a piece of gold,

> The whore grabs the half crown,

170

And leaves the larger but the baser coin!

GLUMDALCA: We don't need a monarch to interpret that!

(HUNCAMUNCA grabs TOM THUMB by the hand, they run off, laughing, EXIT)

GLUMDALCA: So I'm left scorned and rejected

For such a chit of a silly virgin, am I? I feel storms

Now rising in my breast, tempests and whirlwinds

Shriek and roar, I am all hurricanoes! The four winds

Of the world are pent up inside my carcass, where

Confusion horror, murder, guts and death reside.

As you can gather, I am no lamb inside.

Let Tom just wait, I sense a bloody fate!

ACT 2 SCENE 9

(KING wanders on, distraught. Brightens when he sees GLUMDALCA)

GLUMDALCA: Come, love, lay your troubles on my bare warm shoulders.

> What's the matter, my Leigey, I ask only
>
> Because I know you are in love with me.

KING ARTHUR: Sure there was never so sad a King as I.

> My life's a ragged coat like a beggar's,
>
> A Prince, let alone a King
>
> Should throw that garment off,
>
> To love a captive and a tender giantess is best.

GLUMDALCA: Oh, my Love!

KING ARTHUR: What a great Queen you are, my tongue is your trumpet,

> And your music works inside me, unknown to other men.
>
> Oh, Glumdalca, heaven designed you as a giantess
>
> But an angelic soul you turned out to be, help me,
>
> I am a walking multitude of family griefs and burdons of state,
>
> And only on your lips is any comfort found,

172

I'll take nature's cure that will my ills confound

If immediately you lay your garments down upon the ground.

Oh, glory be, what is this I see!

GLUMDALCA: What is this I hear?

KING ARTHUR : Oh, amorous queen.

GLUMDALCA: Oh, randy King!

(KING ARTHUR and GLUMDALCA make love. Fade to violins)

ACT 2 SCENE 10

(HUNCAMUNCA, TOM THUMB, PARSON, as at a marriage ceremony)

PARSON: Happy is the wooing, that's not long a'doing, my children,

> For if I guess aright, Tom Thumb this night,
>
> Will give his being yet another light.

TOM THUMB: All my efforts will be to that end, Parson.

HUNCAMUNCA: Please, Tom Thumb, you make me blush.

PARSON: It is the virgin's sign and suits her well.

TOM THUMB: I don't know where, or how, or what I am,

> I'm so transported I have lost myself.

HUNCAMUNCA: Look to the stars, my Tom, they're so small,

> That were you lost, you'd find yourself no more,
>
> Like the unhappy semstress, who lost her needle in a pin-box in the hay,
>
> She looked and looked, but found the needle gotten clean away.

PARSON: You happy two, long may you live and love and propagate

> Till the whole land is peopled with Tom Thumbs,

Like when in Cheshire cheeses, hungry maggots breed,

And another and another still succeeds

By thousands and the tens of thousands they increase

Till one continuous maggot fills the rotten cheese

Till they are called by their true names - Chief Ministers of State.

God protect you, my children, and all who eat in you.

(EXIT HUNCAMUNCA, PARSON, TOM THUMB)

ACT 2 SCENE 11

(DOODLE, FARR-PARR GRIZZLE in conversation)

DOODLE *(Aside):* Certainly I think Nature herself

Wants to loose her adamantine chains,

Unfix the universe and in a rage

Hurl away her axles, locks and hinges.

All things are confused,

The Queen is drunk, the Princess hitched,

So it's said and not by me,

The whole of nature is reversed.

FARR-PARR GRIZZLE: Rumour and speculation. Doodle, have you heard

Anything of my sweet Honeycombe Huncamunca?

DOODLE: I've heard a thousand sighs today,

But none from that wonderful bitch of ours,

Such is sweet Huncamunca, sought by all,

And the King, the Queen, the entire Court in thrall.

FARR-PARR GRIZZLE: Damn your reports, you make them up,

You pilferer, as you go along, are you drunk?

I do not want to hear a single word – except ' Huncamunca here!'

DOODLE: She is probably married by this time,

To some Brigadier or one or two grenadiers, perhaps,

Or, perchance, O curses, some general Tom Thumb nearby!

FARR-PARR GRIZZLE: Not my Huncamunca, no! Whose fuckin'side are you on anyway?

DOODLE: On your Huncamunca's sweet side! And yours.

FARR-PARR GRIZZLE: Tom Thumb's more like.

DOODLE: Or everyman's, she's strayed so far.

FARR-PARR GRIZZLE: If that is true, then the whole of womankind is doomed.

DOODLE: If that is true, then we are doomed ourselves.

FARR-PARR GRIZZLE: By Jesus Christ, here she comes herself.

I'm not going to believe a word out of that pretty mouth,

Above which sits Innocence on a royal brow ingrained.

(ENTER HUNCAMUNCA, dancing)

FARR-PARR GRIZZLE: Where has my Huncamunca been?

HUNCAMUNCA: O, here and there.

FARR-PARR GRIZZLE: Where?

HUNCAMUNCA: Errands of mercy

DOODLE: For whom?

HUNCAMUNCA: Mankind.

DOODLE: Then god have mercy on us all.

FARR-PARR GRIZZLE: Never! See here, I have the marriage licence in my hand.

HUNCAMUNCA: Poor old Tom Thumb.

FARR-PARR GRIZZLE: Why are you talking about him?

HUNCAMUNCA: Poor little man.

FARR-PARR GRIZZLE: Are you leading me on?

HUNCAMUNCA: Mum, mum! and mum again.

FARR-PARR GRIZZEL: Your every stupid word is 'mum.'

HUNCAMUNCA: Tom Thumb was overcome.

FARR-PARR GRIZZLE: You force me to answer you now.

> No more Tom Thumb, I'm on the wrack,
>
> I'm in the flames! 'Tom bloody Thumb,' you love that name,
>
> So lovely is that word to you, if you were dumb,
>
> You'd somehow find a voice to shout out 'Tom Thumb!

HUNCAMUNCA: Don't be so hasty about my so-called damnation

> My big heart for more than one has room,

178

Heaven formed a beauty like me

For at least two more.

I married him and now I'll marry you.

FARR-PARR GRIZZLE: What! You flaunt your treacheries to my face?

You think that I could fill your husband's place

Because that office needs another officer,

Since you scorn to enjoy one main dish

You shall not have the tainted tiddler fish,

The sole duty of your husband is to your Highness,

But I will bear the pain, but never unrevenged

Wear the slighted willow berry in my lapel,

My brooding gloomy tempests are now confined,

Within the hollow caverns of my mind,

But they will ever whirl along the coasts,

And drown the men of many boats,

And then dip down into the circle known as seven,

To cram every chink of hell with hideous spectres

I have seen on dark and wintery days,

As sudden storms rush down the highway of the sky,

Sweep through the streets' - here comes the deadly simile -

And with terrible ding dongs of pots and pans,

Gush through spouts to sweep whole crews along

Drown crowded shops, throngs of hopping vermin,

The dirty and the clean together,

Even the filthy chimney sweeps are now washed.

So universal hygiene is enjoyed by all,

The future and the past!

HUNCAMUNCA: *(Aside)* Oh, will the crazed Farr-Parr Grizzle,

In the rashness of his fury slay

My hapless bridegroom on his wedding day?

I, who this morn, of two, chose both to wed

Must go tonight alone to bed?

Yes, once I have seen a wild fool with a choice like this,

Try to give preference to both,

Coveting to sit on one, and the other, too,

But the two stools did her confound,

She found herself between them, squatting on the ground.

But Farr-Parr has a silver tongue,

And has my affection sorely wrung,

Shall I say 'yes' or 'no' to either,

Or 'yes' and 'no' to neither?

(FARR-PARR GRIZZLE chases HUNCAMUNCA off stage. EXIT BOTH)

ACT 2 SCENE 12

(FADE ON GHOST)

GHOST: Hail, you black horrors of midnight's noon,

    You fairies, goblins, bats and foul owls, all hail!

    Oh, you mortal watchmen, from whose throat,

    The immortal phantoms dread croakings rise,

    You prancing apparitions who by day condemned to die

    In elemental pyres, now play in church yards,

    Skip over our graves to the loud music of a silent bell!

    All Hail! King Arthur Two, what does it mean to you?

(SPOT ON KING ARTHUR, drinking side stage)

KING ARTHUR : Where is my Glumdalca now? I love her truly,

    Every inch was bliss. But when she rolled off me,

    I was flatter than a pancake really.

GHOST *(OFF STAGE):* Too whit, twohoo!

KING ARTHUR: What bloody noise is that? What swine dares

    At this time of night, profane the peace with cacophony

    Of voice and feet?

(GHOST comes forward)

GHOST: One who defies your empty power to hurt him,

One who dares to walk into your bed chamber, unannounced.

KING ARTHUR: You presumptuous slave, you penurious yob,

You vacant lot, I'll have you put to the stake.

GHOST: Frighten other people with that up 'em OK,

But I am a ghost and am already dead,

Over and done with as a man of flesh and genius.

Bloody heavens above, you stars –

It is better that your last hour had come

For that hour is now extended by at least a tun,

Fifty by fifty times a slow death and all for fun!

Don't worry, I'll drag you forward by your shroud,

Every second squeeze you like a bladder

So you can piss your life away,

Because you do not really matter. Goodnight!

(MAKES TO LEAVE)

KING ARTHUR: So you're running away, is it? Just as well

I was wondering just what courage a ghost might have.

And you can't say I said that, since you have no breath to speak of.

Don't dare walk into my chambers once again,

On pain of being cast away on the sands,

As sure as guns go 'bang, bang! Bang!'

I'll have you on the wrack prepared to hang,

I'll fill that Red Sea full of loathsome gin

The stink alone kills cats from twenty paces,

Ruins mothers and their kin, I'd dunk you in,

I promise, you, the last sodden sample of the lowest races.

GHOST: Ha, says you! Ha, says I, for King Arthur II,

Whose father's ghost I know as well as Thumb's,

Two for the price of one, back in the day well known

As mighty Arthur Number One. Now I see,

It's true, even those who drive a coach and horses

Soon make forgotten corpses.

KING ARTHUR: Not for Arthur Two, for Number one was number two's true father.

I see you now, you really are the honest pere of Number Two,

And I am me twice over and so is Tom. I thought you were kidding first.

GHOST: Here I am, an authentic infinite shade!

KING ARTHUR: Then let me press you in my arms

You spirit multiple, you best of ghosts,

You're something more than insubstantial now!

GHOST: I wish I was something more as well

So we could feel each other in a warm embrace.

But now I have the advantage over you,

For while I feel you, you can't feel me.

KING ARTHUR: But tell me, you fine piece of fancy atmosphere, tell me

What terribly important business brings

You back down here to the baleful earth?

GHOST: Ok, then, be ready, be advised,

The land is full of slaughters,

Enough to send you packing home.

Listen, *(Sound of mob off stage)* hear that?

Your subjects, en masse, are perfectly revolting,

Up in arms, led by the forked-tongue Grizzle.

KING ARTHUR: I suspected all along, you know,

    I shall have him shovelled into dung

    Like a beetle on its back, the bum!

GHOST: I observed it too, when rosy-fingered dawn arose

    To open the revealing shutters of the sky,

    It exposed your royal palace quite a lot,

    So I have seen bees in clusters forming up,

    I have seen regiments of stars on frosty nights,

    I have seen the sands of time on windy days,

    I have seen the shades on Pluto's ghastly shores,

    I have seen daisies dance in Spring,

    I have seen the leaves of Autumn fall,

    I have seen the apples of summer smile on me,

    I have seen the snows of Winter's icy frowns,

    I have seen...

KING ARTHUR: ...Oh, fuck what you have seen!

    Have you come down here as Arthur's phantom next of kin

    To abuse me with endless similes

    To keep me on a verbal wrack.

Bugger off, my mind is full of triple meanings now,

All made worse by two-faced traitors,

I have grizzles to erase, not make.

Go! Or by all the torments of married bliss, I'll run

You through the body although you have none!

GHOST: Watch it, O King, the woods are on the move,

I will leave you now, not frightened

By your voice or temper,

Bless you my son's son's son,

And my son's remembrancer, myself,

And Merlin too. Cherchez la fame, I suppose,

But you're right, where is sweet

Huncamunca Honeycombe...?

KING ARTHUR: ...leave her out of this!

GHOST: Be warned by cockerels such as chanticleer.

I will warn you formally now come what may,

King Arthur Two! Beware! Beware! Beware!

And try to avoid your impending fate

For if you are killed today

Tomorrow all your care will come too late.

KING ARTHUR: Hang on a minute, sprite chappy, misty kin,

Don't leave me in this uncertain state,

So when you tell me what my fate is,

Teach me how to avoid it.

(ASIDE, to audience) A moment alone with you lot.

All of you, join in the universal condemnation

Of 'like' and 'as', as very sick figures of speech.

Curst be the poet who first ever wrote a bloody simile!

Damn every bard who used them publicly, tho' I have seen

Some whose comparisons are both just and true,

While other wordy fools liken all

To a block of rotten wood or Cheshire cheese.

I tell you, Lucifer is happy here, for the whole of creation

Cannot furnish apt metaphors for his wicked situation.

Thanks for listening. Back to the fray.

Now what to do about one Colonel Farr-Parr Grizzle and the nation?

GHOST *(Shouting off stage)*: Good luck, tough shit, my son! Think on it!

KING ARTHUR: I'll give it my most serious consideration, sir.

ACT 2 SCENE 13

(ENTER QUEEN DOLALLOLLA, steals up to KING)

DOLLALLOLLA: Why, my heart's King Arthur Number II,

> Do you sneak away from these my breasts?

> Why do you leave me alone in the dark

> When you know I'm scared of ghosts

> And dogs in the night that bark?

KING ARTHUR: Oh, Dollallolla, blame love, my love,

> I'd hoped the fumes of last night's

> Punch had shut your eyes tight as a stone.

> *(ASIDE)* A moment again. But I have found that there's no potency

> In wee drams for tender horny wives,

> Who wake and ride upon their husbands

> After two quarts of gin or more,

> But what even bigger surprise awaits

> For wives to wake up with the sun,

> To find their Romeos vanished,

> Then reaching out with grasping arms

Finds her deserted for a limp and useless bolster

In spite of her ever willing charms.

Reflect well on that, my Queen,

I have read all about it in Ovid's Metamorphosis,

How Jove in an inanimate form

Lay with lovely Diana, trust me in my myths,

Sometimes I thought the bolster was my Diana,

Or something like that, I think.

Now come back to me, you most virtuous of your sex,

Oh, Dollallolla, if only wives were all like you,

Husbands in their beds would sprout no horns,

Or ladies hide them in a better place;

If sweet Huncamunca inherits just a part of you,

Tom Thumb indeed is blessed in bed and board,

Tom Thumb! Oh, that fatal name,

If only you knew what I knew, you'd know-

-yes, just what you'd know, like a starfish in the sand.

DOLLALLOLLA *(Aside)* : Such sticky pastry metaphors,

Where does he find them? I can't make out one word.

Tell me, Arthur, why do you always announce, like those men

Who travel freak shows about the countryside,

With 'now you will see what you will see,' why?

So, come on, tell me more, now you have told me quite enough.

(ENTER DOODLE in a rush)

DOODLE: Great Arthur Two and sloshed Dollallolla One!

May you both be blessed with ever such long lives,

I beg you now, hear a most dolorous dirge,

News these two bickering physicians bear.

(EXIT NOODLE. ENTER 1st, 2nd PHYSICIANS, Dr C HURCHYARD and Dr FILLGRAVE, bickering)

FILLGRAVE: We attend your Majesty's command, however, lugubrious,

From the fields of ignominious defeat.

KING ARTHUR: 'Defeat?' Never! 'Ignominious'? perhaps...

DR CHURCHYARD: The great Tom Thumb is gone, gone,

In spite of my most prime medicaments.

DR FILLGRAVE : Mine too.

DOLLALLOLLA: Gone!? Woe, woe and woe again!

KING ARTHUR: This is passing sudden. To what distemper did the great Tom Thumb succumb?

DR CHURCHYARD: He died, may it please your majesty, of a distemper called Diarmorphine,

> Spotted by the second Chief Surgeon's sixth assistant, Dr AP Galen, of Rome.

> When the great Tom had, in the heat of battle, sudden bouts of giddiness, I bled him, then

> applied mustard poultices, glister for blisters, the devil's claw for gripes, then a

> purge, a vomit, then came the stools and all that crap. Diarmorphine was the name of the game.

DR FILLGRAVE: No, it was not. I tell you, you're making a big mistake, it was not

> Diamorphine,it was Peripilisis! If he'd broken his arm, I would have cut it off, if he'd

> had a headache, I would have peeled off his scalp, then and only then, I would have

> given my special Emetics and Diaretics. Your Majesties, I assure you the symptoms of

> Peripilisis, are very various, varied, uncertain and doubtful, but I know them like the

> back of my hand. Dead as a doornail. Sorry.

(TOM THUMB rushes on flourishing a bloody sword)

TOM THUMB: Your Majesties, Arthur Two, Dollallolla One, a great victory has blessed our arms.

DOCTORS FILLGRAVE, CHURCHYARD: Jesus Christ, not him!

KING ARTHUR: You still live!?

DOLLALOLLA: You blazing stars above, can this be true, or is it an Illusion I see before my eyes?

KING ARTHUR: And you have not been dead at all?

TOM THUMB: Not one itsy, bitsy little bit!

DOLLALLOLLA: Thank God you have not changed.

TOM THUMB: Hear you! Farr-Parr Grizzle with a bold rebellious mob,

> Advanced upon the Palace, threatening every gate,
>
> But the Princess sweet Huncamunca, I delivered straight,
>
> Triumphant as the Tom who stands before you now,
>
> Without my iron helmet in place maybe,
>
> But I will soon, too, set the people free
>
> Guided by divine right and royal Liberty!
>
> But where is my sweet, sweet Huncamunca?
>
> There was a rumour among the Grenadiers,
>
> She was mistaken for a bride. She stood outside
>
> The fray a moment or two, a bravura bravado!

194

Then sped the bloody field like a lamb from slaughter

Give her my eternal love, however faint the laughter.

DR FILLGRAVE : Hey, what about us?

TOM THUMB: There you still are, you carvers of the dead! Bugger off!

DR GRAVEYARD: We've come all this way...

DR FILLGRAVE: ...and it was costly too.

DR GRAVEYARD: I told you it was Peripilisis...

DR FILLGRVE: ...it was Diamorphine!

KING ARTHUR: Get outta in here!

DR FILLGRAVE: We've lost our reputation, Mr Graveyard, and what is worse, our double fee,

I fear.

DR GRAVEYARD: Damn all monarchs, the trick did not work this time, Mr Fillgrave

DR FILLGRAVE: It will next time, Dr Graveyard, there are plenty left.

(EXIT 1st, 2nd PHYSICIAN, Doctors FILLGRAVE and GRAVEYARD)

TOM THUMB: False physicians to a man, Chief Poisoners

To the State, part of the conspiracy to throw

The people down the drains, with broken hearts and gins,

And cast aspersions on my longevity,

Foul Grizzle, footling rebels, all drowning in their piddle.

I go now, and it won't be long before I return,

Being the protagonist in practically every scene,

Wait for me, in joyousness, of course, but in patriotism also,

Sweet Huncamunca will answer all your questions in a moment.

ACT 2 SCENE 14

(EXIT TOM THUMB, flourishing sword, meets PRINCESS HUNCAMUNCA, they embrace, EXIT, sound of love making)

VOICE of KING ARTHUR: Good lad! Go to it!

VOICE of DOLLALLOLLA: Brave lass! Go to it!

(Sound of love making, with sound of battle. PAUSE. ENTER PRINCESS HUNCAMUNCA, tidying herself. ENTER DOLLALLOLLA, KING)

KING: You look exhausted, my daughter, but satisfied, like humanity at its peak.

DOLLALLOLLA: I know where in the hell you've been and so does your Dad here, so belt up. But where has Tom Thumb gone?

HUNCAMUNCA: Well, I 'm not sure for now, but half a minute ago

He sallied out to encounter the two-faced foe,

Piddle and Co, and swore, if fate has not deserted him,

From his shoulders he'd cut vile Grizzle's head

And serve him up as chocolate in your bed!

KING ARTHUR: Such down-to-earth loyalty! Come Ladies,

Stay with me, as one, we'll wait for Tom Thumb's victory.

DOLLALLOLLA: Tho' giants conspire with Grizzle and the gods,

Tom Thumb alone is equal to all the sods!

He is indeed a breastplate to us all!

While he fights for us, we need not fear at all,

His martial arm performs our very wish

And serves up every foe in many a gravy dish.

KING ARTHUR: Let the mistress of this house have pause

While the cook presents the bill of fare,

Whether cod, that northern king of fish,

Or duck, or goose, or pig adorn our forks

However, many guests appear, regardless of their sex and number,

She sets their dinners now without a single blunder.

Let's go now, and celebrate the decanting of many tops of bottles.

DOLLALLOLLA: You are so insightful, I have the thirst of a Dutchman's dredger.

(EXIT GLUMDALCA, KING ARTHUR, HUNCAMUNCA)

ACT 2 SCENE 15

(TOM THUMB wonders on and off looking upwards)

TOM THUMB: I have never seen such a day as this!

How the weather change with our fortunes,

The still born thunder rumbles overhead

As the gods unhinge the world,

And heaven and earth in confusion hurl

Their darts upon the earth.

Yet will I tread upon thus tottering ball

Until Farr-Parr has his inevitable fall.

(EXIT TOM THUMB. ENTER PARR-FARR GRIZZLE, DOODLE)

FARR-PARR GRIZZLE: So far our arms with victory are crowned,

Tho' we have fought one or two or three or four,

Yet we have found no further enemy to draw.

DOODLE: But I would cheerfully avoid today

To engage our foes, for it is the first of April, as it goes.

FARR-PARR GRIZZLE: Today of all days I'd choose,

For on this day my dear Mum was born,

You watch, I'll make Tom Thumb into such a Fool.

I'll send his wits on errands he's never heard of,

To weep among the flames of hell below.

DOODLE: I'm happy to find our armies are so stout,

By god, they knock the opposition out,

Nor does it move my wonder less to know

How we came to be so strong,

Let's talk about it as we march along,

There are two sides to every confrontat-i-o-n,

Especially mine, the man of common sense,

Partisan of every bleeding fact-i-o-n.

(EXEUNT FARR-PARR GRIZZLE, DOODLE. ENTER TOM THUMB side stage. Shadows of TOM fighting upstage, with battle noises)

ACT 2 SCENE 16

TOM THUMB *(Aside)*: Jesus Christ, my senses are lost in amazement.

Hey, Huncamunca, Glumdanca, come on, come on!

(ENTER GLUMDANCA, HUNCAMUNCA)

Look at your Tom! yet another me. Look!

The ghost of Merlin recalls me at my best!

GLUMDALCA: Ah! No, I do not wish to look on this,

A sight of horror, see, hold back, oh no!

My darling Tom, you are torn to pieces and devoured by

The expanded jaws of a huge red cow!

(GHOST APPEARS SIDE STAGE)

GHOST: Don't let these sights put off your brainy mind, Tom Thumb,

For, see, a sight more glorious hits your eyes,

See, from afar, a theatre rises up,

There are ages still unborn,

And they will pay tribute

To the heroic actions of today

Then this burlesque tragedy

At length shall choose your name

As the greatest Laureate of the Game

Henry bloody Fielding at his worst and best again,

That's the real name of the game!

TOM THUMB: Enough, let no more war-like music sound,

We fall contented if we fall renowned!

ACT 2 SCENE 17

(ENTER FARR-PARR GRIZZLE, DOODLE, with rebels. GLUMDALCA, with TOM THUMB - the two groups confront each other)

DOODLE: At last the enemy advances here and stops!

FARR-PARR GRIZZLE: I hear them with my ear, I see them with my eye. Draw your broad swords, now, curs.

DOODLE: Farr-Parr fights for liberty!

FARR-PARR GRIZZLE: - the very mustard of life!

DOODLE: I battle for both sides of the sandwich!

TOM THUMB: Are you the famous man whom famous men call 'Colonel Farr-Parr Grizzle'?

FARR-PARR GRIZZLE: Are you the much more famous man very famous men call 'Tom Thumb?'

TOM THUMB: The same.

FARR-PARR GRIZZLE: Come on, upon our bodies we will prove our worth. For free Liberty!

TOM THUMB: For free love! Charge!

DOODLE: For everyone everywhere! Charge!

(A general melee, DOODLE stands aside, FARR-PARR GRIZZLE, GLUMDALCA and TOM THUMB pause)

GLUMDALCA: Turn, you coward, you wouldn't fly from a mere giantess, would you?

FARR-PARR GRIZZLE: You're too coarse, too full of cellulite to fight.

GLUMDALCA: Stop this my thrust to your heart then.

FARR-PARR GRIZZLE: No, I'm thrusting at yours.

GLUMDALCA: Fuck, you've pushed too hard, you've run me through the guts.

FARR-PARR GRIZZLE: Then that's the end of one at least.

GLUMDALCA: No, it's not, I'm tough as shit, and still got lines to speak.

TOM THUMB: And when you're dead, Farr-Parr Grizzle, boy, that's the end of two,

Both rebels to the cause – the cause – myself, not you!

FARR-PARR GRIZZLE: Don't you come all triumphal over me!

DOODLE: Under all the bombast I was true to King Arthur II of the Brythons.

See how I'm standing at your side,

Ready to repel any creeping marine commandoes inside!

FARR-PARR GRIZZLE: Sweet Honeycombe Huncamunca is still mine!

TOM THUMB: Take that! (*Stabs him, GRIZZLE falls*)

FARR-PARR GRIZZLE:

>You won't enjoy the Princess undisturbed,
>
>I'll send my ghost to fetch her to the other world
>
>As mere bait for heaven, then she shall return.
>
>But Oh! I feel death rumbling in my brains,
>
>Some kinder sprite knocks softly on my soul,
>
>And gently whispers me to haste away;
>
>I come, I come, most willingly I come,
>
>As when some city wife longs for country air
>
>To Hampstead or Highgate does repair,
>
>Her husband in a hurry implores her at the door
>
>And cries, 'my dear, the coach is at the door.'
>
>With equal wish, desirous to be gone,
>
>She gets into the coach and shouts 'Drive on!'
>
>And so do I! Aaaah! *(DIES)*

TOM THUMB: With these last words he vomits up his soul,

>Which, like whipped cream, the devil swallows whole.
>
>Bear off the body now and cut off the head,
>
>Which I will to the king in triumph lug;

The rebellion's dead, their goose is cooked

And now my breakfast is prepared.

(DOODLE salutes TOM. TOM THUMB, GLUMDALCA, EXIT. GRIZZLE, dead on floor)

ACT 2 SCENE 18

(COURT, KING ARTHUR II, QUEEN DOLLALOLLA, GLUMDALCA, MUSTACHA waving. COURTIERS)

KING: So Grizzle is no more!

Open the prisons, set the wretches free,

Order our treasurer to disburse six pounds

To pay their debts. Let no one weep today,

Come, Dollallolla...

– aside - curse that stupid name,

It is so long it takes an hour to speak.

By heavens, I'll change it to 'Fido'

Or some other civil monosyllable

That will not tire my tongue,

And Glamulca's just as bad.

Come, dear, sit you down,

And from my throne right here,

Let's watch the courtiers bow in fear.

Tell them to come forward.

This is the wedding day of our dear Princess and brave Tom Thumb,

Tom Thumb, who wins two victories today,

And this way marches back, bearing Grizzle's head...

(DOODLE dashes on, in a sweat)

DOODLE: Oh monstrous, terrible, dreadful, heinous!

Deaf are my ears to it, and my eyes blind,

Dumb my tongue, feet lame! all senses lost!

Howl wolves, grunt bears, hiss snakes, shriek, you ghosts...

KING: ...what is this blockhead talking about?

DOODLE: I mean, my Leige, only to lace this tale with a little decent horror.

Well here goes - while I was in my garret two stories high,

I was no turncoat ever, I looked down into the streets below

And saw Tom Thumb surrounded by a mob -

Two hundred apprentices out for blood, twenty-one shoe-boys,

Hackney coachmen in a line behind the whores,

Assorted chimney sweeps, fish wives, swearing at themselves,

And born on high, aloft, the very bloody head of Farr-Parr himself.

When, all of sudden through the streets there came

A big red cow, of larger than usual size,

And in a moment... or guess,

You can guess the rest,

Tore up Tom Thumb like a rat

Between a terrier's paws,

And before you could say, Oh, No,

Swallowed the pieces whole!

The dead body of Tom Thumb is now no more.

GLUMDALCA: Woe, woe, I was dead right, spot on, sad too say!

KING ARTHUR: Let it be, let it be, this night has cured

Your love for me, and mine for you, no doubt of it.

Dollallolla is my only hope.

Lock up all the lock-ups all over again,

Order my Treasurer not to give out a single farthing.

Hang all the culprits, guilty or not, it doesn't matter.

Ravish the virgins in the streets,

Schoolmasters whip the boys, and more.

Let bankers, lawyers and estate agents loose

To cheat and rob and ruin the world,

Bury the babes as they poke their noses out

Of their bloodied wombs

Of this crook'd and silly universe...

...Christ, I think her Majesty's going to faint...

DOODLE: Not yet, gracious Dolallolla, peerless Queen, I have no more news.

ACT 2 SCENE 19

(GHOST OF TOM THUMB APPEARS)

GHOST: Yes, Tom Thumb, I am here again, but hardly alive,

My body is in the cow but my spirit in here thrives.

(GHOST OF FARR-PARR GRIZZLE appears)

FARR-PARR GRIZZLE: Mine too. O you stars, my vengeance is restored,

You'll never get past me now, for I will kill your ghost!

(GRIZZLE KILLS TOM THUMB'S GHOST)

GLUMDALCA: Barbarous felon! You've gone and killed the best ghost in the land.

HUNCAMUNCA: I shall still dream of him in my bed!

GLUMDALCA: No you shan't! Take that! *(Kills HUNCAMUNCA)* And that! *(Kills FARR-PARR GRIZZLE)*

DOODLE: You great big fat murderess! Take that!

(KILLS GLUMDALCA)

DOLLALLOLLA: My champion gone! And with my own fruit knife! Take that!

MUSTACHA: Save me, my Doodle!

DOODLE: Save me, my Mustacha!

KING ARTHUR: I knew Doodle for the filthy double agent he always was! And your waving was always third rate! Come on missus, stand by your man!

(DOLLALLOLLA, and KING kill DOODLE, MUSTACHA)

DOODLE *(Dying)*: Take that! The end of kings!

KING ARTHUR: End you too! Take that!

DOLLALLOLLA: For all your fucking around!

(Stabs KING. KING ARTHUR, dying, turns knife on himself, to himself)

Only myself can do royalty like me!

(Stabs himself)

As when the child whom Nurse from mischief guards,

Sends Jack the Bastard with a pack of cards

Kings, queens, knaves and all are at instant risk

And mow each other down,

Till the whole lot of them

Lie scattered and overthrown,

    (To AUDIENCE) So are all our packs upon the floor are cast,

All I can boast is that I fell the last!

(KING ARTHUR DIES. CUT LIGHTS. CAST LINE UP FOR CURTAIN CALL. ENTER SIR ROBERT WALPOLE, in a rage, flourishing cane)

SIR ROBERT: Stay where you are! *(Shouts to off stage)* Secretary, call the Constable and take all this down! Which one of you said it, yes, that even I 'had my price?' do I? And our royals live in 'sties?' Who said that? You! *(ACTOR falls on knees. SIR ROBERT Thrashes him. ACTOR whispers)* O, it was an ad lib, you say, can't remember. You mock *me*, you mock my office of Prime Minister, you mock the king, you mock the kingdom! The last straw! Too many plays, too many libels. Never again! I'll soon see you out of work, not only will I now strictly control you vagabonds through my Office of the King's Revels, and my licenses to perform plays, you can now add texts to that, the scripts submitted to my department before any license is even considered. The stage will be cleansed of these criminal slanders, especially against me! *(Listens)* Where? Yes, well, the Lord Chamberlain's Office will do. Who's in place there now? *(Listens)* Yes, oh, yes, Odell, didn't he write a poem or two in praise of my Bills and Acts. Yes, he'll do too. He can be my first official departmental Reader of Plays. Yes, close this Hay theatre forthwith, ban that burlesque and put this Fielding out to fallow. And so great is my influence, I will see that this censorship lasts until 1968, such is the misplaced toleration of our people. Why, you ask - because I said so. Don't any of you decent folk worry, I have legions of patriotic spies to watch over you, down to your very naked thoughts, pounds, shillings and pence. Off with the play! And so to bed, *(winks)* if you see what I mean! *(CUT LIGHTS. EXIT SIR ROBERT WALPOLE SHOUTING)* Secretary, call my constables! *(YELLS)* Curtain! (To AUDIENCE, nastily) And I mean it.

CURTAIN

CASTAWAY (A PLAY)
A dream play in one act or so

The action takes place in the imagination

CAST

Gerald, 35, a visitor

Ceridwen,30, Gerald's wife

Girlie, 23, Gerald's girl friend

Geoffrey, 30, his brother in law

DANIEL, Gerald's father-in-Law

1st, 2nd MAN IN MASK

Chorus of masked ghouls

Parts can be doubled

(Stage hung with transparent curtains, gauzes, sound of wind blowing through them, distant thunder and lightning, a bugle calling Last Post, words of military command, echoes of distant traffic, horns, motor bikes, ambulance sirens, bombardments, collapsing buildings, distant shrieks and howls, all mixed and irregular; eerie twilight, odd shadows images flash on and off on screen, rows of phantom masks, of extraordinary hideousness, (these are to be selected from the Swiss Valley of LOTSCHENTAL'S TSCHAGGATTA Festival, see 'masks', internet) On higher level, backstage, stands GERALD, 35, strongly built, dressed in working man' clothes with gardener's belt with secateurs, boots, mobile and note book; he gazes around in awe, townscape flashes past; when Gerald 'flies' he uses his arms as a bird, whooping and dipping in mid-air. He holds onto an (imaginary) boom as he mimes flying. His mobile sounds)

GERALD (*Listens*): O, Hello, Ma. Yes, always lovely to hear your voice. Yes, I'm on the roof of the trolley bus again, yes, number twenty-seven. No, no danger. I'm hanging on to the electronic boom, as usual. Just whizzing past the college now, where I might get a job. God, they've changed everything all round here. The wreckers with their tanks. Streets, houses, obliterated. Apt armageddons in the van. And I was only here yesterday. Listen to the bedlam, they'll never end that. Huge new block towers up to the clouds, imitation Gothic piles, gargoyles as big as your ass; new ruins on old, Jesus, what an enigma; Christ, the Colisseum just flashed past; prisons of the Fleet, execution blocks! 'Blood streams in the firmament!' Where have all the grottoes gone, the havens, bowers, rotundas, auberges, sanctums? O the follies of it all. Pardon, Ma? "And where are the ideal locations in model form?" you ask, Ma? Well, there's Avalon, the Garden of Eden, the Happy Hunting Grounds, the Land of Apples, Brigadoon, Shangri la, El Dorado and my favourite, Ma, Parnassus, the Mount of the Bards! – could be anywhere. And what is my job in all this, you ask – I am the Guardian of Lost Chords, Warden of the Golden Mean, in short Ma, I am the Chief Imagineer of the ancient Demetians! What…? Now don't worry, I'll soon have a proper job after this little adventure in foreign parts, and who knows, I might end up in the conker trees behind the old family homestead. After all I am in love with all things sylvan, dingles and copses, even down to the underbrush. No, my sleep is no longer troubled by masked succubi, I sleep like an old-born babe, really I do, I do not exaggerate, and I'll be home for the jolly hols when this is all done, I swear. Listen, Ma, this is the Guardian–Warden himself speaking. No forked tongue in sight. "Where..?"(Listens, looks around, swooping) Yes, at the traffic lights opposite the Clinic, where the girl masturbates, she's there now, so it must be Saturday morning. She is banished, you know, there is no bed for her in the family annals. They say they don't know, but I suspect. They pretend no girl whatsoever masturbates on the pavement in the centre of town, route 27, especially since the girl is from a decent family, but everyone knows she does - the jerky movements alone are a dead giveaway. Not a word against her, I try to tell them all, but they just jeer and mime wanking. Shameful. Let her alone, I cry! They cast her aside, so she does not even possess the status of a black sheep. The girl can't help it, and why not? All she's doing is what we're all doing, isn't it, trying to squeeze a bit of pleasure out of this unbelievable and bloody turmoil called life! On a common wrack, the lot of us! Bunch of wankers! (Aside) I mustn't talk to my Ma this way, must I? Yes, Ma, still on the roof, enjoying the view, wherever it is. Christ, the voices again from between the clouds, all clashing, just snatches, some boastful, some new Towers of Babel, bugger off! - can you hear the bugle call? (Listens) "Take no notice?" OK, Ma. No, Ma, me? Yes, in a dream, nor in a dream – in between. Now Ma, tell Dad this. (Reads from notebook, in broad Welsh accent) 'the Llangollen Whitebeam 'sorbus cuneifolio' is restricted to the cliffs of Eglwyseg Mountain in Dinbych, whereas in Merthyr Tydfil the motley whitebeam 'sorbus motlegiana' is really a hybred of Llew's Rowan and grows abundantly in all edgelands." Tell him. Ta , Ma, located the old herbal but yesterday. Fresh knowledge! Dad won't laugh, will he?

217

Well, if he does, tell him this, that yesterday I had the honour of promenading at noon along the margin of a sunny field of ripening oats. Yes Ma, Quaker I imagine. That should calm him. You know what my epistemological episodes do to him. And emphasize the fact that I may be still only an apprentice tree surgeon, but with fantastic prospects, marvellous foliage, the budding historian of each and every growth of mistletoe of the old oak trees of the fucking Druids. (To audience) But in truth I know I am basically just an extremophile, survivor of the red hot lava ocean flows from the smoky vents of the earth's crust, on the midnight hour! Nothing pacific about that! Ha! (To himself, gripping his forhead, swaying) Damn, through the mists again, extraneous thoughts do come... "The Coelabites of the...Thespiad were assaulted by numerous naked... demons...."

(Yell off stage) : "For God's sake say something we understand!"

GERALD: 'Take no notice', as you say, Ma. Now where do I get off, how to get down? Like a swimmer of the skies, I have to swoop! The bus-stop there, by my girlie. Coming in to land! *(GIRLIE in mask appears side stage. GERALD 'swims' off his perch and lands on the pavement. Smile at each other. GIRLIE has a rapid orgasm, to GERALD'S nods of approval. GERALD speaks Into mobile)* Yes, Ma, I think she's come, I can see her fingers, all glistening, more relaxed too. She's nodding back to me! Lovely local vestal virgin, Ma, and all nympho, not a fake orgasm in her whole body. *(Shouts)* Hi, there, lovely, girl, let me tell you again - you, like me, I am proud to be associated with your frankly self-services in the open air. We, for example, constantly appear to be in a state of existence, don't we, and will anyone give us an explanation?! No, they just show us the door, so many times, before slamming it in our faces. *(Into mobile)* No, Ma, 'extremophile', that was a joke, not meant for Dad, just the leafy bits and the page numbers for him. Tell him I love the visions and that I feel so much safer up here among the vultures, you immediately know a human flesh-eater when you meet one.

(Listens. Sound of bell of 27!) Yes, cling, cling, off you go number 27, till we ride again. Bye, bye, Girlie. You have swum into my ken again! *(GIRLIE faded off. To mobile)* OK. Love you Ma and Pa. Never not to be in touch. Promise! Cheers for the day!

1st VOICE, off stage, female, mature, screams in agony: Mother, dead! Dead! Dead! Now father, die, die, die!

(GERALD does not hear, wipes his brow, peers around, sways dizzily, pulls himself together, consults note book. Ghoul faces, masks flit, sound of sobbing, cracks of whip, grinding machinery. Image of MAN IN HOSPITAL BED, DIRTY OLD DANIEL, wrinkled, spotted, toothless, white-bearded, in hospital nightgown, torn and stained, he drools, farts, burps, splutters, scratches, spits, wanks, drinks from bedpan)

DIRTY OLD DANIEL (Shakes fist): I issued no orders. There wasn't a hint of evacuation there! I alone will decide when to hit the piss-pots of paradise. I gave no orders from myself alone!

(Image flickers on and off; distant music, a three-second snatch of ABBA's 'Fernando', fade to cacophony. GERALD 'wakes' and does one or two dance steps. A smart suit in plastic Cleaner's cover on a hanger appears back stage. A figure in the gloom. GEOFFREY, 35, dressed like a bank manager, shakes the suit at Gerald)

GERALD: Where's Ceridwen?

GEOFFREY: You married a slut, didn't you?

GERALD: The forks are still dirty after she does the washing up. Not me.

GEOFFREY: You have a slut for a wife and I have a slattern for a sister, Bro.

GERALD: I am not your brother by any length of the imagination.

GEOFFREY: 'Half-brother.' Got this suit from your now sick Pa-in-law, dirty old Dan in his den of sinners - us, you, everyone, that is, this time. Better watch it, you could get blamed for everything, after all you are not from our street. Said to give this to you and not to cancel the show

GERALD: What 'show'?

GEOFFREY: The theatre one, in town or the Clinic

GERALD: But I'm not involved on stage in either.

GEOFFREY: That's what you think. *(Shakes suit)* Fresh from the Cleaner's. Gerald, dear Bro, what is this really all about?

GERALD: Drooling dirty old Dan shoved it under my very nose three months ago. "Take it!' He insisted, 'not my size,' I insisted back. The five-foot miserly dwarf! 'I can't give it away,' he goes on, 'still lots of wear in it. Your size doesn't matter, you can use it when you paint the garage walls, or do those bits in the weeds you call 'gardening' a casual labourer about the place, I suppose. It takes all sorts, as my religion says. That's where I am so lucky, I always have the right answer. But, look," he goes on, "don't you see, there's still wear in it, there, there and there. Don't put it in the bin if you don't want to. I can't deal with it, I can't rub it out, it could go on for months. You do the dirty deed yourself! The show must go on, or not, as the case may be.' Then he marches off leaving me holding the glossy three-piece. I chucked it behind a tree and fled, but he followed me and now he asks everyone to give it to me for 'the final solution.'

GEOFFREY: Every time he opens that leaden vault he calls his mouth, the trees for mile around shed their leaves.

GERALD: Reversal of nature, eh? Not bad! I didn't suspect it at first. Leave him to Lucifer, in his deadly claws. Heard they're doing tests on disgusting old him as we speak.

GEOFFREY: You know after his last by-pass op, the nurses found him in the bog having a smoke.

GERALD: What a smoke-screen is this world.

GEOFFREY: Well again, welcome Bro-in-law. My foul old half-Pa told me to say that all the time, and keep you occupied like mowing the lawn for your bread, show you round the estate, make him, that's you, Gerald, jealous of him like the rest of the human beings in the shitty toilets of the endless, farting globe. Tell him about my religion and how I dominate it, with my seraphim and cherubim, and, what's more, manipulate Lady Luck herself, by the very labia! That's me at my highest!" That's what he said. "But be cool about it, Geoffrey," he went on, "I'm in the process of making my last will and testament, but the Man-with-the- Scythe won't get me until he's got my say so, I've got some vicious connections in the heavenly pastures, so watch out, Mr Scythe! And bend the knee to your truly here, who is so much me!" Dirty old Daniel and his foetid pen, always on the lookout for a testicle or two to crush, smear a nipple ring, pull a Tampax string... I quote of course...

GERALD: ...sounds about normal for his circle of Hades.

(Image of DANIEL in hospital bed, flashes on. Goes into repulsive body noises, scratches, as at first appearance)

DANIEL: 'Normal?!' Don't count your chickens! Who am I before? Whoever I will be, I was' I was never a door without a hinge, never a soul without a sin, never a rape without a blessing,

221

you'll be pleased to hear. To put it honestly, I am a secret agent from Heaven on direct orders from the Saviour. My personal Handler is the Archangel Gabriel himself, I hold congress with the greater and lesser prophets of all time, Moses and his bush, Abraham and his altar, etc, etc, I am not named Prophet Dirty Daniel Senior, for nothing. My task is to obfuscate all the deeper mysteries of the Bible, which sometimes, not even an owl can understand. My insights are immortalized as windows. As for you, the renewed good boys, by their own choice, go to many heavens, 77 in fact, and those who choose the evil path go to a multiplication of hells, mostly girls. The signs also lurk in ordinary things, on the pavement in black bubble gum blobs, as you wash yourself between your legs, suck your socks. How I abhor the abominations of the sycamore and the filthiness of the locust honey trees! There are endless wickednesses in gardens and allotments too, and I have been elected to recognise them at a glance, however hidden, like gooey Girlie sometimes, hidden in plain sight. I cast her out because, unlike Ceridwen, she did not confess to her multifarious sins of grunt and grind. Out, and show the world just what you are made of, I declared! And she did, like an arrow, such shame. What a film noire, threatening my bunk in Paradise, my little holy dens of gold under every dung-heap! Whereas Ceridwen was always up for it, and confessed her naughtiness to strangers in the night, and have it on from anyone, especially in the backseat of my Rolls. She recognised my exultation and gave freely. And why? Because the presence of the Second Coming is here and now and is happening all around us all over the place. You are not flesh and blood any longer, you are actually all spirit, sloughing off your sins like snakes. Ordinary things, handbags, cigarette lighters, lawn mowers all have their special spoors of good and evil, even a 'U' bend in the lavatory or wipe of the arse, have their sacred esoteric message. I know that among other chores, I am God's holy instrument for flogging by hand, as well as for bliss and manna and crab-meat, yes, the hairs in your nostrils and the wax in your ears, will not be spared. I can see it, yes, over there, stop that, sir, or I shall depress you to the seventh hell, or you madam, hands where I can see them, the Second Coming is not called that for nothing, either, and you are still under holy orders, by ME, yes, ME the mightiest of all the Serviteurs of JC, Daniel Senior, victor of all battles with the Guardian-Wardens, the so-called 'Imagineers.' Barbaric! And, yes I have to say it – jejune! Pass the word, stop casting the castaways, they're so pathetic! They will only cancel the show when I tell them in the theatre or the Green Room! As it stands, it will be all right on the night! Call the Surgeon-in-Chief, tell him to bring his sharpest scalpel, there's some tough old birds among the leathery arseholes out there tonight. Call for the Surgeon! (SCREAMS) Call for the bloody Surgeon and his scarlet fucking knife before I flat-line him with a single glance! Tell him, I'll tell him that I'll die when I like it, in theatre after theatre, cast after cast! I will give the order, me, myself, "Upstairs! Beyond the blue horizon!" Me. Upstairs! The Messiah has kicked the Archangel Gabriel off his perch so I can sit at his right hand, forever. God, I am so understanding. Eden, that's what it comes down to, all mine again, but only when I say so, and only for the likes of me, Agent Daniel Superb, Senior! Not now, not yet, not ever now or yet!

(FADE repulsive DANIEL to cacophony)

GERALD: "The show must go on or not go on," he said, the rotten old perv. GEOFFREY:... a public show? Just a self-glorying pustule with himself centre stage, and the rest of us in our proper place, hammered shut. (ASIDE to audience)

GERALD: Why does no one ask about the possible contents of his will?

GEOFFREY: This location seems to get stranger and stranger, you notice that?

GERALD: Yes, even the trolley buses do not 'ding, ding' as they used to. And they've changed their number to 27 'A'. And most of the quartier has been demolished.

GEOFFREY: You don't say so?! *(To audience)* Heard the latest, have you? No? Well, I'll tell you – Joe Blob has fallen in love with Jenny Taylor. Geddit - Jenny Taylor...'? Laugh, go on, laugh, laugh! *(Encourages audience to laugh. Sudden hideous screech of laughter off stage. GEOFFREY immediately cowed)*

(ENTER CERIDWEN, GEOFFREY'S sister, GERALD'S wife, a sexy thirty year old, in ultra mod gown)

CERIDWEN: Hello you two old farts.

GERALD *(Aside)*: Ceridwen, great Hag of night. *(To audience)* My wife.

CERIDWEN: That fucking suit! Why didn't you incinerate it for him?

GERALD: There was still wear in it.

GEOFFREY: Not in him, I hope.

CERIDWEN: Oh, shut up, you desiccated prick.

GEOFFREY: When did you ever say 'no'?

CERIDWEN: Don't you start. Have you decided who's who yet?

GEOFFREY: What about Brendon for King Arthur?

CERIDWEN: Brendan! The guy who shambles around Aberystwyth dressed as a monk?

GEOFFREY: He was the victim of an uncontrollable nuclear fission reaction, rod overburn R.P.O. He was a top surveyor of the

224

atomic nucleus before he became an opera singer. As a result of that dire RPO accident, he suffers from the serious distemper of impromptu laughter, of which I alone have the antidote.

GEOFFREY: And what is the antidote?

GERALD: The antidote is...there is no antidote.

VOICE *(OFF STAGE):* Fucking incomprehensible!

CERIDWEN: Why in the hell didn't you shred the threads. The Holy Father, a dismal pater, a vile groper, tell you later, might have let us stay for free in the garage garret and come up with the cash for this stupid show he's always jabbering about.

GEOFFREY: He'll put himself in the programme as both producer and director, you'll see. He'll fuck you.

CERIDWEN: Enough of you and your and Pa's primal ordure - fucking stupidity!

GERALD: True, he wanted the show to go on in the first place.

GEOFFREY: Why do you still clip his hedges and shorten his grass for him, all by yourself?

GERALD: I am the great undiscovered warden-guardian of the Demetian diplomatic corps.

GEOFFREY: Belt up, you penniless, linguistic prat.

CERIDWEN: I could have used the cellar as my boudoire. Shitty family scraps. And shopping last week, he refused to pay for the crab-meat in the shell, said I'd have to pay half of it. And there in the shop, on the counter, he divides the crab meat into two portions, in the shell, and we each paid for the his/her half. The butcher was agog. "Better than charades,' was our Pa's parting words to him.

GEOFFREY: Is the old sod dead yet? - he's had enough bloody near-death scrapes.

CERIDWEN: He's lying flat on his back in emergency, so no one can tell.

GERALD: What about Geoffrey here as Lancelot?

CERIDWEN: Bollocks! Have neither of you noticed yet that I am flowing with shiny red hair this morning?

GEOFFREY: You could do Guinevere.

CERIDWEN: That old tart!?

GERALD: Something's troubling you. Come on, out with it, no mask this time! No, on second thoughts...

CERIDWEN *(she dons a mask, in pseudo posh voice. GERALD and GEOFFREY go into tortured routines of shock/horror at the story)*:

Yes, your daughter here, the Marchioness of Maida Vale, turned up at the Boodles' Summer Solstice Verve Cliquot tennis party at Windrush-Bossingham Hall, and first person I saw was Princess Yasmin, with the Countess's daughter's best friend Lady Amber, and she was wearing the self-same porcelain sky-blue dress as me! A downright fashion nightmare!"

GEOFFREY: Get it off your chest, Sis, that's the thing.

CERIDWEN: Leave my tits out of this, dirty old poo, too.

GERALD: In spite of his critical condition, couldn't your shite-hawk Pa give us the cash flow for the show?

CERIDWEN: He wouldn't give you the shit from under his finger nails. Hell, he's still putting it about we're staying for free in that stinking garage garret of his. So drop it, buster!

GERALD: Couldn't we put down Geoffrey here as a deposit, after all, he is a genuine step- son.

GEOFFREY: I just received this letter from the chief Surgeon, he asks us to restrain all unnecessary screams, especially the onanistic howls from the girl known as 'Girlie,' who, the Surgeon warns, is gravely threatened with all those digital agitations and is in danger of dislocating her tibia...

CERIDWEN: ...excuse me, I have to go into a toilet to laugh at a joke that shitty!

(EXIT CERIDWEN, kicking the suit ahead of her)

GERALD: 'Slut' - the understatement of the era. (*Dons a mask)* I was spontaneously chasing vagaries last night when I saw her, with her mates, reeking specialists in regurgitation, in the act of vomiting in the gutter, stuck gluttonously together like male strippers in drag, self-loathing, self-pitying shrews running to fat and flatulence in well-known plazas, spoiled narcissists, foul-mouthed, immature, with piss-stained, skid-marked, sperm-soiled jokes. Later, I spotted her giving revellers 24 blow-jobs all in a row, in the market square, so much so that all the priests were alerted and had to go to the back of the queue.

CERIDWEN (*off stage, in loud whisper*): God how you must hate yourself.

GERALD: God, Jesus C, I used to love my wife, I chose her... I can't believe it. Where the fuck am I? Where have all the great cathedrals gone with their grand confessionals?

GEOFFREY: The Great Hag of Night has them in her thrall alright.

GERALD: I never suspected my ghastly Ceridwen lived in such a nest of vipers. No offense.

GEOFFREY: None taken. I should know.

GERALD: You'll inherit. He's got property all over the mediaeval City and the old countryside.

GEOFFREY: He won't cut me out. No, he can't ...he'll demote me, though, pennies not pounds, all tied up in complicated trust funds with well-paid trustees by the dozen. When he's gone, it's the lawyers for me, and I know a few ripe villains there who'll do him in, in bed or out of it. He'll die as well as decay, if I have anything to do with it!

GERALD: Everybody swears he'll survive. They blame his religion.

GEOFFREY: The fading sadist, I'll see about that.

GERALD: I wish it would rain more, it has a calming influence on the wall flowers. I'm off now, to mow a lawn or two, take in a bow or two. Ceridwen's seen dear dirty old Dan four or five times till yesterday, and she's not giving away a thing. Same for you. She won't get a bone out of him. She's keeping an eye on the whole theatre staff, in town and clinic, in case they operate on his wallet before the Xmas panto.

GEOFFREY: Cheers.

(FADE GEOFFREY. ENTER CERIDWEN, dressed in fashionable gown, waving a document)

GERALD: He's sent us a demand from his bailiffs, for three-months rent, I bet! Topsy bloody turvey turd! We've only been here three weeks.

CERIDWEN: Then do something about it. Your fault. If only you'd sent that suit away, to the salt mines, to Auschwitz-Birkenau, Hampstead, anywhere. A small thing to ask.

GERALD: Did you bring my sandwiches?

CERIDWEN: No, but I didn't forget your socks. *(Throws them at him)* And do something about that ugly cold sore on your lip. I can hardly look at you. And my boy-friends are a symptom, a trigger, not a cause.

GERALD: Trichomonas vaginalis can also affect the anal cavity.

CEREDWEN: You're always peculiar after you've been thinking. Last time it was cystitis.

GERALD: The honeymooner's affliction.

CERIDWEN: Nothing to do with me.

GERALD: Passion's piss disease.

CERIDWEN: Never for the Marchioness!

GERALD: Hah!

CERIDWEN: I don't know anything about that. I'm not ashamed of my boy-friends. I was never unfaithful. I just lay there. When I'm watching TV and want a fuck, I don't go to the street for cheap pick-ups. Basically I don't want any of them But I've got a block over you. When your hand's on my belly, it's like a tarantulla. And why should I deny myself the pleasures, you're older than me and done it all. You'd begrudge me a fuck with the guys who turned me on for the first time in my life. You do everything wrong as far as I'm concerned. They try every position. Buy yourself a book, yes, go out, 'How to Win Friends,' 'The Joy of Sex!' You might learn something. And I hate the curtains you chose and the forks are still dirty after the washing up...

GERALD: ...that is you!

CERIDWEN: No one helped me. I was equal to it all.

GERALD: That is not what you told me. You father...not so long ago....you're fond of telling it...go on.

CERIDEN: ...he drove me to the pine woods after the birthday party of my crazed sister and stopped in the shade of an old ash tree, leaned over to close my window, slid his hand onto my crotch and held it there, squeezing, up and down, then flipped back my skirt, ran his hand up to my cunt, which was moist already, I heartily confess it , and then with his middle finger right up, sent me to paradise, back arched in ecstasy, huge grunts, slipped off my panties, pushed me down in the back seat, I heard the zip of lust, widened my thighs, he bent over, and pushed and pushed harder, 'such little blood', he said, and up and down for forty five minutes to the second. And came I came back again and again. I had no choice, he was expiating his sin and mine too, together, intercourse was one of the Saviour's favourite signs, he said, and came all over my belly. He did the same to Ma on the same nights... GERALD: ...regular as...go on...

CERIDWEN:... as All Bran.

GERALD: If there is a God, Jesus should have cut off his balls – right?

230

CERIDWEN: I didn't do it on purpose. It was such a long time ago.

GERALD: Years later, you found the Book of Family Laws open on his desk at the page on rape and incest and penalties for such, and if you'd said one word about it, he'd still be doing ten years by. And your mother...

CERIDWEN: ...she didn't want to die. She yelled on her death bed, I was there, "I don't want to die. That devil will be there in hell waiting for me. I don't want to die. Die him! Die him! she cried and cried.

(Flash of DIRTY OLD DANIEL tossing, turning in hospital bed)

VOICE *(Off stage):* The nunc dimittis rehearsal now! *(In plain song):* 'Yes, O Lord, let your servants go in peace according to your holy word, for my eyes see the light you have prepared for all the nations and for all the glory of your true worshippers, here, corporeal, in person, never the dirty Jews, to dwell at your right hand forever, with no other soul, sprit or ghost in sight, except yours truly, here, me and myself! I alone know! After all, I have only ever taken half a dozen lives in my life, and they all deserved it! Bless you all, but much, much later."

(FADE DIRTY DAN. THE LAUGHING MAN *erupts onto stage, laughing, giggling, chortling. LAUGHING MAN points into audience occasionally laughing maniacally)*

LAUGHING MAN: Now who laughed that lying laughter out there then? I heard. There, there, there! You're not amused, are you, just embarrassed. There again and again. You all even laugh when I say the words, 'skid marks,' there see, not amused, or 'sperm', sperm always gets a laugh, it so leaps about the place, like shit always 'plops' about, doesn't it. I don't know – somehow too many genitalia hereabouts to night for any fun. Just piss off the lot of you, you, prime mirthless human disappointments! Bah! You're worse than me!

(EXIT LAUGHING MAN)

GERALD: That's telling the world. *(GERALD reads)* "Marriage is just another timidity system foisted on women for sex..."

CERIDWEN: I knew it!

GERALD: Your sentiments exactly. This plan...which you assert has taken you ten thousand years to detect, is all around! Let me tell you from where I stand, men are too stupid to have thought up such a sophisticated plot, and are far too lazy to execute it.

(CERIDWEN throws a punch at GERALD. ENTER GEOFFREY)

GEOFFREY: No fisticuffs, gentles. (CERIDWEN EXITS in a huff) She'd do a marvellous Guinevere. But don't be too hard on her. She went to the cemetery with flowers for her grandfather's grave but yesterday, but the grave had gone, quite dug up, according to local laws, to make room for the next occupant, the skeleton dispersed, didn't leave even a finger-bone as a memento, and that's allowed, every twenty years, the time for grief over here, so she threw the flowers into the old plague pit, and still hasn't quite got over it. A bit hard to take, I must say, even for a heart of granite. The old granpa had left her strictly alone, never touched up her tities or clit, she adored him for that, and that alone.

(FADE OUT GEOFFREY. FADE IN backstage 1st, 2nd MAN IN MASKS, with judges' wigs and black cap)

1st MAN IN MASK: Kill the autopsy, your Honour, but do not mention euthanasia except in the Maker's presence. Did they plan to 'terminate' him, you ask, 'nil by mouth' him? The Nurses seemed reassuring, although one insisted that he had given her a launching party, tho' to what end no one knows exactly. And

232

there were many visitors, visible and invisible for many thousands of terminally ill patients.

2nd MAN IN MASK: So, you heard, your Honour?

1st MAN IN MASK: Many times.

2nd Man: The mourners were there.

1st MAN IN MASK: But no question of tears.

2nd MAN IN MASK: He was terminated.

1st MAN IN MASK: By whom.

2nd MAN IN MASK: By himself.

1st MAN IN MASK: Which one?

2nd MAN IN MASK: The one in the mirror.

1st MAN IN MASK: What about a period of grief, your Honour?

2nd MAN IN MASK: He'd just had one, your Honour.

1st MAN IN MASK: Did you go and visit him?

2nd MAN: I did indeed.

1st MAN IN MASK: Day or night?

2nd MAN IN MASK: Backwards and forwards.

1st MAN IN MASK: Cherchez la femme?

2nd MAN IN MASK: Your Honour?

1st MAN IN MASK: Yes, your Honour?

2nd MAN IN MASK: Christ, you are so fucking ugly!

1st MAN IN MASK: Watch it, buddy!

2nd MAN IN MASK: Look, like I was telling you, your Honour, I left Beth and took up with Lucy, so cheerful but she couldn't cook and she a West Indian. You like black girls? Yes, white is best, nothing like one, all lily-white, like swans. Lovely. But Lucy...Women, always want something, money, see, sex, romance, 'After Eights.' Well after what happened with Lucy, all women are deadwood to me now, deadwood! Know what happened, we were having a drink in the pub, me and Lucy. Mac came in, he'd had his eye on her, he just marched across to her, went on his knees, and said, "I love you, Lucy. Marry me!" She got up, hugged him and said "Yes, yes, yes!" and they both left of the Registry Office. That was the end of that. I tell you, women, all deadwood now.

1st MAN IN MASK: 'Cept Girlie.

2nd Man IN MASK: 'Cept Girlie.

(FADE 1st, 2nd MAN IN MASKS. ENTER CERIDWEN, GERALD)

GERALD: I tell you, when I woke up this morning, there was a wonderful tree in the garden.

CERIDWEN: You do not say.

GERALD: I take great comfort in the continuance of the Douglas Fir.

CERIDWEN: Who the fuck killed cock-robin? He was breathless and hateful when last I saw him. In that condition, he only had hours to go. And you?

GERALD: Same. *(Consults note-book):* Let me tell you now of the plant 'uva ursi', now this one has many anti-septic properties, by virtue of a gloyoside known as arbutin. This is absorbed by the body and broken down into hydroquinine and glucose. When the hydroquinine is excreted, it exerts a benign antiseptic action on both kidney and bladder, but your urine has to be alkaline, so be sure to eat plenty of fresh fruit.

CERIDWEN: Well, there you go.

GERALD: Who do you think is finally going to do the old swine in?

CERIDWEN: We were a happy united family, you know, especially from the outside, he made sure of that.

GERALD: His arteries were clogged with tar, his lungs rotted with nicotine, his mind deranged with God.

CERIDWEN: Rumours! Kids' stories!

GERALD: From the exterior only. Did you question the surgeon-in-Chief?

CERIDWEN: In his very theatre, no one escapes.

GERALD: Who authorized the certificate?

GERALD: Death.

CERIDWEN: What a wicked thing to say.

GERALD: Just trying to keep in touch with my feminine side.

CERIDWEN: Pardon?

(Consults note-book)

GERALD *(Reads)* : 'Anima', the dominant household being, is the female essence or directive which flits around the subconscious ambiance of the home...'

CERIDWEN: ...when I was out shopping yesterday, I saw a row of flower pots outside the shop, "Ideal for graves," the assistant said, making the sign of the cross, but I didn't believe a word of it.

GERALD: When did you last hear your sister scream?

CERIDWEN: Don't look at me.

GERALD: How agèd are you, Ceridwen?

CERIDWEN: For my last birthday, I got champagne and – thrush, fuck it!

GERALD: Look, ignore the drunken kangaroos and the weeping nuns, you're right, the key to the secret of life lies somewhere under the toilet bowl. *(Consults note-book)* I feel I'm on an endless wrecked, merry-go-round loaded with the uneasy, unfamiliar corpses of all the ages I have never known. How in the hell can you feel sorry for everyone if you live next door to a graveyard? Did you know beehives are said to be the final retreats of departed spirits - while all the time, what we search for so heartbreakingly is for just little golden corner, in nature or in human nature, where we can sit and muse and drink every day with no hangover. A little golden corner. That's all. *(Reads)* "...the interlockings of knowledge, the objective correlative, come from familiar feelings of finality, and the actualisation of their inchoate nature - then, and only then, will the post duende beacons of truth shine out...'

CERIDWEN *(Mimes pulling chain):* All your bloody useless jaw should be heard to the sound of toilets flushing, there's so much shit in it.

(Sound of genuine loud laughter)

GERALD *(Reading):* 'To us sons of exhortation, religions, Moses, eg., are merely history distorted between layers of false language. You must burrow between these obscene layers of lies and you will discover the Mysteries , the real repositories of human truth.'

CERIDWEN: Did you get that useless idiot's job at the College Geoffrey arranged?

GERALD: 'Come back when you're famous, come back when you're dead, come back when the moon is a glorious red.' *(CERIDWEN mimes pulling chain)* No. But I will never be guilty of the sin of worldly sorrow. Totus mundus agit histrionem. What does that vulgate mean, you ask. It was a sign up outside the Globe Theatre, and it means 'we're all players.'

CERIDWEN: Darkness and Diarrhoea, we have this tragedy on our doorstep and all you do is talk in filthy riddles and disgusting innuendo, you douch bag!

GERALD: And for your birthday, did I not create for you an enchanted dream world, it opened with a glistening red apple, remember, hanging over the head of a bust of Sir Isaac Newton, with a sequined fox looking out from a cabinet of curiosities, as a child whispers nursery rhymes from inside the wax-work model of the life-size palace bog. And when the sickly boy prince, who kept a feral urchin as a pet, died, London ran out of black mourning crepe...'

VOICE *(Screaming)* : Let him die. Now! Now.

CERIDWEN: He is fucking good as dead, you cretin, we're on the whodunnit and who-gets-the-dosh bit now, so ease your stupid joints and piss off with your silly screams. (SCREAMS CUT ABRUPTLY) You count your curses, I'll count my blessings, lovers, husbands, even thrush made me think. He did it in the backwoods, dirty toad. At only nine, I learned as much as twenty harlots a night, a sin forgiven every second, he said. God, I was brought up behind my back, so I never knew what was going on, and they knew that. And now I've got too many dicey tastes to stop one inch of it.

(FADE OFF CERIDWEN. FADE ON GIRLIE)

GIRLIE: When dirty old Daniel tried it out on me, I screamed his name a thousand times in the specious streets until and he had me sectioned, which was exactly my plan for getting out of that infested sty of a house, and I've been doing my five-finger exercises vigorously on Saturdays ever since, to ensure my little retreat in paradise kindly stayed where it was, in the mad house. They left me alone to rot, but actually I was left alone to live. You should see my encyclopaedias and DVD's, so many friends, like the Laughing Man, my disembodied voices, Fernando, allies and all so heedless, without a single belladonna or a garrotte as far as eye can see. Friends that fly to you like that please the heavens. But no one noticed me, except you, dear Gerald, thank God, Gerald, all in a half-dream, you said. True?

(FADE ON DIRTY OLD DANIEL in hospital bed, surrounded by machines bleeping, tubes, drips on stands, attached to his body. Mutters, shakes fist, gives orders, masturbates, stops, frustrated. Cacophony of sounds, as at beginning. GEOFFREY, CERIDWEN appear out of shades, approach DANIEL, hands stretched out like claws, they reach for him, fiend-like)

DANIEL: God, no! I gave no orders. No... no...not yet! No...no...

(Sound of tram, 'ting a ling,' general cacophony as long as fight lasts. CERIDWEN, GEOFFREY swoop down on dirty old DANIEL. DANIEL fights them of. As they tear at the tubes, DANIEL hangs on to the tubes, tug of war, tubes snap; DANIEL threshes about, tearing down tubes and wires. They tear off DANIEL'S gown, slash his body, beat, hammer his head, hurl

him to the floor, stamp him to death. DANIEL is still. FADE. The gory panorama FADES with CERIDWEN, and GEOFFREY still stomping. 1st and 2nd MASKS and GERALD fade on. (Masked VOICES (also in judges' wigs) 'interrogate' GERALD)

1st MAN IN MASK: So you went to see him then?

2nd MAN IN MASK: I went to see him, yes, your Honour.

1st MAN IN MASK: And the lady known as 'Girlie'?

GERALD: Yes, your Honour, she went to see him too.

2nd MAN IN MASK: You were mowing the grass outside as an employee, Girlie was moaning and groaning, as a relative inside, so you didn't have to sign the visitors' book.

1st MAN IN MASK: So there is no evidence that you were really there.

2nd MAN IN MASK: Spot on, you Honour. None of us were really there.

1st MAN IN MASK: Did you see Ceridwen?

GERALD: She was alone with Daniel for a while.

2nd MAN IN MASK: Did you see Geoffrey?

GERALD: He was alone for a time with Daniel too.

2nd MAN IN MASK: Did you know about Ceridwen and Daniel?

GERALD: Ceridwen told me.

1st MAN IN MASK: And Ceridwen and Geoffrey?

GERALD: The one thing I hoped would never be fact, your Honour.

2nd MAN IN MASK: Did you tell Girlie all this?

GERALD: No.

1st MAN IN MASK: Why not?

GERALD: She knew already.

2nd MAN IN MASK: What have you to say in your defiance?

GERALD: Ceridwen, Geoffrey, Daniel, the Holy Trinity – the final solution, there you have it! 1st MAN IN MASK: At last!

2nd MAN IN MASK: I think that is more than enough, *(Bangs gavel)* The guilty are over there!

1st MAN IN MASK: But Gerald, what was dirty old Daniel's point? Why did he drag it out for so long?

GERALD: If I may venture a last word, your Honours - the unspeakable Daniel wanted to breathe one more time in order to commit one last blast, one full, final fell black order - like - 'Fall out the maggots! Fall in the sinners! We in the end are the glorious winners'" What are the two nutters up to now?

1st MAN IN MASK: Ceridwen and Geoffrey are in illegal congress, and have hired a battery of lawyers behind them – they have decided it's all dirty old Daniel's money in their grimy palms, or their own deaths on the line. They've cleared up the mess at the hospital, concealed the evidence, the remains are decently interred already, no bones about it. They've set up home in Daniel's former bedroom and adjoining chambers. They have each other again, in bed and out of it, till nil-by-mouth doth them part, they think. They said you could now stay out late without their permission, to take your gardening tools with you – and - fuck you - generally!

(FADE OUT 1st, 2nd MAN IN MASK. FADE OUT GERALD. FADE ON GIRLIE. Fade on *GERALD, 'flies' down to join GIRLIE)*

GERALD *(Bowing)*: Your very own favourite Imagineer has returned.

GIRLIE: Straight from King Arthur's Court, no doubt.

GERALD: I played all the parts. I am guiltless on every count.

GIRLIE: Of course you are. They are my friends after all said and done.

GERALD: Semper fi!

GIRLIE: So I am very glad to see my darling extremophile back this Saturday morn, and looking so cool.

GERALD: And I didn't forget the mistletoe, I promise. Carry on.

GIRLIE: I'm being shown the door as well, aren't I?

GERALD: Slammed shut again, thank god.

GIRLIE: Still with no explanation for our existence.

GERALD: Yes. And you?

GIRLIE*:* Are you going home?

GERALD: No.

GIRLIE: Why not?

GERALD: Ma, Dad, I love them too much.

GIRLIE: What are you going to do then?

(GERALD spreads out his arms to her. Cacophony up as at beginning; fades, sound of ABBA's 'Fernando' song, just a few bars; GERALD takes GIRLIE's hand, they embrace, begin dancing to 'Fernando', a few bars only. Dance into the shadows, a loving couple, gazing into each other's eyes. Cut lights, music up with house lights, 'Fernando' again as audience exit)

CURTAIN

The Prophylactic Conspiracy

Death. In May 1427 a 'brigand' was hanged in Paris. At his public execution, the Great Treasurer of the Regent of France appears. He shouts curses at the criminal, climbs the ladder behind him, beating him with a stick, preventing the priest from hearing his last confession. The Regent then turns on the masked Executioner who is also exhorting the unfortunate to beg for forgiveness, and beats him as well. The Executioner tries to finish his grisly work - the final shackles and then the rope, but he is nervous and bungles the job. As the miscreant is about to be dropped into the final void, the rope snaps and the victim falls, breaking a leg and a few ribs. But the Regent, not a whit discouraged, forces the hapless man to climb the ladder to the threshold again. This time he is expertly tied up by the Assistant Executioner and despatched.

'Withdraw the Widow in Weeds.' 'Too distressing. Disgusted, Tonbridge Wells.' 'The Loved One,' rouged death, too dark. Bring on the Chapel of Peace, with Mantovani. 'Put down, passed over, laid away, gone for Burton, on the other side,' will the line never end? My God, divert me! Sex!

In the main square of the City of Brussels, a youthful firebug and murderer is fittingly punished. A funeral pyre is prepared for him. He is tied to a stake with a chain. The executioner torches the pile of faggots soaked in oil and tar. As the flames leap higher, the penitent addresses the awed and trembling spectators. His pleas prove so eloquent that 'many burst into tears.' The records add 'the death was the finest ever witnessed in the square.'

So, my young friends, let me tell you now, death by homicide, death by disease, death by famine, death by immolation, death in childbed – these were common, often public, and always unconcealed. There was a fascination with every aspect of death, especially in the physical effects. Tombs in town cemeteries were decorated with stone corpses, mouths agape, eyes wide open, torsos twisted in agony, the bowels slashed open, crawling with maggots, alive with worms. It was accepted widely that decomposition took exactly nine days, and that Lazarus, after his miracle, lived a life of terror in anticipation of his inevitable second death, more dreaded because of his first experience of it. Death was elongated, from physical death, bodily decay to the resurrection – if the priests had been sufficiently paid for their prayers – a stay in Limbo, the last judgement (by St Peter) and all in just a few days. The wrongdoers of the community were soon erased without trace. Dante's multi-circled hell was an everyday reality, but a short one. Public slaughter and depictions of same, were a sort of morality-action drama of the day, with room for all.

One of the greatest artists of the age, Peter Bruegel, summed it all up in ghoulish and terrifying detail in his masterpiece 'The Triumph of Death.' This painting showed death at his busiest, again on his black charger, scything through mobs of defenceless sinners, riding over cart-loads of skulls, scattering phalanxes of immobile skeletons, even hacking at the throats of his victims. He shows, hideously enough, a female corpse in a coffin, her tiny bony baby hanging over the side. This whole army of God was accompanied by Death's follow up – the merciless apostolic reserve, an arrayed mass of grinning, greenish skeletons in black cloaks and shrouds on the march against all worldly sinners.

Withdraw the widows!" keep them off the roads! keep them out of bounds, keep them off anywhere, death cells are not immune to the uses of gas, the rope and the axe – no! Auschwitz proves otherwise, in accordance with some law or other. And no penalty for the chimneys either. For what? Do not remind, just withdraw, like Eichmann with pipe and slippers. Millions just demised, deceased, disappeared. No flowers, no disgust again. My God, divert me! Sex!

But fear of death oppressed the living. Louis XI of France was so afraid of the taint of mortality, he tried to expunge it from his presence – he had that part of the Forest of Loches cut down where he had received news of the death of his newborn son. He never wore the same garments in which he received tidings of anyone's passing. There were manuals to assuage the fear of expiring. 'The Art of Dying' was a favourite. Its pages were crammed with depictions of death, the agonies of the damned, the hords of hell pitchforking sinners into fiery furnaces, but scenes of forgiveness and redemption were popular too. All these scenes stared down from the walls of the churches of the day, day in, day out. The main theme was The Triumph of Death. It was all a kind of tableau, everyone a skeleton, with Death mounted on his accustomed spectral charger, dragging off his victims to the flames. This tableau was often performed in court and market place. No on escaped the still, straight stare of death.

Would you like to wash away your hands, again and again, of everything, blood and discharges from the nether regions. Like that! Toilet tissue, double absorbent. Talc. Modesse, yes! Down with anti-deodorants I say. Understains. Lotsa water. Fire hazards, no burns please, except in trailers. And ever so odourless. Twenty-four hrs a day. Twenty-four hours a night. BBC forever! Try a twenty-four hour wank. Shag a bag. No teen-age VD epidemic. Do not forget the twenty four hour YOU! Death? No fear! It is nowhere. What is there, you ask. Sex is there, for God's sake! Pass the talc, the tissue – empty the tombs, shroud the goons. Divert me, Lord! Sex!

Let me explain, in some detail to you, my cowering friends, - especially, the future of Mediaeval man, or woman, earthly or heavenly, was not exactly promising. The Day of Judgement was the only future that mattered and that was always close at hand. It would bring with it grotesque upheavals and 'revenge is mine saith the Lord' stuff. No one was exempt, for all, Pope and peasant alike, were tainted with original sin. It was a long arduous and bloody road to Paradise, but death was much closer, clearer, so much more attested, palpable. Society was compact, exact and static. The notion of 'social progress' never saw the light of day. What was the point of a future when the Day of Judgement was so near? Similarly, for the 'present,' all signs pointed to one sole certainty, the Triumph of Death? The 'future' therefore, on earth forever contained the elements of terminal futility. So it was to the mythological past that people looked for solace. The legend of King Arthur was revived. It was perceived at once that men could live courteous, virtuous and valorous lives and face death with equanimity. The chivalric code attempted to promote this vision of a good life. It was expressed daily in the meticulous ceremonial of courtly etiquette. This applied to every occasion. The Cup Bearer of a noble household took precedence over all other servants, for the Cup signified the Grail itself. Acts of courtesy abounded. It was a sign of different levels of respect to pass the cup to the right or the left. Church services were often delayed by protestations over precedence at the entrance gates, no one wishing to offend the other, as laid down in the Code. Communion was likewise delayed. On leaving church, similar prolonged exchanges were obligatory.

Extraordinary, my friends! The desire to symbolize every action was taken to amazing lengths. The saintly Susa, for example, eats an apple. He first cuts it into four pieces. He eats three quarters in commemoration of the Trinity, and the last quarter in memory of the Heavenly Mother who gave Jesus a cox's pippin to eat. But on the day after Xmas, Susa eats no apples, the Christ child had not yet had time to grow teeth. Susa drinks wine in five draughts, out of respect for the five wounds of Christ, but with two final swallows because water as well as blood flowed from the gashes.

"Buy this statue of Jesus," the market vendor cries, "it glows in the dark!" "Come forward for Jesus, the five-second stadium fervour is behind you! Never in vacuo, always in gorgeous uniform. Holy cow, 'tis the rightful anointed Queen who reigns over ourselves, no less, no doubt of it. Bread and circuses. Never a second of boredom, never a second of doubt! Just bow and curtsey in the direction of Windsor, and you're done! Bingo! Rule Britannia. Build this Lego crucifix! Do it yourself revelations, genuflect like mad. Just do it alone, selfie orgasms, do anything. Never together! Your Majesty, divert me. OK. SEX!

Births, deaths, and mournings provided spiritual treasures too and were suitably dressed up. Queens in mourning were expected to wear black at all times and live in one darkened room for one year. The victims of executions had their distinctive garb as well, mostly tattered shifts. The trappings of these gruesome 'morality plays' were treasured, especially if they had a religious dimension. In 1231, the mourners at the lying-in-state of local saint Elizabeth of Hungary, tore the linen off her face, plundered the rags, cut off her hair and even sliced off her nipples. In 1100, Umbrian peasants wanted to murder their parochial holy man Saint Remuald, to be sure of obtaining his precious, miraculous bones. On his death, Henry V of England had his body boiled down, the heroic bones extracted and dispatched home. What remained of the King in the pot was buried on the spot, and, the records are in a hurry to point out, "not without ceremony."

Clothe me in Prince, or even in Cliff. Celebs are holy too. Worth a penny or two, defy time! Flesh fur and faeces, terminally tinned. Look, a lock of virgin hair. More! Outta the window. Look! Goldilocks in jackets, musical shrouds. Shit locks. No joke locks. Silence discs, loneliness discs, cowshed, supermarket and folly discs. All crap, however costly. Fortunes see to that. Or bargain God discs. Pluck a blade of grass from His cemeteries going free, and buy a doll that urinates with it all, right here. No, even? Seek sex then. Open sex, closed sex, queer sex, very queer sex, flat on the floor sex, wall to wall sex, down and out sex. See, handsome, feel better now?

A touch about weeping now. No shame was attached to the expression of public emotion in those days. In 1412, the volatile Parisians gathered outside the royal palace to express, for all to hear, their prayers for the victory of their King in his latest wars. But riots broke out between the peace and war factions, and the demonstration was called off. Nevertheless, every day, from May to June, 1455, processions were once again out on the streets. These consisted of artisans as well as aristocrats, the highest and

247

the lowest of society. They paraded "weeping piteously with many tears, showing great devotion for their monarch." At the funeral of Charles VII, 1425, the royal mourners in the cortege showed such sadness and sorrow that many tears were shed amid acclamations for Charles." Another Charles, this time the Bold of Burgundy, at his father's death-bed, "wept, moaned and howled so as to make everybody wonder at his unmeasured grief." Tearfulness was not reserved for the exalted and their interments. A newly arrived English Ambassador to the French Court frequently interrupted his own self-introductory speech with "violent fits of weeping" to attest the overwhelming honour at being present at such a renowned spot. He was all the more respected for his lachrymose outbursts. At the Peace Congress of Arras, in 1435, Jean Germain, Bishop of Chalons, during his passionate sermon, induced his congregation "to hurl themselves to the ground, sobbing and moaning the while." Welcomes and farewells, greetings and au revoires, helloes and goodbyes provided the opportunity for many such emotional fits. Religious gatherings were especially prone to them. In 1429, Richard, a Fransciscan friar, preached in the centre of Paris for ten consecutive days. On the tenth day, his license to preach ran out. When he took his farewells, "the great and the small wept as touchingly and bitterly as if a dear friend had died." A fellow preacher Antoine Fadin, was so powerful on the Day of the last Judgement, "that he had to pause all the time to allow the sobbing, breast-beatings to subside." Emotions constantly spilled over into violence. At the burial of yet another King of France, a fight developed between the pall-bearers and the chanting monks as to who was to have the pall off the bier and the sacred vessels with it. At the royal cortege of Charles VII, the coffin-bearers called a halt to the whole ceremony, and refused to go on unless they had a pay rise. In 1431, the banqueting Hall of the King of France, prepared for the royal visit of Henry III of England, was witness to marvellous and shameful scenes. Half the populace of the area, which was starving, driven on by the smell of cooking food, invaded the Hall. The state victuals laid out on the huge tables, were snapped up and borne away. The Provost Guard tried to restore order, but "as soon as they ejected one or two, a dozen others would come in through the broken windows of the chamber." At another feast such a horde broke in that the Constable of France and his Marchal had to serve guests from horseback. At this same event, the King himself had to intervene in a fight between royal siblings as to who would have the honour to sit at his right hand. At the crowning of Louis XI in 1511, "there was such a crush in the Cathedral that the bishops and nobility could hardly budge and the Princes of the Blood almost squeezed to death in their seats of honour." Royal presences always seemed to promote the worst emotional excesses.

However, the urge to live a decent life lived on. The desire was direct, immediate, complex, and it touched everyone, man, woman and child for they were all still sinners locked into the ineradicable filth of their wickedness, to be removed only by redemption, which was rare since the priests always wanted their cut. The Arthurian Code of Courtesy persisted for a century or two, especially on the bloody fields of jousting and personal combat, final forlorn bleeding attempts to embody the ideals of the round Table. But whatever the hopes, whatever God's mercies, The Triumph of Death remained fresh as a daisy and nasty as sin. There was no hiding the daily ministrations of the monster, no removing his loathsome, murderous sting. And everything attached to his deeds were done in close-up, no air-brushing for his dark Majesty and his grinning minions. The celluloid pieties for vacant consumers, the commercial illusions, the re-packaged palliatives, manufactured by remote parasites in distant corporations, were absent; those fantasies of fantasies, were not yet the global scourge of later years. Those degraded puppets, the celeb virgins and princes were absent, those coteries of mongrel Facing-Both-Ways, the TV magnates were absent; the faceless corporation removal men, the advertisers, were absent; those self-congratulatory blanket makers, the Press Lords, were absent; those who take living man and make him his own prophylactic, who take the poor forked creature, us, and degrade

249

even our last dignity, death, were absent. And being absent, there was a great void and death remained inviolate.

"That is all philosophy," observed Adelaida, "You're a philosopher and you've come to instruct us."

"Perhaps you're right," he replied with a smile, "I dare say I really am a philosopher, and who knows, perhaps I really have the intention of instructing people...yes, that may very well be so – indeed, it may."

And now, a few additional notes on the Englishman, the Emotions and the Queen. No, please!! Emotion is embarrassment. Tears, delight equals scuffling of feet, blushes, stiff upper lip. TV audiences, empty bellows speaking vacant minds. Indiscriminate laughter, the hollow mass. Echoes of authority. The Queen, Head of the famous English Expressionless Movement. Nonstop. Tedious, repetitive, ceremonial smiles, fixed, repetitive, insipid, timid, regality alive, awful at race tracks, horse shows only. Semper frigidity, the good breeding mob, best side only. Now ref Federika Affair, the state visit, of Holland, radiant, glamorous pix page 34567 etc, alive, vivid. Sidekick hostess Mrs Windsor, jowly, very plain. Who allowed that!? BBC hushed, obsequious, rambling, nauseating common places, toothless, inane officialise, my husband and I, exhausted, ugly. Whole nation sheathed, unmoved, bugged by self. Who booed the duo? Five pound fine. 'Only booes for Federicka' pleads boo booer. Public nuisance. Five thousand coppers, dicks in morning suits search royal box with mine detectors. Britannia! Never national, never self-suffocation, never shall be dead. Go, ye whingers of England. Variety is abroad. Adventure overseas, opportunity knocks elsewhere. Gesticulators there, song and dance! "Rise like lions after slumber" sang the poet. Brawls after soccer. For whom? For what? Why. For political party bogs, social morasses, account raiders, money mobbers, bosses of super expenditures, of bankrupts, patriotic scoundrels, hedge-fund pilferers, gay treacherites breaking out all over, secret services in the punts, Cambridge colleges on the lawns, top-drawer perverts, Master of

250

Queen's Pix, politicians progress quite stationary; priests ejaculate privately, clandestinely, God! a preventative Dean and Cathedral! In super safe streets of our imperial capital, vice rackets, fellatio pimp and ponce, flagellation sermons in the pulpit. Moral foundation is all wank, sins stroked, regardless of expense. Spiritual re-armament, by puppets. Crested Glebes take precedence, near extinct. Weep ye grass lovers, weep! Child beating, academic misnomers. Turn the other way. Newspapers, we are all like stuffed St Bernards in a taxidermist's Parlour, begging for brandy. Above all, forever HER! - Top Nanny of our Grateful State, Monarch of Queenshine, Mistress of Prophylacteria, Empress of Opiates in the Land of Chloroform, Keeper of Dormant Statues, Shepherd of Countless Contessas, Mistress of Ladies in Waving by the thousand, Boss of the Brats in Wailing, for years and years, such as these, apart, glow in her, by, with and from her and her glorious Kingdom of Hypocrisy! Flow on! and if all fails, shine, baby shine – never forget – SEX, brilliant stuff at the end of every pleasant reign, bless her!

A quick passing look at ghastly Dr Ward and slapper Keeler then. Why not? Ward and his degenerate pasty middle-aged face! Twelve million readers saw it. Sunday broadsheets frank, vile. Pix of the traitors, the Ruski fuckers, cabinet making the beast, regardless of race and school. Coppers observed on urinal roofs. Boy's walking clubs. Fuck them if you can. Life proposes. Ward and Keeler, no harm, never fornicated so much with abroad males, that's life. It can happen to the best of us. Listen, Syphilis is the only classless thing in England. Randy Fathers of the Faith, what is this country coming to? I ask, so I'll tell. It's coming to **me**! Doctorates of Dry Shit, Master Minds of Saxon Dung, garnished with Scarabs, from the very Commonwealth, hers! - weird behind it - the empire of evil, Ward and Keeler, even if dead. Look, I opened the cupboard. I took up the egg, lion stamped. Marginal leftovers of the orgy. Invites again and again, the Old Bailey. Moments of truth. Decent farce in court. So many peelers. Shame! I threw that egg, stamped with lions. Hit the upright cop. I put my Times under my arm, marched off to Bow

Street. No humiliation. "I got kids too" said the cop and winked. "This will help with my little girls' education." A family man's comment, kids, and do not you ever forget it. Ward still baleful even as a corpse on the scullery floor, by his own twisted hand. His spirit still presides over reefer 'n flagellate encounters in the powers of corridor, Whitehall. But Death can never excuse sin or wipe away emotion. "Bless you, Englishmen and your Sovereign!" I suddenly burst out. In a day or two, the entire nation had forgiven me for that single, singular outburst. 'With my hat upon my head, I stepped into the Strand, and there did meet another man whose hat was in his hand.' Here endeth my brief views on vile Ward and worse Keeler. Shame on you, bless our courts, save our Queen and all who kneel on her! Divert me! Sex! And so, to bed.

END

POEMS

A Modern Cross

It was a marriage of true lies I knew,

She, soft as the dawn, a liar born,

Birds of a feather

Liars together.

He, bold as a hawk, all feather talk,

Birds of a feather

Liars together.

"I say I have a wife, and truly this is true,

And truly she would have you think it too."

Birds of a feather,

Liars together.

"I have you, and you have me,"

"I say to her and she to me."

Birds of a feather

Liars together.

"I play the tune, I whistle up the lie

But now you're here, the lie's a lie."

Birds of a feather

Liars together.

"For you, for us, for love, for truth I'd truly die."

Birds of a feather

Liars together.

"And this account, for our account, just this one time"

"You were meant and I was meant, for us, we're mine!"

Birds of a feather

Liars together.

"And you will teach me, still a wife, of life, sweet life?"

Birds of a feather, liars together.

"I have, I will, I am. I mean...let me next time."

"No, let me again, our love's so pure, so fine."

Birds of a feather

Liars together.

"And you're such fun! Our future is all wine!"

Birds of a feather Liars together.

She bound by vows, in marriage was she clad.

He knew no laws but what in payment had.

Birds of a feather

Liars together.

He had no wife; she, no cash.

Birds of a feather

Liars together.

New Year's Eve

I celebrate the year that is passing us by

The late day's barrenness done

When we lay first below the sky

To love afraid in the waging sun.

Though now the light is dim at noon

And snow controls the sky

Though now a clearer death has grown

And harvests sown uneasily,

I grieve no love as the last nights fly

For we leave the year and the raging fear

That bled us in the sun. Without a tear

I celebrate the year that is passing us by.

Death Watch

Was it a Winter even

I waited by

A snow becoming hospital?

Was it a summer down

I passed

A sun-recalling festival?

There was a different grief

Not brief or tall - to do with hours outside

The sisters' watch,

A dumb dimension at the heart of pain,

Where pain is painless, time undone,

Where death takes time for time to turn again,

A central thrall

Where seasons have no remedy

Where Winter is no memory

And summer no recall.

The Parting

There is no remembering, it is too late to remember

In the worn day along the cruel river we walked

Less alone, we were less alone in the island wind,

In the shifting sun no blade burned or died.

By twisted waters

And by barren shoals of light

The widows of the river, the willows,

Hung their limbs and wept among the heat

And as we walked below grave shades of ash

We did not know the isolation

In cold families of trees or the coldness

Of the sun that lay so golden on the leaves.

There is no remembering, it is too late to remember

The staring veil of a widow along the cruel river,

The trial of two solitudes, the slow guilt of return,

The burning and death done in the shifting sun.

Last Night

There was no cry, love, then was no sound,

Slow moths around their death

The candle's motion

Or the breath

Of ocean

From the cliff's loud ground.

There was no shadow, love, then was no shade,

The falling of the light on darker light

The sighted sea-waves

Wreathing glade

Made white

Below the open moon, below the lowing caves.

There was no loss, love, then was no death,

A laboured son without the heart of age,

The crowded rage of breath

Gone over its cry

And I

The coming joy embrace from this blind stage.

Fragment

We feared the shock of the cold church closing,

The alarms of light on the river going,

The city's angular night

And the cascading moments of the clock in our ears

As we lay down deathly to fear the end of day

And the immemorial loneliness coming.

For an Angel

Welcome, Angel, to the bed

Where the both of us belong,

Welcome to my heroine,

Welcome to my song.

Welcome to my heart,

Welcome to my cock,

Welcome to the start

Of loving hard and long.

Never mind the dirty sheets

A loving heart between them beats,

Never mind the piss-pot just below,

My angel's back, that's all I know!

The White Months

The white months land by my window,

Down noiseless lawns the robins listen,

Ice cracks in the misty porch,

The dog limps in blind coldness.

We sit listening

The naked wind sweeping

The flat flakes falling

To hiss-touching flames.

Sitting, listening, the ice-mailed gloom

And outside fade

To the frigid elocution of the moon

Shutting its snow-falling face.

Winter and Time becalming

The green subjects of field

And youth do not fearfully

Hold me alone, I know

Love's coming together will burn

The conspiring mansions of snow

And silence the turning

Of the unuttered hours.

When we

Lie listening

The white months weather moving

There is no reasonable death

Wishing at our door.

Lightning Source UK Ltd.
Milton Keynes UK
UKOW05f0225250417
299829UK00001B/101/P